Coming Home to Mercy

COMING HOME SERIES - BOOK ONE

MICHELLE DE BRUIN

Copyright © 2021 by Michelle De Bruin

Published by Scrivenings Press LLC
15 Lucky Lane
Morrilton, Arkansas 72110
https://ScriveningsPress.com

Printed in the United States of America

All rights reserved. No part of this publication may be reproduced, stored in a retrieval system, or transmitted in any form or by any means—for example, electronic, photocopy and recording— without the prior written permission of the publisher. The only exception is brief quotations in printed reviews.

Paperback ISBN 978-1-64917-143-6

eBook ISBN 978-1-64917-144-3

Library of Congress Control Number: 2021942837

Editors: Elena Hill, Linda Fulkerson

Cover by Linda Fulkerson, bookmarketinggraphics.com

All characters are fictional, and any resemblance to real people, either factional or historical, is purely coincidental.

All scriptures are taken from the KING JAMES VERSION (KJV): KING JAMES VERSION, public domain.

To all the dear people in my life who have ever welcomed me home.

*Surely goodness and mercy shall follow me all the days of my life,
And I will dwell in the house of the Lord forever.*
Psalm 23:6

ACKNOWLEDGMENTS

What a fun story this was to write. The early 20th century was a time of innovation and progress. To write this book, I researched all kinds of items from telephones, to flying machines, to Model T Fords, bandstands, and even the art of building a ship in a bottle. The attitudes of the era fascinate me. People felt the same way one hundred years ago as we feel today about new inventions and the changes they make in our lives.

The freedom to invent and sell, to drive and to pioneer is so American. Writing a story highlighting these many inventions gives us a nostalgic glimpse into the perspectives and the bravery that has made us what we are today.

I watched many videos, read books and articles, and visited websites. Among the diverse materials I learned from, there are three sources that I would like to mention.

The first one is the NOVA documentary from PBS about the Wright Brother's Flying Machine. This show gave me a fantastic window into history so that I could write this story more accurately. The crash in the trees was a huge disappointment to the team of builders in the documentary, but it was a great help to me in increasing my understanding of the early biplanes and the dangers.

The second resource is *The Curtiss Aviation Book* printed in 1912 by Glenn Hammond Curtiss. This manual was published for pilots of the Curtiss brand of flying machines and was helpful in learning about the overall field of aviation.

The third resource is the website of the Wright Brothers Aeroplane Company. There is a vast collection of fascinating information on this website including photos and descriptions of the aircrafts manufactured by the Wright Brothers.

I would also like to thank some people, including my family, my husband, and my readers. Thank you for supporting me in so many ways.

Thank you, Tom, for answering my questions about motors and about machinery, and for listening to me read sections of the story to you. I appreciate your help in developing the plot line for this story.

Thank you to Linda and Elena at Scrivenings Press for helping me get this book ready to publish.

The writing and the reading of a book is a conversation. The messages of faith found in this story are ones I have lived and feel are worth sharing. They are my side of the conversation giving testimony to God's work. I trust that the words you read help you move deeper in your conversation with God as you pray and listen to him.

I also like to keep in touch with my readers, so please stop by and visit my website at michelledebruin.com Let's continue the conversation about life, about faith, and about the work God is doing in our lives.

LIST OF CHARACTERS

The Millerson Family from Chicago

- Margaret—Margaret Millerson
- Henry—Henry Millerson, Margaret's brother
- Fran—Fran Millerson, Henry's wife
- Julia—Julia Bauman, Margaret's youngest daughter
- Arthur—Arthur Bauman, Julia's husband
- Ben and Sam—Julia's two sons, Margaret's grandchildren

The Citizens of Oswell City

- Matthew Kaldenberg—the town's doctor
- Logan De Witt—the local pastor
- Karen De Witt—Logan's wife and Margaret's oldest daughter
- Paul and Lillian Ellenbroek—the town's mayor and his wife
- Artie and Cornelia Goud—the owners of the jewelry store
- Alex and Mildred Zahn—the owners of the bakery

- James and Grace Koelman—the town's lawyer and his wife
- Jake Harmsen—the editor of the town's newspaper
- George Brinks—the owner of the hotel
- Helen Brinks—George's sister-in-law and housekeeper at the orchard
- Clara Hesslinga—an elderly woman who lives alone
- Eva Synderhof—the owner of the dress shop
- Conrad Van Drunen, Markus and Betje—a widower and his young children
- Ezra and Martin Barnaveldt—the brothers who sell Ford cars

1

Chicago
April, 1913

Margaret Millerson glanced away from the mountain of buntings on the table and sought encouragement from Julia. Bright, cheery Julia. She always had a positive word on her tongue and a happy look about her eyes and mouth. If anyone could assure Margaret she hadn't taken on too much by providing decorations for the Library's Charity Ball, her younger daughter could bolster her once again.

"You'll finish in plenty of time, Mother. Look how far we've gotten this morning." Julia smiled, melting away a degree of Margaret's tension.

Margaret shifted her attention to the white rosettes piled on the drawing room sofa taking shape under Bertha Reynold's skillful hands. The woman looked up and smiled at her friend.

"Yes." Margaret couldn't quite smother the note of hesitation in her voice.

"And look at all those tablecloths Isabel hemmed." Julia gestured to another of Margaret's close friends serving on the committee.

Isabel paused her work with the needle and thread. "Only five more left."

"But the ball is tomorrow." Margaret held her breath against a sigh and looked at Julia.

"Which gives us the rest of today to finish, and tomorrow morning to set up." Julia picked up a candlestick and polished it.

"I haven't heard from the florist. I need those flowers for centerpieces." The idea of hosting the grand event with no flowers to provide the perfect touch of elegance stole her breath away. "How will I know they will be ready in the morning if I haven't heard from them?"

"I'll stop and check in there this afternoon. But, Mother, don't worry. Everything will be just beautiful." Julia smiled again and worked on another candlestick.

The sigh slipped out. Margaret smoothed her hair and gathered a length of blue fabric into a swag. She must put her energy into her work and not into fretting.

The grandfather clock ticked away the minutes. Sounds of traffic in the street drifted through the open window on this mild spring day. Clatters of pans and the general hum of a well-run household echoed from the back part of the house. Margaret's breathing returned to normal. Life would somehow go on, even if her part of the charity event failed.

The telephone rang. Margaret glanced down the hall where the wooden box hung near the kitchen door. To think of talking into a wooden box. She was still trying to grow accustomed to the new device her brother Henry had installed last winter. Most calls were for him on the subject of some business matter or another. Margaret returned her attention to the fabric in her hand. This call was probably another one for Henry, and someone would have to tell the caller that he wasn't home.

Hurried footsteps grew closer. Ida, the housekeeper, stood in the doorway. "It's Logan."

The announcement stilled Margaret's movements. She couldn't think why her busy preacher son-in-law would call long distance on a Monday morning and ask for her, unless he delivered bad news. Surely nothing had happened to her daughter or to that precious baby the whole family anticipated. But Karen's due date lay three weeks into the future. Logan couldn't possibly be calling about anything related to the baby.

Margaret roused from her concerns, laid the fabric down, and hastened down the hall. "Hello?" she said into the receiver.

"Mother." Logan's warm voice held a hint of urgency.

"Yes, Logan. What's the matter?" Margaret licked her lips and glanced into the kitchen of the Millerson mansion. Household staff ceased their work and watched her.

Logan chuckled. "Nothing is wrong. I have good news."

Margaret's eyes widened. "Really? What is it?"

"Karen has had her baby. It's a boy!" Logan's voice rang with enthusiasm.

"What? Already?"

"He arrived on Thursday. Karen and I haven't had a chance to tell our families until today because the doctor has been keeping a close eye on him. You remember Doctor Kaldenberg, don't you, Mother?"

Of course she remembered Matthew Kaldenberg, the handsome and professional-looking man who shook her hand in the receiving line at Logan's and Karen's wedding. Later that evening, he'd engaged her in conversation at the reception. Few days had gone by in the past year when she didn't see him in her thoughts.

Logan spoke again. "The doctor has been monitoring the little guy because he hasn't been eating enough. Dr. Kaldenberg wants to make sure he's gaining weight."

"Is he? I can understand, with such a premature birth, why a baby would be underweight."

"The baby is making progress even though it's slow. But here's the best part. He didn't come alone. He brought a brother with him." More enthusiasm rang in Logan's voice.

Margaret clutched her throat. "You mean—"

"Twins!"

Margaret knew her son-in-law well enough to believe that if he stood here with her delivering his news in person, a huge grin would claim his face and he might even lift her up and spin her around. She wanted to say something to let him know she shared in his joy, but no words came. Attempting to absorb this astounding news, she stood in silence staring at the wall.

"Mother? Are you still there? Hello?"

She must respond before Logan assumed a disconnection and hung up. "Y-yes, I'm still here. Your news surprised me. That's all."

"Understandable. The arrival of two babies has surprised all of us." Logan chuckled again.

"But they are well? Both babies?"

"Healthy as can be."

"And Karen?" Margaret's voice trembled.

So did Logan's. "Fine. Karen made it through the labor and delivery just fine."

"Oh, thank God." The whispered words slipped from her lips. She roused from her shock and turned practical. "What are their names?"

"One baby is named John after my father. The other one is named Simon after Karen's." Logan's quiet voice brought tears to her eyes.

Out there in the world lived a tiny infant with the name of her late husband, a man whose right to respect was debatable. Now he had a grandson bearing his name. And Karen had chosen the name. Logan's bit of news spoke volumes about the healing that had taken place in her daughter's heart.

"Listen, Mother." Logan's voice now held a serious tone. "We're having a special church service in two weeks to celebrate the birth of John and Simon, and we'd really love for our families to come to Oswell City for the occasion." Logan paused. "In fact, if you wanted to come a few days early, we'd appreciate it. Karen has to spend time with the doctor when he comes for examinations, and I need to be available at church during the day, so another person around to help out will really come in handy."

"Oh! Why yes, of course." Logan's plea cleared her brain and roused her to action. "You may plan on me Thursday afternoon. I'll leave Chicago as soon as I can that morning."

"That's great, Mother. Thanks so much. I'll tell Karen. She'll be glad to know." He told her "good-bye" and hung up.

Margaret stared at the silent box on the wall for a moment. Theirs was a party line. Nothing that came through on that telephone was private. The whole of Chicago would soon know that she was a grandma twice over and that she'd be traveling the end of this week. She'd better get busy spreading the word to her family.

The kitchen staff no longer stood watching, but their movements were quiet enough to allow them to easily overhear the phone conversation. She smiled at them and raised her voice.

"Julia. Bring everyone to the kitchen please."

Within minutes, the decoration committee crowded around Margaret alongside the staff. A question hung in Julia's eyes.

Margaret clasped her hands together and faced the group. "Friends, I have an announcement. That phone call was my son-in-law, Logan. He called to say that Karen gave birth to twins last Thursday. They are named John and Simon after their grandfathers. I am leaving on Thursday to go be with them until the following Sunday."

The room erupted in cheers and congratulations, hugs and well wishes. A quick and light lunch gave the group more time to discuss the details Logan had shared over the phone. The women settled in to more work on the decorations in the afternoon while their conversation centered on Karen, Logan, and their life in Oswell City.

At the evening meal, Margaret shared the table with her brother and his wife. They'd been out of town on a trip for Henry's steel business and had arrived home late that afternoon. She laid down her fork, took a deep breath, and looked up.

"Henry. Fran. You'll never believe the telephone call I received today from Logan. He called to say that Karen gave birth on Thursday to twin sons."

Fran's eyes widened and she paused in drinking tea, her cup hovering in midair. "Twins. Oh my goodness. Is the poor girl all right?"

"Logan said she pulled through just fine." A smile spread across Margaret's face. The shock of the news had worn off and now excitement took its place.

"Amazing news, Margaret. How are they? What are their names?" Henry stopped cutting his meat and glanced at her.

"Logan says they are doing well, but one baby is underweight. It sounds like the doctor is giving him extra attention. Their names are John after Logan's father and ... well, um, Simon after Karen's father." Margaret gulped in some air. Henry had lost respect for her husband after he'd committed the crime of gambling with money that wasn't his.

"Simon, eh?" Henry grimaced. Then he glanced at Fran and shook his head. "Well, a little tyke could do a lot worse than that for a name. He'll be known to the world as Simon De Witt, won't he? I guess carrying on his grandfather's heritage will make up for the man's mistakes." Henry returned his attention to the food on his plate.

Margaret's next breath caught in her throat. Henry hadn't exactly pardoned her husband of his misdeeds, but her brother had been willing to see the reconciliation taking place in their family. Mention of baby Simon's surname erased for Henry the possibility that the new baby would be a replica of his corrupted grandfather.

The smile claimed Margaret's mouth once more. This announcement of the births was such good news. Better than she could have imagined.

"You'll want to travel to see them. Did Logan invite you?" Fran refilled her teacup.

"Yes, he did. I told him I would come on Thursday."

"You'll go as soon as the charity ball is over." Fran sipped her tea. "I'd love to see the babies too, and Karen as well. Her wedding was so long ago. We should make another trip to Oswell City."

"Logan also invited you and Henry, as well as Julia and her family, to come. They are having a special service to celebrate the birth of the twins in two weeks. Logan and Karen want us all there. His family from Silver Grove will probably come too." Margaret's pulse sped up. How she'd love to see Logan's mother, Sandy, again.

"Oh, yes of course. We'll go, won't we, Henry?" Fran turned to look at him.

"Karen has always been special to me. I wouldn't miss it," Henry said, a moment before poking a bite of meat into his mouth.

"I'm so glad. Thank you, Henry." Margaret gave him a smile.

Henry nodded but kept his focus on his meal.

Margaret's tense muscles relaxed. Henry's opinions and preferences ruled in this household. He valued many good things, but if they should differ from Margaret's priorities, he knew she would not speak up or act out against him. Her brother wasn't a tyrant, but neither was he open to exploring new ways of thinking.

The effort of convincing him to do so had never proven worthwhile. He sulked or criticized until his world fell back into its predictable and comfortable order. Margaret wished to avoid unnecessary tension with her brother, but his quick acceptance of Logan's invitation smoothed her way and heightened her excitement. She glanced at Fran and shared a smile with her. Their plans were made. Henry and Fran would soon follow her to the small town where Karen and those new grandsons lived.

"Mother, the florist is here." Julia's voice rang through the ballroom of the Blackstone Hotel shortly before ten o'clock on Tuesday morning.

Margaret turned from the table spread with one of the tablecloths Isabel had hemmed and went to meet the visitors.

"Where would you like these, Mrs. Millerson?" A young man in a brown jacket asked from behind the fronds of a bushy palm.

"Right over there." Margaret pointed to the corner near the table. "Let me help you." She moved ahead of him and held the delicate trunk as the man settled the tree on the floor.

"Four more are coming. Show me where you would like those," he said as he walked to the doorway.

Margaret followed him and gave directions on the placement of the small forest.

Another member of the florist's company brought in lovely bouquets of flowers in hues of reds and creams. Julia directed the arrangement of these flowers in glass bowls on the tables.

"But where are the flowers for these pedestals?" Margaret pointed to the tall urns on each side of the doorway.

The helpers frowned at each other and shrugged. "Don't know," one of them said.

"But we must have them. They were a part of the order I placed last week."

"We'll check the truck." The young man bolted out the door. He soon returned with a report. "There aren't any more flowers included in this delivery."

"Oh, dear." Margaret smoothed her hair.

Julia grasped her arm. "Don't worry, Mother. We'll find the flowers. Everything will be just fine."

"Let me check back at the shop. I'm sure we can get two more bouquets made for you." The young man smiled at Margaret.

A nervous smile accompanied her nod as the florists hurried away.

"What do we do?" Margaret turned to Julia, hoping for more cheery encouragement.

Julia steered her to the refreshment table. "Help Bertha lay out plates to fill with these nice slices of white cake."

Bertha looked up from the knife in her hand and gave Margaret a smile. She tried to return it, but her thoughts of the missing bouquets lingered.

Isabel placed more tablecloths on the tables while Julia attached the buntings to the woodwork. The ballroom took on a festive appearance and would have looked perfect, if not for those empty pedestals near the entrance.

Jobs completed, Bertha and Isabel went home. Julia stayed and kept watch at the window. "I see them coming." She glanced at Margaret with a happy expression on her face and raced to the door.

The same young man, hidden behind a grouping of red roses and white glads, entered the room. "Here you are, Mrs. Millerson. Sorry for the delay. We are providing flowers for a wedding this evening and got their order confused with yours." He set the bouquet on the pedestal and helped his friend situate the other bouquet.

"Thank you for bringing those." Margaret clasped her hands before her.

The young man saluted and left with his coworker.

"Looks nice." Julia stood with her hands on her hips and studied the room. "I think it will do just fine. We got it all done in time, didn't we?" She smiled at Margaret.

"Barely." She shared a laugh with Julia.

Margaret went home to put on her purple evening gown with shimmers in the fabric. Then she returned with Henry and Fran as strains from the string ensemble warming up filtered through the room. Friends of Margaret served a red beverage from the punchbowl and offered guests slices of cake.

City officials and colleagues of Henry arrived and milled about with their wives. Library staff and patrons joined the gathering as everyone enjoyed themselves dancing to waltzes, eating, and sipping punch.

Margaret stood near the entrance with Bertha and Archibald Reynolds, friends of the Millersons and business associate of Henry.

"Congratulations on the arrival of the new grandchildren." Archibald smiled at Margaret. "Bertha arrived home yesterday all aflutter with the news. We are very happy for you."

"Thank you." Margaret settled her heartrate with a sip from her punch glass.

"When do you leave?" Bertha asked.

"The day after tomorrow. I can hardly stand to wait that long, but the delay will give me time to help you, Isabel, and Julia clean up from tonight's ball." Margaret gestured at the guests filling the ballroom.

"It is a wonderful success. The library will benefit greatly from your efforts. Well done." Archibald praised her.

"Thank you. I felt as though I had taken on more than I could accomplish, and now that I must leave right away after the ball, I fear I am too distracted to do a very good job." Margaret's cheeks heated.

"Not at all. You've made us all proud of you, Margaret." Henry gave her a brief smile in between sips from his punch glass.

The evening offered her many more chances to share her news with others from her social circle. Few of her friends had already heard about the birth of Karen's babies. Margaret delighted in telling the story over and over again. Perhaps the new telephone was more private than she first believed. If Henry could carry on somewhat confidential business conversations on it, then perhaps she could trust it too.

THE NEXT DAY, she worked with Julia and the other women packing the decorations away. The flowers still looked nice, so Margaret set one of the centerpieces aside to take with her to Oswell City. Karen would enjoy a bouquet to brighten her dining room table.

Some cake was left over as well, so Margaret carefully laid several slices in a dish towel. These would also get packed so they could travel with her.

That evening, as Margaret selected various pieces of her wardrobe, a visitor arrived. She descended the stairs to find Miss Rose, her seamstress from the downtown dress shop, waiting in the foyer.

"I've brought something for you." Miss Rose's brows rose as she smiled.

Margaret hadn't placed any orders for clothing, only for one baby gown to be ready three weeks from now. "What is it?"

Miss Rose lifted the lid off of a rectangular box. A white gown with delicate little pleats and embroidered designs across the bib lay in the tissue.

"Oh, Miss Rose, you don't mean to tell me that you finished it!" Margaret rested her hands on her cheeks.

"Not just one, but two." Miss Rose lifted the small gown out of the box to reveal a second, identical one, nestled in the tissue underneath.

"Oh!" Margaret drew in a long breath as caressed the gown in Miss Rose's hands. "How ever did you get these both sewn in time? I didn't tell you until Monday afternoon."

The seamstress smiled. "I had some spare time last night."

Margaret gave her a mock frown. "Don't tell me you stayed up all night."

Miss Rose laid the baby gown back in the box. "The point is, they are both finished. Now take them along to your grandsons and enjoy dressing them in their new clothes."

Margaret shook her head. This woman before her was a wonder. "I don't know how to thank you."

"It was all my pleasure. Have a good trip." Miss Rose let herself out the door.

In a state of awe, Margaret reached into the box. Holding each little gown out before her, she imagined an infant outfitted in them.

Ida walked by. "Aren't those just darling?" She lifted the hem of one gown and admired it.

"I can't wait to see them on those new babies. The moment that I get to meet John and Simon can't come soon enough." Then she'd hold both babies and know for herself that they were healthy.

With Ida's help, Margaret packed the new little garments carefully away. She returned to her suitcase and added a few more garments to her collection, envisioning the activities that would fill her remaining hours in the city.

In the morning, Hank, the family's chauffeur, would drive Margaret to the station. Then she would board the train and settle in. Only a few hours of travel across the vast Midwestern farmlands stretched between her and her family in Oswell City. The train ride would go fast, and then she would be with Karen and the new grandchildren.

2

Margaret leaned forward for a better glimpse out the speeding train's window. Oswell City would soon appear on the horizon. She remembered the look of the outlying countryside from her last visit. The intersection of the roads she just now passed and the cluster of trees around a pond were familiar. Farmsteads with their trim, solid buildings guarded by protecting borders of trees alerted her that she was only minutes away from her destination.

As the train climbed a low rise, there in the distance she could make out the little town's brick buildings. Flat tops of the main street's stores and peaked roofs of houses became more distinct. A church spire rose above them into the afternoon sky.

Clasping her hands, Margaret leaned back. She'd arrived. Very soon she'd be in Karen's home getting acquainted with those new babies.

"Next stop, Oswell City." The conductor walked the aisle announcing the location.

In haste, Margaret arranged items in her satchel and closed the top. Like a child eager to open her Christmas gifts, she watched above the heads of the other travelers for the moment when the train would finally stop. Buildings whizzed past the windows. The piercing whistle blew, and the train slowed. People stood along the tracks and inched by her window as the train came to a halt. Margaret studied them in search of her son-in-law.

Everyone around her crowded the aisle. Margaret stood, brushed her skirt, and checked her hat. The minutes dragged as she crept to the door, her eyes always on the people outside. She had yet to spot Logan. Surely he'd come. Maybe a visitor had detained him at the church or some other urgency had developed. Her stomach fluttered as she stepped off the train.

"Mrs. Millerson." A man rushed toward her. His face looked familiar. After a moment of mental consultation with the list of names of the people she knew in this town, she matched his appearance with Paul Ellenbroek, the mayor and a friend of Logan.

He shook her hand. "Welcome to Oswell City. Logan couldn't meet your train as he'd planned. The doctor is at the parsonage right now and needed Logan's assistance. I'll help you gather your luggage and drive you there."

Margaret nodded at this startling bit of news. She'd have to wait to see Logan. Of course he wouldn't have brought any babies with him to the noisy depot where soot contaminated the air. But a glimpse of him would have brought her closer to her grandchildren. Now the connection was delayed.

The discovery of the doctor's presence at Logan and Karen's home caused a flutter. She may meet him again after all these months of memories of the evening they'd spent together.

Mr. Ellenbroek assisted Margaret into the front seat of his car and motored down Main Street. Such a charming town. The jewelry store, the bakery, and the bank moved by her window. Customers walked along the street looking in windows and shopping. Two men lifted their arms and waved to her driver. A dress shop displayed a sign between two of the stores. That was new since her last visit to Oswell City. She must check into that business sometime and see what the seamstress kept in supply.

They traveled three more blocks and turned the corner. Mr. Ellenbroek parked his Model T Ford in front of a brick house and got out. He came around to Margaret's door and opened it. He then collected her luggage from the back seat and led her to the door.

Logan answered the knock. "Good afternoon, Mother. So glad to have you." His bright smile welcomed them.

The boy was adorable. She must remember that he served as the local minister. People older than him looked up to him and respected him. But that didn't change Margaret's perception of him. From the wave of his blond hair on his forehead to the tie that slanted across his dress shirt due to a baby squirming at his shoulder, Logan would always appear to her as a soul as honest and trusting as a child's. Her regard for him included a degree of motherly love independent of his age or status.

She patted his cheek. "I'm so glad to finally be here. Is this Simon or John?"

Logan adjusted the baby's position so Margaret could get a better look at him. "This is John. The doctor is with Karen and Simon. Come with me. Let's get you settled in your room."

Mr. Ellenbroek followed Margaret and Logan down the hall to the guest room. He set Margaret's suitcase on the bed, gave Logan a good-natured slap on his arm, and left the house.

Logan turned the baby in his arms to look at her while Margaret removed her hat and laid it on the bed next to the suitcase. "Hey, John. How would you like to meet your grandma?"

She was correct in her assessment of him. Totally adorable. The high soft voice he used with his infant son and his movement of John's hand in a wave to her confirmed Logan's permanent place in her mother's heart. She hardly knew which boy to hug and kiss first. Given the fact that hugging Logan would squish the baby, she started with John.

"Come to Grandma. Let me have a good look at you." She reached to take her tiny grandson from Logan's arms.

The murmur of voices from another room caught her attention. One voice lilted calm and peaceful. Karen. The other voice droned deep and fervent. It must belong to the doctor. Margaret glanced into the hall. The consultation couldn't be happening too far away for as well as she could hear their conversation. Maybe they visited in the nearby dining room or in the other bedroom.

Margaret gave a shrug. What did she care that Dr. Kaldenberg happened to conduct his examination at the same time she'd arrived in town? She barely knew a thing about him. Just because he'd spent one evening giving her a bit of his attention didn't mean she had a right to expect any more. He may not even remember her.

A part of her wilted. If the town's doctor didn't remember her as well as she did him, sadness would settle in, but she'd accept it.

"He likes you already." Logan stroked John's faint cast of dark hair.

Margaret tilted her head to smile at John. Large, dark eyes gazed up at her.

"Anything you'd like put away? I can help you unpack." Logan pointed at her suitcase.

"There are some dresses I would like to have hung up, but I'll take care of them later. Maybe you would rather hold John." She hated to give up the warm little bundle, but she couldn't blame Logan for preferring the baby to unpacking.

"He needs someone to help him get to sleep. Karen and I have been using the rocking chair in the parlor. It might be the quietest place in the house at the moment since the doctor is with Karen in our room."

"I would love it. Unpacking can wait." Margaret shifted the baby in her arms.

"Fine. If there is nothing you need me to do, then I'll slip over to the church for the rest of the afternoon." Logan straightened his tie so that it properly hung in place covering the buttons on his shirt.

Margaret shook her head. "I can't think of anything. Go ahead and return to work. I'll take care of things here."

Logan offered her a smile. "See you for supper." He gave his small son a pat on the back and left the house.

Margaret drew in a deep breath. Sitting in the parlor put her in the doctor's path. She couldn't prevent a meeting if she sat out in the open like that. She should have asked Logan to move the rocking chair to her room. Then she could shut the door. Pacing the floor of her room with her new grandson in her arms, Margaret allowed her thoughts to turn to the doctor.

A meeting with him would not signal the end of the world, but it would open up in her life a compartment she'd kept sealed off. Ever since Simon died, Margaret had enjoyed pursuing her own life and growing in independence. She lived with her brother as a member of his family, but his provision for her didn't come with a tight rein on how she spent her time, or on her relationships.

Margaret cultivated many interests, as her involvement in the variety of clubs and organizations confirmed. An expansive circle of relationships resulted offering her friends and groups of friends who hosted social engagements galore.

Life was a round of luncheons, parties, charity events, and quiet talks over cups of tea. Giving her affections to one man would change everything, throwing her off balance and narrowing her gregarious path. She'd spent nearly twenty years of her life revolving around Simon's whims, Simon's schedule, and Simon's health. These years she'd spent living with Henry and Fran had been the time of her life. She was having fun, and she had no intention of it coming to an end.

John fussed, so Margaret patted his bottom. Maybe the movement would help him rest. Her efforts didn't work. He stayed awake. She gave in to Logan's suggestion and sought out the rocking chair in the parlor. The change immediately effected the baby. He snuggled in the blanket she wrapped around him and relaxed.

They rocked for a long while until John fell asleep. She must lay him in a crib. Margaret scanned the room in search of one. Maybe Karen kept the crib in her room. Margaret would ask when the doctor finished the examination.

Voices from the bedroom grew louder. The doorknob clicked. Margaret held her breath. The moment arrived to once again welcome the presence of Matthew Kaldenberg.

He emerged first and stepped into the hall, focused on his conversation with Karen. Dressed in his suit, he looked as professional as she remembered. His dark hair was trimmed close to his head. His face appeared clean-shaven. He stood straight and confident.

Karen held a baby in her arms as she glanced Margaret's way. "Mother! I thought I heard you come." Her face lit up.

The doctor's speech died away at the interruption. He turned to look at the guest who had captured Karen's attention.

"You remember Dr. Kaldenberg from our wedding reception, don't you?" Karen asked as she stepped closer.

Margaret's throat went dry. "Why yes, of course I do."

"Do you remember my mother?" Karen smiled and turned to the doctor.

"Certainly." A thoughtful look softened the doctor's eyes. He reached to shake her hand.

Margaret accepted his handshake and gave him a quick nod.

He held eye contact for an instant and then turned to Karen. "I'll check back with you tomorrow afternoon. Make sure to try the method I explained to you for feeding Simon. I'd like to see him gain half a pound by next week."

"I will."

He looked at Margaret again. "Good afternoon, ladies."

Karen flew to the sofa.

"Mother, it is so good of you to come early. Logan has been willing to get up in the night with the babies, and to come home when I need him, but he's busy, and he needs his sleep. I'm glad to have you here now."

"I'm happy to be here. Couldn't wait to come. This must be Simon." Margaret pointed to the newborn in Karen's arms.

"He is. Meet your other grandson." She held him closer so Margaret could see him. "Looks like you got John to sleep."

"I did. Where do you want me to put him?"

"The crib is in the bedroom. You can lay him down in there."

Margaret left the parlor and laid John down gently so he would stay asleep. Then she returned to the parlor.

"Oh, that reminds me. We need another crib. Would you please go ask the doctor if he could help us locate one? Logan and I talked about it last night, but I forgot to mention it. Maybe he hasn't gone too far for you to catch him." Karen claimed the rocking chair and worked to put Simon to sleep.

"Uh." Margaret's mouth dropped open. Fulfilling Karen's request meant running down the street and yelling as she chased after a man. Her face heated. None of those behaviors belonged in her repertoire of proper manners. They certainly were not the way she wished to make her first impression on the doctor or on any neighbors along the street who might be watching. Surely Karen could come up with another way to snag Matthew Kaldenberg's attention.

"Please hurry, Mother. He might have reached downtown by now, or someone else may have called him to an emergency. He's a very busy man." Karen's brow furrowed as she glanced at Margaret.

She had no other choice. Karen needed Margaret's help. That was why Logan invited her here in the first place. If being of true assistance to this household meant a departure from dignity, then Margaret may have to swallow a bit of her pride.

"I'll try to find him." Margaret retrieved her hat and hastened out the door.

MARGARET FOLLOWED the sidewalk to the intersection Fifth Street made with Main Street. A straight, tall man carrying a black medical bag strode past the bank. A man wearing a white apron came out of the bakery and waved to him. He stopped to talk with the man from the bakery.

Now was her chance. If she hurried, she might catch up to him and avoid making a scene by calling his name and grabbing the attention of the entire business district. Margaret lifted her skirt and crossed the street. She kept her rushed pace as she passed the Koelman Law Firm and the Oswell City Savings Bank.

The doctor disappeared into the bakery.

Margaret sighed and slowed down. At least she knew where he went, but he might have a new crisis to attend to, making him unavailable. She entered the bakery and looked around.

Loaves of bread lined a shelf near the door. Pastries were on display in a glass counter. Cookies, doughnuts, and rolls filled another glass counter. The place smelled deliciously of sweet dough, inviting anyone with even the smallest appetite to believe they were famished and in desperate need of everything the bakery had to offer.

"Good morning. May I help you?" A clerk glanced at Margaret.

"Uh, yes. I'm Pastor Logan's mother-in-law, and I'm looking for the doctor. Is he here?" Margaret checked her hat. It had loosened from its place on her head when she hastily donned it, and now needed secured.

A smile broke out on the clerk's face. "Congratulations on the new twin grandsons. That's the biggest news we've had around here in a long time." The clerk moved from the counter. "The doctor is right back here. I'll get him." He disappeared to a back room.

Customers milled around in the store with their attention on the baked goods and not on her, so Margaret took advantage of the quiet moments to straighten her hat.

"Press that bandage to your hand until I return." Dr. Kaldenberg called out over his shoulder as he followed the clerk. He turned and nodded at Margaret. "Good morning, Mrs. Millerson. Nice to see you again so soon. What can I do for you?"

His presence so near and his forthright gaze unsettled her. Karen's request slipped her mind. Margaret forgot why she'd pursued him. When her brain started to work again, it prompted her to ask him a question. How she'd love for him to take her to an intimate dinner similar to the one they'd enjoyed together on the night of Karen's wedding reception.

Margaret shook her head to clear it. Those were hardly the words her daughter had given her to speak to the professional doctor in public. A woman entered the store pushing a baby in a carriage. The image brought Karen's words back to her.

"Karen would like your help locating another crib for them to use. Is that possible?" Margaret asked.

The doctor gave her a slow nod. "Yes, I believe I can find some sort of bed for them to use. I'm headed to the children's home in Clear Brook tomorrow. They might have an extra crib we can borrow."

Margaret smiled. "Thank you. Karen and Logan would appreciate it."

"I'll bring it by their house when I return to town."

She nodded as she backed away from him and left the store.

At Karen's house, Margaret removed her hat and sat on the sofa as Karen emerged from the bedroom. "Simon is asleep now. Did you find the doctor?"

"I did. He will check at the children's home and bring a crib with him when he comes back."

"I knew he could help us. Logan and I tried to be as prepared as possible for the new baby, but two babies have caught us a little off guard. Everyone has been so kind with their offers to help us." Karen sat in the rocking chair. "So, tell me all about

Chicago. How is Julia? How did the charity ball go Tuesday night?"

"I'm told that the ball was a success. The library was pleased, anyway. I brought you one of the floral centerpieces and some leftover cake. We can eat it for supper if you like."

"Where are the flowers?" Karen stood.

"In my room. You may get them."

Karen left and soon returned with the glass vase and the flowers with their stems carefully wrapped in a damp towel. "They're beautiful. I'll put them in water right away." She went to the kitchen, put the full vase on the dining room table, and reclaimed the rocking chair.

"I want to be sure and tell you, dear, that your uncle Henry approved of your names for the babies. He thought the name Simon was a good choice for your little boy." Margaret clasped Karen's hand.

"I'm so glad. Uncle Henry's acceptance of Logan was slow at first, but it has been growing. Maybe he can look past Father's failures and accept baby Simon for who he is." Karen spoke in a low voice full of feeling.

Margaret nodded. "Your son will have a different surname from your father's, so that will help. Simon De Witt will grow to be a very different person from the man we knew as Simon Van Deursen."

They visited while John and Simon napped. The quiet lasted for an hour. Then the babies woke up, both of them hungry and in need of a change of clothes. Karen took John and fed him giving Margaret a chance to get acquainted with Simon. They traded so Simon could eat. By this time, the hour had arrived to prepare the evening meal. Margaret headed to the kitchen with a baby on her arm and looked around.

It had been a long time since she'd cooked a meal by herself. She looked in a few cupboards and glanced in the ice box.

"Use the ham, Mother," Karen called from the other room.

Margaret found the meat and started cooking it. At least ham was a simple food to prepare. It would break her in easy on this first night of review on the subject of cooking. Karen soon arrived in the kitchen and set the table.

While they worked, the infants lay on a blanket on the parlor floor. They stayed content until Logan came home. He entered a house filled with baby cries while Mother and Grandma worked in the kitchen. Margaret watched him pick up a baby and rock it in the chair. She couldn't say if he held Simon or if he held John. She hadn't yet learned how to tell her grandsons apart. They looked identical to her inexperienced eye.

Logan's attention settled the baby down. Margaret drew in a breath. Three adults should be able to manage two babies.

But the evening proved challenging. John and Simon required constant attention. Logan, Karen, and Margaret needed to eat their evening meal. The kitchen needed cleaned, and she still had a suitcase to unpack.

Logan left the house again after he ate to call on a sick woman. Not until he had returned, the kitchen was clean, and the twins were asleep did Margaret finally get the chance to look after her suitcase. She worked in her room, enjoying the quiet. Living with Karen and Logan in the mild chaos of doctor visits, baby care, and housework without the help of any servants would be much different from the serene existence she took for granted in Chicago.

3

Matthew worked in his office in an unsettled state. Memories of the previous afternoon tortured him. He should have expected the inevitable meeting with Logan's mother-in-law. Any woman would want to be on hand following the birth of her grandchildren. Margaret Millerson was no different.

But why did she have to arrive in the middle of his examination? If she would have come to town when he was at his office or out on a call, he could have heard the news of her arrival and had time to prepare himself to see her again.

The way the meeting happened left him with a serious case of light-headedness that set his world spinning. He'd tried his best to cover his reaction with measured words and controlled actions before he left the house, but Margaret probably saw through them. He'd never been good at concealing his strongest feelings even though his medical profession called upon him to make the effort each day.

Meeting her again at the bakery had only prolonged his discomfort and challenged his ability to hide his feelings. How he wished he could have had a nice talk with her alone. But the store had been full of people. The Zahn's bustling bakery was not the place to renew his precious acquaintance with Margaret Millerson.

Today was the day of his monthly visit to the children's home in Clear Book, and he must get an early start. He hitched his horse to his buggy, loaded his supplies, and followed the road out of town.

Some of his colleagues drove cars on their travels. He should probably break out of his old-fashioned ways and pay a visit to Martin Barnaveldt at Oswell City Auto, but the investment seemed risky. The spring season had been a soggy one that kept the country roads quite muddy. He couldn't take the chance on a car that might get stuck in the ruts and fail him in an emergency.

His horse and buggy had served him well for years, and he couldn't imagine why he would want to tamper with a dependable system. He tapped the horse with the whip in a gentle show of appreciation and put his best effort into enjoying the scenery.

He may have succeeded if those memories of the parsonage would leave him alone. Margaret stayed on his mind. She wasn't Mrs. Millerson to him. Her name attached itself to the comforting picture of her he carried in his thoughts. Margaret. He shouldn't think of her in such an informal manner. She was a woman of class and elegance, and therefore deserved the best treatment a gentleman could give. His thoughts strayed to her appearance. The burgundy traveling suit she wore set off her auburn hair and brown eyes with perfection.

An oncoming truck arrested Matthew's attention. He veered the horse wide to the right to avoid a collision.

"Hey, Doc!" The driver waved through his open window. The greeting sounded friendly enough, but Matthew couldn't tell. Irritation may have infused the man's words.

Snapped out of his reverie, Matthew took a few deep breaths and shook his head to fully awaken. At least he'd missed a splattering of mud from the truck's tires. Another reason why he preferred horse travel. His horse was much less messy on the road and more respectful of fellow travelers than a heavy and speeding delivery truck.

The road to himself once more, Matthew fell back into contemplation. The bachelor life had worked just fine for twenty years. He didn't need a woman in his life. His heart probably couldn't take it anyway. He'd loved and loved well until his dear wife died during her labor bringing their first child into the world.

At a crossroads, Matthew brought the buggy to a stop. A Model T Ford and a set of work horses pulling a farm wagon passed in front of him. Looking both directions, Matthew guided his horse onto the main road heading south.

Driving failed to keep his mind off the past. Memories still tore at his heart. After laying his family to rest in the grave, he'd left the storekeeper life he'd shared with his father and went to medical school. The training taught him how to save lives so that he might spare others the anguish he'd endured.

Twenty years of a rewarding medical practice separated him from devastation. He'd done well living his life alone, safe from any more tragedy. His heart had accepted the changes in his life and given him peace until the night of Pastor Logan's wedding. Margaret looked queenly and stylish as the mother of the bride. In that moment, a fire was kindled in his heart and had burned with a steady glow ever since.

He knew where that glow came from. Love. He'd felt it before when he'd married the first time, and now after all these years, he felt it again. The pastor's mother-in-law, one of the finest women who lived, had kindled this steady burn of love.

She must not discover this secret affection he felt for her. No one must ever know. He was the town doctor, the conqueror of his own pain and the champion of others who suffered. For the sake of his profession, his well-being, and his patients, he must continue standing strong and undefeated.

As he drove through the countryside, he passed the homes of so many he'd known for years and cared about with deep concern. If he fell to another pain like the first one, he'd fail them. He'd managed to survive and drag himself back to stability and wholeness. The next time he may not get so fortunate.

But he loved Margaret Millerson. If he knew what to do about it, he could go on his way and do his job with the same confidence he'd always relied on. He'd just have to keep the fire concealed the best he knew how. There was no room in his life or in his community for it to get out of hand.

A river, swollen with spring rains, flowed under the bridge he crossed. The Clear Brook Children's Home occupied the bank on the other side of the river rolling along the edge of town. Matthew turned off the road, parked his buggy, and tethered the horse in the shade of a tree where she could feed on grass while he worked.

He took the elevator up to the third floor and walked the length of the spacious, sunny wing. A cluster of children sat on a sofa and chairs near a window working on puzzles.

"Good morning, Doctor Matt," a little girl named Ruby called out.

He smiled back. His last name had too many letters and syllables for the smallest children to spit out, so his identity had been shortened to "Matt."

Matthew entered a room with a slim bed he used for examinations, a desk with a chair, and a cabinet of supplies in the corner. He went to the window and lifted the shades. Sunlight streamed into the room glowing on the white tiled floor and reflecting from the white painted metal of the furnishings. He opened his bag and organized the supplies he'd brought along.

Miss Worley, a young teacher on staff with the home, entered the room. "Dr. Kaldenberg."

"Yes?" He glanced up.

"Shall I bring in your first patient?" she asked.

"Please." He settled on the stool ready to begin the day's work.

Miss Worley left and soon returned with a girl who introduced herself to him as Jane. They had a pleasant conversation about the friends she'd made since her arrival at the children's home and about the help Miss Worley gave her with her schoolwork.

He gave Jane a routine examination, and found the girl to be in good health. "You may let Miss Worley know to send Albert in. I believe he is next on the schedule."

Jane's face fell. "Albert hasn't been feeling well. He can't come today."

Matthew drew in a deep breath. Albert had been his patient for a long while. The young boy suffered from a physical disability that affected his walking as well as a hint of a mental disability that hindered his speech. Poor Albert did not need any more difficulties.

"Where is Albert?" Matthew asked the girl.

"In the room he shares with Lance, but Lance had to move in with Bernie. Albert needs the room to stay dark, and he can't stand any noise."

Matthew rose from the stool and held a hand out to Jane to assist her from the chair. "Come with me. Let's find Miss Worley and see what she can tell me about Albert."

Jane smiled and accompanied him into the hall. A consultation with the teacher informed Matthew that Albert lay in bed in a room in the adjacent wing. She led him there and Matthew entered. The room was dark as night. Matthew went to the window and lifted a corner of the blanket keeping out the sunlight.

"Ow! Quit that." A yell sounded from the nearby bed.

Matthew looked down into the face of Albert. Pain etched lines in the boy's features. His eyes were scrunched closed.

Matthew sat on the edge of the bed. "Good morning, Albert. Tell me, what is the matter?"

"That you, Dr. Matt?" one of Albert's eyes peeked at him while he spoke with a distinct slur between his words.

"It's me. I'm back and I want to help you. Do you have a headache?"

"Terrible."

"How long have you had it?" Matthew felt the boy's pulse as he talked.

"Since yesterday. One of the teachers has been lookin' after me, but I don't feel any better." Albert rubbed his forehead.

"Lie still. I'll get my bag from the other room and examine you." Matthew left to complete his errand and called Miss Worley to join him in Albert's room.

Matthew worked over the boy for a long while coaxing for a look in his eyes which Albert protested in the worst way and applying pressure to various places on his face. He noted the eye was red and watery. "Albert, does your eye hurt when you blink?"

The boy nodded slowly.

Satisfied that he'd found answers to Albert's sufferings, Matthew sat on the edge of the bed, crossed his legs and settled his wrist over one knee. "It looks to me like Albert has a corneal abrasion," he informed Miss Worley. "It can be quite painful and causes sensitivity to light."

Albert's brows rose indicating he'd heard the announcement too.

"Oh, my," she whispered with a concerned glance at Albert.

"I'd like to move Albert to the examining room and apply a pressure patch to his eye." Matthew stood and settled his hands on his waist. "Could you please help me get him out of bed?"

Miss Worley bent over Albert. "Did you hear what the doctor said? He'd like to move you."

"I heard." Albert kept his eyes scrunched shut. "Will it hurt?"

Matthew patted Albert on the shoulder. "Not long. And your eye will feel much better in a few days."

"Just wrap your arm around my neck. The doctor and I will help you walk so that you can keep your eyes closed." Miss Worley scooped Albert's head off of his pillow.

"All right." The boy's voice shook but he allowed Miss Worley to help him.

"Steady. Take it slow." Matthew helped Albert to his feet.

Albert hobbled out of the dark room and with the assistance of his helpers, worked his way down the hall to the examination room.

"Just help him lie down up there." Matthew pointed to the bed.

Miss Worley nodded and followed Matthew's instruction.

When Albert was settled, Matthew laid a towel over his eyes. "That will keep the light out until I'm ready to place the patch." He glanced at Miss Worley. "I'll need your assistance. Could you please stay?"

She nodded.

"Good. Thank you." Matthew moved to the cabinet to collect a supply of sterile gauze and tape.

Miss Worley stood at Albert's side, talking to him in quiet tones. Albert appeared relaxed as he held the towel over his eyes.

"We need to move the towel from your eyes, Albert. Just keep them closed. You won't feel a thing." Matthew organized his supplies as he talked.

Miss Worley followed Matthew's instructions as they worked together to apply the pressure patch to Albert's eye.

"That should make him feel better." Matthew reached for a roll of bandage.

"Will he go blind, Doctor?" Miss Worley asked.

"I don't think so. The cornea should heal in a few days." Matthew cut a strip of bandage and wrapped it around Albert's head to secure the patch.

"The patch needs to remain on the eye for 72 hours. Thank you for your help." He smiled at Miss Worley.

"You're welcome. We all care about Albert and want him to succeed. I will see to it that the patch stays in place." She left the room.

Matthew checked the clock. He had enough time to eat

some lunch. After washing his hands, he went to the dining room, asked for a sandwich, and brought it back to the little desk in the examination room. If he ate his lunch here, he could watch Albert.

The boy stirred as Matthew ate his last bite. Matthew went to him.

"Do you have any pain?" Matthew asked.

"Not too bad," Albert murmured.

"Lean on me, and I'll help you back to your room." Matthew slipped his arm under Albert's head.

The boy pulled himself up and allowed Matthew to take him back to his bed. Once he was settled, Matthew drew a blanket over him.

"You did well, Albert. I'll give Miss Worley the medication that will help with headaches and then come back to check on you tomorrow. How does that sound?"

"Fine." Albert sounded sleepy, so Matthew made sure the curtains were doing their duty of keeping light out of the room and went in search of the young teacher.

The remainder of the afternoon he spent with the children on his examination schedule, but Albert stayed on his mind. He couldn't resist another peek at the boy before he left, so he went to Albert's room and found him resting very comfortably.

He finished with his last appointment of the day and went to a café for his evening meal. A flier for Saturday's exhibition hung from the bulletin board near the door. It told the details of the show. Flying machines of all makes and models would be flown by experts from the Wright Company in Dayton, Ohio. Matthew's breath streamed from his lungs and a smile tugged at his mouth.

The dream of flying had helped him function in these years following the death of his wife and child. He'd learned about the mechanics of flight in a science class he'd taken in college. From hot air balloons and parachutes to airships and the Wright brothers' experiment at Kitty Hawk, the excitement of lifting into the air had taken hold of him.

With no family to support, he'd saved his money for the day when he could afford his own flying machine. A biplane or a monoplane or a glider, it didn't matter which model he bought. He was in the market for anything that could lift him up above the trees where he might fly free in the endless blue sky.

Matthew ordered his meal and took the flier with him to his table. While he ate he studied the information in the announcement and meditated on what it might mean to fly. His years of saving, of waiting, and of dreaming were nearly at an end. Tomorrow he'd get to watch airplanes take to the sky and make the decision of which set of wings would make this dream come true.

4

Albert had too much pain on Saturday morning to satisfy Matthew. He instructed the teacher to administer pain medication, and finally, by midday, the young patient rested more comfortably.

Matthew packed his bag and went downstairs with the promise to return in the evening to check on Albert. A glance at the clock in the lobby alerted him that the exhibition would start in less than thirty minutes. Matthew tossed his bag into his buggy and hastened through town to the fairgrounds.

The place swarmed with buggies and cars. People crowded the walkways and thronged at the gate. Matthew parked his horse and buggy and allowed the mass to absorb him as he walked to the ticket booth.

A man in a straw hat and a striped vest stood near the entrance. Beside him on an easel a poster displayed the same information as the flier in the café.

"Step right up," the man said in a clear, demanding voice. "Witness the marvel of flight. Purchase your tickets and enter right here, folks. Nineteen thirteen is the glorious year of flight. Come see why. You won't want to miss it. Talk to the experts after the show." Then the man began his speech over again while a ragtime tune played in the background.

Matthew bought his ticket and went through the gate to the grandstand. Every seat appeared to be taken. With so many people gathered outside, he couldn't imagine where all the spectators would fit. He climbed the steps near the center and squeezed into a seat between a large man smoking a chubby cigar and a group of enthusiastic youths. They pointed to the sky yelling and cheering as they took turns describing nosedives and daredevil stunts. The other man complained to a crony about the crowded grandstand.

Matthew settled back the best he could in the cramped arena and removed his hat as the national anthem played. When it finished, three airplanes zoomed overhead until disappearing behind the roof of the grandstand. The crowd roared with cheers. The planes came back and split up, each one going a different direction.

One of the planes spun until the pilot hung upside down from his seat on the wing. The crowd roared again. Another plane spiraled in a free fall and lifted back into the air again an instant before hitting the ground. The third plane twirled in loops across the sky as the other two airplanes dipped and spun behind it.

The youths at Matthew's side jumped to their feet and cheered. People in front of him and those standing in the aisles who hadn't yet found a seat pointed at the sky, waved, and called out in their excitement. The entire assembly vibrated with the awe and the longing for flight.

Matthew's heart took turns beating in joy over the magnificent sight before him and pounding in fear of the images that formed in his imagination. What if one of those planes hit the ground or collided with another plane? Yet the daring risk is what made flight so fascinating. It satisfied the drive deep within his doctor heart to defy death.

The control of a flying machine looked the destroyer in its

ugly face and declared mastery, rising above susceptibility to injury or attack. Flight ascended to the heights of freedom and victory, offering a brush with eternity. He must find a way to achieve this phenomenon for himself. As the exhibition progressed, he resembled many others in the audience with his gaze on the sky and his mouth hanging open in wonder.

A new set of airplanes took to the sky. These machines were a little larger than the first ones but just as agile. With the help of their cloth-covered wings, they floated through the air, soaring with a bird's instinct for height, balance, and grace. He envisioned himself at the controls, entertaining a passenger with a leisurely tour of the heavens as he guided the biplane with ease and confidence. This model was for him.

The planes dipped and twirled much to the delight of the audience. The third plane cut across their paths at a daring speed headed directly for a set of telephone lines on the far borders of the field. Matthew held his breath. Now was the moment when the biplane should make a sharp turn to the left if it wanted to avoid the lines. The plane kept following a straight path as if it flew out of the pilot's control. It turned, but not soon enough to avoid contact with a line. The plane sputtered and nosedived to the ground.

A gasp of horror rose from the audience. The other two planes landed and then everything fell silent.

Matthew jumped to his feet and raced down the aisle. On the ground near the racetrack he spotted two policemen. "I'm a doctor. I can help the pilot if he is injured."

The policemen glanced at each other and then one nodded to the ambulance. "Try and catch a ride."

Matthew sprinted away and leaped onto the running board as the ambulance pulled away from its parking place. A fire truck followed with its siren blaring.

"I'm a doctor. I want to help," Matthew repeated to the ambulance driver.

"Hang on!" The man yelled with his focus straight ahead.

In the absence of his medical bag, Matthew inched onto the fender and poked his head inside the window. A stethoscope hung on the wall. He took it down and looped it around his neck. He jerked a drawer open and discovered supplies that would help him form a cast, if needed. They jostled around in the drawer due to the vehicle's speed over the uneven ground, but Matthew managed to grasp enough material to serve the emergency. He stuffed them in his coat pocket and jammed the drawer shut.

The ambulance jerked to a halt. Matthew jumped off and knelt in the fray of torn fabric, splintered wood, and bent metal. People milled around everywhere. One limp body lay on the ground. Matthew gave it his full attention.

"The man's a doctor. Back away!" the ambulance driver announced.

A degree of calm descended on the scene as if the presence of a professional guaranteed a positive outcome. Matthew used the stethoscope right away. The man had a heartbeat. Good sign. Next he examined the man for broken bones. There were several. The scant supplies Matthew pulled from the ambulance wouldn't go very far in correcting the problem.

He stood and called out to the driver. "He lives. He has a good heartbeat but several broken bones. Load him up and get him immediate attention."

The driver and two other men extracted a stretcher from the rear of the ambulance. With care, Matthew helped them move the injured pilot from the ground to the stretcher. They carried him into the ambulance and stood by as Matthew prepared him for travel. One of the other men offered to stay for the ride to the hospital so Matthew jumped out and waved them off.

A crew had already cleared away the wreckage of the broken plane, so the exhibition resumed with stunts and tricks from the two surviving biplanes. Matthew followed the fence back to the grandstand. It trailed far from the attractions of the show, providing Matthew with a path out of the view of the audience.

He welcomed the chance to walk alone. It allowed him to catch his breath and settle down. Concern for the pilot filled his mind. The man may have more serious injuries than an impromptu examination on the ground could reveal. Matthew uttered a brief prayer for the unknown pilot that he might heal and lead a normal life in the days to come.

Matthew glanced over his shoulder at the show. The plane that crashed was the same model he wished to own. Maybe he should view this wreck as a sign that flight was too dangerous, and he'd only waste his money if he purchased a biplane.

He shrugged off the idea. Those pilots were performing daring stunts. Matthew would fly a straight line using all the safety precautions available to him. Any sensible pilot would act responsible and keep himself out of danger. He'd do whatever he needed to in order to fly like an expert. Arriving at the grandstand, he veered in the direction of the booth with a sign advertising it as the place to gather information and place orders.

"What model are those planes that are flying right now?" Matthew asked the representative behind the table.

"They are the Wright Model B pusher biplane. It is a two-seater manufactured at the factory right there in Dayton." The man picked up a brochure and handed it to Matthew.

He took it and studied the pages. With the money in his savings, Matthew could afford a flying machine. The purchase of the airplane was much easier than he had expected. He could pay cash and not have to take out a loan or delay his purchase until he had more money

"Lessons at Huffman Prairie flying school are mandatory for all owners of Wright Brothers airplanes." The man pointed to the page that explained about the flying school.

Matthew would need to allow a month away from his medical practice in order to attend flying school. That meant finding a substitute to provide care for Oswell City during his absence. He'd visit with Dr. Hayes, a colleague in Clear Brook, when he checked on Albert that evening.

The plan held possibility. He nodded his thanks to the representative and headed for the concession stand. The remainder of the exhibition he'd spend on the ground level enjoying a snack instead of trying to claim his seat. Some other person who'd gone without a place to sit could use it.

That evening, Matthew returned to the children's home to find Albert awake. He complained of a hammer pounding his face.

Matthew smiled at the complaint as progress. At least the boy felt well enough to sit up and talk. Matthew gave him another dose of the medication and instructed the nurse on his care overnight.

"While I'm thinking about it, could I borrow a crib? It is for a family in Oswell City that recently announced the birth of twins," Matthew said to Miss Worley.

She tapped her chin. "I believe we have a spare bed for babies on the third floor. It is more of a bassinet. Do you think that will work?"

"Yes, it should."

"I'll ask the matron. Please wait just a moment." She turned and left the room.

Matthew gathered his supplies and packed his bag. Then he straightened the covers of Albert's bed and engaged the boy in talk about his friends.

Miss Worley returned with a large basket. "Here it is, Doctor. You may use it for as long as you like."

"Thanks." Matthew took the bassinet with him and stowed it on the seat beside him in his buggy.

As he made the trip back to Oswell City, he thought over the information he'd gathered that day about biplanes. Did he really want to spend his savings on a biplane? What if he crashed?

He had to stop second guessing himself. He'd always wanted the chance to fly. Now it had come. Some men raced cars. Others owned boats or went fishing. Flying was a perfectly respectable hobby to enjoy for recreation. There was no reason why he shouldn't pursue this interest. He'd waited and he'd saved. He could feel good about the planning he'd done over the years to make this dream happen.

Matthew guided his horse down Oswell City's Main Street, turned onto Fifth Street, and parked in front of the parsonage. Following the sidewalk, he carried his awkward load to the front door and knocked.

Logan answered. "Hi, Doctor. Come in."

"I brought another bed with me as your wife asked. It isn't a crib, but it should work for a newborn." Matthew hauled the bassinet into the dining room.

"It will work fine. Thanks for bringing it." Logan reached for the oversized basket and put it in the parlor.

Margaret and Karen moved between the kitchen and the table, setting it for the evening meal and placing dishes of steaming food on it. A bouquet of red and white flowers sat in the center. A platter held slices of cake. The family looked as if they were preparing for a special occasion. Perhaps today was someone's birthday or some other day of celebration.

He should have thought to wait with his delivery so that he didn't interrupt the dinner hour. But the family would want the extra bed before the newborns fell asleep for the night. Matthew stood in one corner of the room watching the activity and formulating a plan for a smooth escape.

"Good evening, Dr. Kaldenberg." Karen greeted him. "We are just getting ready to eat. Please join us."

The invitation punched him. "I couldn't possibly. It looks to me like you are celebrating a special occasion. I would only be intruding."

Karen frowned. "You mean the flowers and cake? Mother brought those with her from a charity event she hosted last week in Chicago. They are for us to enjoy as part of our very ordinary supper. We'd love to have you join us."

"Well." Matthew shrugged. Millie, his housekeeper, hadn't left any food in the icebox for him to heat up tonight. He knew this because he'd told her not to wait for him to return from Clear Brook. Refusing Karen's invitation meant scrounging around on his own at home for the items to construct a cold sandwich. The thought didn't appeal to him.

Not near as much as the succulent scents of roasted meat coming from the kitchen.

Logan pushed another chair up to the table. The action spoke as an unquestioned indicator that Matthew was included.

When the preparations were completed and the glasses were filled with water, everyone found a seat. Logan occupied the head of the table. Karen sat opposite him. Matthew claimed the chair to Logan's left, and Margaret sat across from him. She offered him a shy glance as she bowed her head for Logan's prayer.

The meal had barely begun when a knock came on the door. Logan went to answer it.

Alex Zahn from the bakery stood on the front step. "Good evening, Pastor. I'm glad to catch you at home. Could you please come to my house? Mildred is asking to see you."

"I'd be glad to." Logan reached for his hat and coat.

The conversation caught Matthew's attention. "Is that hand I stitched giving her troubles?"

Alex shook his head. "No. She has the pain under control thanks to those pills you gave her. She just wants to talk the accident over with Pastor Logan."

"Sure, I understand." Matthew turned his focus back to the food on his plate when the men left.

The meal continued with easy conversation until a baby's cry sounded from the bedroom.

Karen scooted her chair away from the table. "Time to feed the twins. I can usually get most of my meal eaten before one of them awakens, but we were running a little behind tonight."

"I'll keep your food warm for you." Margaret left her chair and gathered up Karen's plate as well as the one Logan had left behind.

"Thanks, Mother. Don't wait for us. You and the doctor go ahead and keep eating." Karen left the table and went down the hall to the bedroom. The door closed, and soon the cries ceased.

The sounds of Margaret working in the kitchen reached Matthew's ears. He poured more gravy over his potatoes and took a bite while he waited for her to return. She came back and settled in directly across from him. Their eyes met for an instant before she looked down at her plate.

Matthew watched her cut her meat. The grace and the elegance of her movements mesmerized him. He loved her refinement. Everything about her was beautiful from the flush of her cheeks to the way she held her fork.

She looked up. A question hung in her large eyes. "What is it?"

"Does this remind you of anything?" He swept his hand in a large arc over the table.

Her gaze took in the flowers, the cake, and the white tablecloth. Even the glow of the lamp was reminiscent of the candlelight from their first evening together.

"Karen's reception." Margaret's gaze settled on his face. "I believe the colors of the flowers are even the same."

"I met you for the first time that night." Matthew's voice slid low and quiet. It was the voice he used when he shared confidential information with a patient. Margaret wasn't his patient, but the memories he shared with her of that evening were secret and precious.

Her lashes fluttered. "I remember."

"Do you?" Her response gave him hope that she might hold that first meeting as sacred as he did.

"Oh, yes." Her voice was little more than a whisper.

He wrestled with the sudden and strong longing to reach across the table and hold her hand. But he mustn't do that. This dinner so unexpectedly meant for two had fanned the flame deep in his heart that threatened to burn out of control. It needed no extra fuel to spread into territory where it didn't belong. Matthew raised his napkin to his lips and wiped his mouth. Maybe if he concentrated on eating, the fire within would die down to a manageable size.

The meal continued in silence as Margaret finished her food. When she reached for the cake and served him a slice, she opened a conversation about his clinic and the sorts of cases he treated. They talked of his work until their slices of cake were gone.

Karen still hadn't returned to the table and Logan was still at the Zahn's. How Matthew hated to waste this quiet evening with Margaret all to himself. But he had no reason to hang around and delay his departure. Besides, he needed to do some research for a surgery he must perform in the morning. The medical journals in his library were calling to him.

But before he left, he might find a way to continue the pleasant experience of spending time in Margaret's company. As the meal came to a close, Matthew cleared his throat. "The annual Sunday School picnic is this week. I'll be attending, and I'd really enjoy having you as my companion that afternoon. Will you meet me at the orchard?"

Margaret's eyes grew wide and she nodded.

A smile pressed against his mouth, but he held it back. Smiling might allow the steady flame to burn unmanageable. He'd better not risk it. He nodded instead. "Good evening, Margaret. Thank you for sharing dinner with me." He left the table and exited the house.

5

Margaret opened a bleary eye. The quiet of the house in the early morning hour startled her. Perhaps the silence is what jerked her awake instead of noise. At least one baby, and at times both of them, had been awake for much of the night. Logan had gotten up with Karen and insisted on helping her keep the babies settled, but Margaret had chased him back to bed.

This was Monday, and she only had until Sunday afternoon to hold and cuddle her grandsons. She intended to take full advantage of the hours in the days that stretched before her, even the ones in the middle of the night. She could catch up on her sleep when she returned to Chicago. The most important thing right now was helping this new family get off to a strong start.

She rolled over and listened. Birds chirped in the tree outside her window. A dog barked in the distance. In the house, all was quiet. She eased to a seated position and reached for her slippers. After wrapping her robe around her, she left her room.

A glimpse of the parlor revealed Karen dozing in the rocking chair with a sleeping baby snuggled in her arms. Margaret touched her shoulder. "Karen, my dear," she said in a low voice, "you should go back to bed. Let me take him."

Karen roused and looked at her. "Oh no, Mother. I must get dressed soon. We need to go to the orchard today and help the Ladies Mission Society set up for tomorrow's Sunday School picnic. They are all counting on us. I promised them your help as well as mine. Logan will come, too, after he gets the garden planted. I think he wanted your help for that project."

Karen's speech produced an ache on Margaret's insides. She wanted to spend the day holding babies, dressing them, and rocking them. Not trailing around outdoors focused on projects that would steal time away from caring for her grandsons.

"But who will care for the twins? Someone must stay home with them."

"We'll take them along." Karen waved a tired hand. "There will be plenty of ladies at the orchard willing to offer help if we need it."

Margaret stiffened. She didn't want any other ladies looking after the twins. She was their grandmother. That fact made her the most deserving of time spent with John and Simon.

Logan emerged from the bedroom dressed in farm clothes. He appeared more ready to milk a herd of cows than to spend a day working with the townspeople.

"Good morning, Mother." The cheer in his voice gave no hint of nighttime disruptions, and the smile on his face made him look as if he'd enjoyed ten hours of uninterrupted sleep.

She nodded in response, unable to voice the proper greeting. His whole appearance and demeanor caught her so completely off guard.

He approached the rocking chair and kissed Karen's forehead. "Good morning, sweetheart. You must be tired."

Karen answered him in quiet, affirming tones. The scene hinted at an intimate family moment, one that Margaret shouldn't impose upon. She slipped away to the kitchen and worked at making coffee.

Logan entered the kitchen in time to fill a cup with the fresh brew. He took a seat at the small table in the corner. "Do you have time to help me plant the garden after breakfast? I'd like to get it planted before we head to the orchard."

Margaret cracked eggs into a bowl while her mind churned. She hadn't planted a garden in years, not since her own girlhood in the Chicago suburb where she grew up. Her mother had kept a bed of roses and occasionally a few tomato plants. Never had Margaret been dependent on a plot of ground for sustenance. Vegetables had always been delivered in wagons or carts for her choosing. Logan's request opened a new realm of existence.

He sat at the table sipping his coffee with his honest gaze on her.

She must give him some sort of an answer. "Why, yes, of course. I will help you. Just show me what to do."

She may also need pointers on what to wear in a garden. A woman didn't wear an evening gown to dig holes for potatoes. Even the afternoon dresses she'd brought with her would make her overdressed for the occasion. She certainly would not ask Logan for a worn pair of trousers such as he had on. One of her gowns would have to get demoted to apparel for menial tasks. The day's activities, including the garden planting, required it. Margaret stifled a sigh and scrambled eggs for their breakfast.

While Margaret cooked, a knock came on the door. She glanced into the parlor in an effort to learn who might call at such an early hour. But she remembered this was a parsonage. People came looking for Logan at all hours of the day and night. Emergencies knew no respect for a household adjusting to newborn twins.

"I'll get it." Logan bounded out of his seat in a swift movement he'd perfected in his years as a clergyman.

Margaret peeked into the parlor once again and watched as Logan opened the door. Standing on the front step, dressed in his suit and looking every inch the handsome specialist who so often captured her thoughts was Matthew Kaldenberg.

Logan greeted him and welcomed him into the house.

Memories of last night's dinner flooded her mind. Margaret glanced down at her attire and her cheeks flamed. The doctor must not discover her in robe and nightgown. Oh dear. What a catastrophe.

Last night she'd been properly attired on the outside, but her heart had been open and vulnerable on the inside. His presence at the table, and his deep intimate voice had reduced her to a tender condition, putting her in danger of abandoning her independence.

She reached to smooth her hair still frizzed from contact with her pillow. How she'd love to escape to her room and throw on a proper dress. But she had no way of reaching her bedroom without passing through the dining room in full view of the doctor. She transferred the eggs to a bowl and shrank into a far corner on the pretense of gathering plates to set the table.

The doctor conversed with Karen and Logan as he examined the baby he brought from the bedroom. The expression in his voice reached Margaret's ears but he spoke too softly for her to catch the words. The table was almost ready for breakfast when Logan called out to her.

"Dr. Kaldenberg says Simon surpassed his weight goal this week. Isn't that good news?"

He probably waited for Margaret to answer him, but she couldn't without moving closer to the door and revealing her attire. She kept her back turned and stayed in place near the cupboard. Maybe he wouldn't need a reply.

"Mother?" Logan called again. "Isn't that good news?"

She wouldn't get by this time without a response. Margaret swallowed her pride and poked her head into the doorway. "Yes. That is very good news. I'm so relieved."

Logan smiled. Karen nodded, and the doctor glanced her way. Of course he'd seen her. He couldn't have avoided it with the way Logan had waited for her to answer. She couldn't think how she would ever conquer her embarrassment of getting caught in her robe and nightgown.

Social decorum might not be quite as formal in this small town as in Chicago, but that didn't mean Margaret must lower her own standards of propriety. She searched for the muffins Karen had made earlier in the week and set them on the table.

The examination was soon completed, and the family gathered for breakfast. Margaret's insides quivered as she stole through the vacated dining room. The doctor had shared a dinner with her last night, and now he'd seen her in yet another of her most unguarded moments. She didn't want to think what else could possibly happen to her tomorrow as she spent more time with the handsome and eligible doctor.

An hour later, the house emptied of any doctors, the dishes done, and her plainest dress in place, Margaret stood with her son-in-law in the plot of grass separating his house from the neighbors. A square of black earth lay at her feet. A blue spring sky stretched overhead.

Logan approached with a hoe in one hand. He handed her a packet of seeds. "Those are the beans. I'll hoe a trench and you come behind me and drop them in."

Margaret nodded. This time of working with him in the garden when no one else was around offered her the perfect opportunity to question him on a subject she found unsettling. The most astonishing rumors had reached her ears on Sunday when she attended the church service with Karen and the twins.

A cluster of women had stood in the hall chatting. Logan was the subject of their conversation. Enough fragments of their conversation floated to Margaret's ears for her to realize these women set him up as a hero. Surely he didn't encourage these perceptions.

During her marriage to Simon, he attempted to get people to

view him as a bigger man than he was. Margaret rejected the idea that Logan functioned in the same way. She'd celebrated Karen's accomplishment of marrying a man who was worlds different from her husband. How she'd grieve the day if Logan joined him in hypocrisy and deceit.

She ventured into deep waters. "Logan."

The hint of motherly sternness in her voice halted his work. He turned those honest blue eyes on her.

She swallowed. A young man with that air of vulnerability about him surely wasn't capable of pulling tricks. "On Sunday, I heard some astounding talk about you, and I've been wanting to ask you about it." She resisted the urge to settle her hands on her hips.

A flash of concern crossed Logan's face. His eyes held questions.

"Some women at church were talking about the birth of the twins and how it happened. I overheard them say you delivered the babies." Margaret's gaze bore into him.

A red flush worked its way up Logan's neck.

"Is it true?" Her hands went to her hips.

He nodded. "Yes, Mother. It's true."

"Those ladies weren't making up stories?" Until this moment, she hadn't been entirely sure.

Logan gave his head a solemn shake.

Margaret crossed her arms. She'd probably sound like she would accuse him of wrongdoing with the words waiting to spill from her mouth, but she must take the risk. She had to know he was different from Karen's father.

"Simon would have welcomed the opportunity to get set up on a pedestal. How do I know you weren't fueling the fire of this story by taking advantage of the heroism these women assign to you?"

Logan must have seen the tears threatening to fall because he reached out and clasped her elbow. His voice dropped low and soothing. "The doctor was stranded on a farm outside of town the night Karen went into labor. Heavy rains washed the bridge out over the river, so he didn't return in time to deliver our sons." Logan took a deep breath. "There was no one else to do it. Only me. Jake put all the facts together and ran a big article in the paper."

"So that's how those women found out, from reading it in the paper." A softness replaced the hardness around her heart.

Logan nodded. "They didn't hear it from me. I didn't tell anyone."

"Not even the doctor."

"No. He came to the house as soon as he got back to town, but even then, Karen was the one who told him. I'd been too afraid during the birth of something going wrong. I could hardly even think." Logan ran his hand through his hair as though talking about his terrifying night made it happen to him all over again.

She gazed at him with motherly affection overflowing from her heart. He was still adorable and still full of integrity. She didn't have to suffer his fall from her own little pedestal she'd constructed for him. Thank goodness. She reached to hug him. "That night must have been quite traumatic."

"It was. But Karen was strong. She did well and the babies are healthy. I count my blessings." The slightest tremble shook in his voice.

She released him and looked into his eyes. "I'm proud of you, Logan. I'm proud of your bravery, and of your humility. Don't ever change, my dear."

He gave her a good-natured grin. "Let's get this garden planted. The Ladies Mission Society will be looking for us, and I know better than to let them down." He grinned again and handed her a rake.

THE AFTERNOON at the orchard went much as she expected. Other women swarmed around the infants giving them so much attention Margaret and Karen were free to do as they pleased. Karen took advantage of the freedom and showed Margaret the house and barn.

"You probably remember from my letters that the church offers the house to people immigrating to Oswell City. They are invited to live here until they find housing of their own."

Margaret remembered Karen's explanation from previous letters.

Karen waved to a woman carrying a basket filled with eggs. "That is Mrs. Helen Brinks, the housekeeper. She makes cheese, soap, and baked goods to sell in town. Cider is also made here with a press Logan discovered in the barn last fall." The women continued to walk. "The orchard is turning a high enough profit to completely sustain itself. Logan and the other church leaders are quite relieved. That was their goal from the beginning."

Karen took her to the parlor that functioned as the classroom where she taught English to the Dutch children who came to Oswell City with their parents. The students and their teacher had started an early summer vacation since the twins were born sooner than expected.

After taking a brief break in the kitchen to feed the babies, Karen was off again leading Margaret to a group setting up tables and chairs on the lawn. They spent the rest of the afternoon working with the women preparing for the large group that would attend the picnic.

THE NEXT MORNING, Margaret arrived with Logan, Karen, and their infant sons while the same women who helped with setup the day before arranged food on the tables. She found a seat among the other women as they visited about the twins. Margaret held Simon, and Clara Hesslinga held John.

She felt quite at ease seated in the circle and conversing with these women. If she wasn't leaving at the end of the week, she'd find these ladies to be good friends. Many of them were her age or a little older. They had much in common with her, and she would value their companionship. Maybe she could share her grandsons with them after all. These women shared her concern about Karen and Logan making the adjustment to parenting twins.

Logan gathered everyone together and prayed to begin the meal. Margaret was in no hurry to get in line for the potluck lunch. She'd stay right here holding baby Simon for as long as necessary. The only person who could convince her to give him up drove his buggy onto the lawn and parked it near the others.

Margaret had been keeping watch for him all morning. When he'd mentioned at the dinner they shared that he'd meet her at the orchard, she wasn't sure what to expect. Maybe he would have an emergency that would prevent him from attending. But here he came. Walking straight toward her with his attention on no one else.

"I'm sorry I'm late. I got called out to deliver a baby at four o'clock this morning." Dr. Kaldenberg pulled a chair up next to her and sat down.

"Is everything all right with the new baby?" Margaret asked.

"Yes. It's a girl. I'll go over there and check on the baby and the mother after the picnic." He patted the infant in Margaret's arms. "Looks like this young man is filling out nicely. The dangers have passed."

"Yes. He appears to be nearly the same size as his brother." Margaret held the baby away from her to look in his face. He fussed and sucked on a hand.

"I would say that assessment is accurate." Dr. Kaldenberg patted the newborn's head and then turned his attention on Margaret. "You look very nice today."

"Thank you." His words startled her. They brought to mind the previous morning when he'd made his house call and caught her in her nightgown. Her cheeks flushed from the memory. But she didn't wear a robe and nightgown now. She was quite properly arrayed in a tea gown, most appropriate to an afternoon spent in an outdoor setting.

"Would you like to join the others in line for some food?" He pointed to the people filling their plates from the dishes on the tables.

"I would. This baby is ready for another feeding. Let me give him to my daughter, and then I will join you." Margaret stood. Simon continued to fuss as though he was no longer content in Grandma's arms.

Dr. Kaldenberg nodded and left his chair.

Margaret looked around as she jiggled the squirming baby. Where had Karen and Logan gone? She didn't see them anywhere. Those two had become quite practiced at disappearing alone together. Margaret went in search of them, whispering soothing words to Simon and shifting his position in her arms as she walked. His fussing grew louder until breaking into a cry.

A glimpse of a dark pink skirt clued Margaret in to Karen's whereabouts. She walked the lane with Logan and held his hand.

Margaret hastened toward them. "There you two are. Simon is fussing. I've tried everything to calm him, but he wants his mother." She handed the newborn over to Karen.

"Thank you for looking after him so long. I'll take care of him. Why don't you go ahead and get some food?" Karen patted Simon's back.

Now that Simon had found his mother, and John still seemed to do well in Clara's care, Margaret hastened to find the doctor. She mustn't keep him waiting.

She found him watching for her under a tree on the lawn. He led her through the line for food and then to a picnic table that still had space for two more. The meal passed with pleasant conversation with the doctor and with the others at the table. Margaret learned more about him as she listened to his end of the conversation and watched him interact with his friends and neighbors, all of whom had likely been his patients at one time or another.

"Time for games!" The call rang through the gathering from Mayor Paul Ellenbroek. He stood near the edge of the apple orchard with his hand raised in the air.

People glanced at each other with questioning looks.

"The first competition is the three-legged race," Paul announced as he strung a red ribbon between two tree trunks.

"Would you like to pair with me?" The doctor looked at Margaret.

She laughed. "I fear I'm too old for those sorts of games. Let the younger people compete."

"We play this one every year. People of all ages participate. Even me." His eyes twinkled at her.

Margaret observed the gathering. People stood and sought out partners. Everyone paired with another person in the crowd.

She sighed. "I suppose. But I don't want to get hurt."

He patted her arm. "Don't worry. I doubt that anything will happen to you. But if it does, you couldn't find a better partner."

Margaret laughed again. "I suppose running a race with my ankle tied to the leg of the doctor is pretty safe."

"So you'll do it?" He held his hand out to her.

"Oh, why not." Margaret allowed him to lead her to the starting line where Lillian Ellenbroek, the mayor's wife, handed the doctor a length of twine.

They lined up with other couples. Karen and Logan bent over the starting line a short distance away. The lawyer and his wife were next to Dr. Kaldenberg. Artie and Cornelia Goud, the owners of the jewelry store, occupied the spot at Margaret's side. The Barnaveldts, the Brinks, and the Zahns completed the lineup.

The doctor bent down and placed his foot next to Margaret's. He threaded the twine around his ankle and then handed the end to Margaret so that she could run it beneath her skirt. When the twine was tied securely around their legs, they stood and waited for orders from the mayor.

"Ready to start?" The mayor asked the group.

Much teasing and laughing answered his question as people straightened and looked toward the finish line.

"All right. On your mark. Get set. Go!" The mayor shot a small gun into the air, adding to the excitement.

Dr. Kaldenberg wrapped his arm around Margaret's waist and pulled her forward with him. To keep her balance, Margaret wrapped an arm around his waist. Together they hobbled across the grass. Logan went down a few feet away from her. He rolled on the grass laughing and dragged Karen down with him. She landed on top of him and shared in his laughter.

Margaret shifted her attention away from the couple. She'd better not watch them, or the same thing might happen to her. More pairs tumbled to the ground around her. Margaret managed to stay on her feet, but only for a moment longer.

Matthew stumbled and quickly corrected himself. On the next step, he stumbled again. This time he fell. Margaret didn't have a chance to stay standing with her partner lying on the ground. She sprawled headlong in the grass next to him.

"Are you hurt?" His voice asked near her ear.

She shook her head. "No. Just winded. Give me a moment to catch my breath."

Someone in front of her cheered. "Good job, Mrs. Millerson. Look at your hand. You reached the finish line!"

Margaret lifted her head and glanced toward the voice.

"Would you look at that." Dr. Kaldenberg murmured.

Even though her body lay flat on the ground, the fingers of her right hand rested on the red ribbon Paul Ellenbroek had strung.

The doctor untied her leg from his and helped her to her feet while Paul Ellenbroek announced the winners. She didn't catch the names of first or second place, but she did hear him say that third place went to Dr. Kaldenberg and Mrs. Millerson.

Margaret didn't care. She was too mortified about her fall in the grass. Of course, it had happened in a game played for fun, but it had happened in front of Matthew. First, he caught a glimpse of her heart at that impromptu dinner, then he witnessed her in her nightgown. Now he saw her take an undignified tumble in the grass.

When the ribbons were handed out, Margaret tried her best to accept it graciously, but all she wanted was to run somewhere and hide.

The group broke up as people sought their chairs and settled in to visit. Children gathered in the shade for more games.

"Would you like a drink of lemonade?" Dr. Kaldenberg asked.

"That sounds nice." The idea of a refreshing drink soothed her irritations.

He nodded and led her to the table with the lemonade. Then he poured two glasses for them and found seats in the shade.

"You make an excellent partner," he said in his low voice between sips of lemonade.

"Thanks, but I'm quite embarrassed."

"Why?" He studied her.

"I didn't ... well, I didn't want you to see me fall in the grass."

"If you remember, I went down first. I pulled you down."

Margaret shrugged. "It was still embarrassing."

"I'm sorry."

She glanced at him. "Oh, no. It wasn't your fault. I had fun. I'm glad we did it. I'm just ashamed that you saw me so soon after I'd gotten up yesterday morning. Today I fell in the grass. This isn't how I'd hoped our reunion would go."

He gazed at her with fondness in his eyes. "You are still the most beautiful and elegant woman I've ever met."

The compliment stole her breath. She would never have guessed he saw her in that way.

"Come on. Let's go join the hymn sing." He clasped her elbow and led her to a group gathered around a trio.

The afternoon passed with the singing followed by watching

the children play games. The doctor stayed at her side until the end. His compliment stayed with her long after she went home with Logan and Karen and the twins. A vital friendship had sprouted between her and the doctor. She would miss him when she returned to Chicago.

6

Margaret hastened into her plain blue dress. A baby cried in another room demanding his breakfast. Margaret rushed through fixing her hair and making her bed. Soon the rest of the household would be looking for their breakfasts. Simon and John slept better last night than they had earlier in the week, but they still awoke early.

The household established a routine during Margaret's stay. She cooked breakfast while Logan dressed and Karen fed the babies. Then, once the twins were content, the adults sat to eat their breakfast before Logan left for the day. She couldn't imagine what Karen and Logan would do when she left.

Logan would probably end up improvising on his own or run late because he'd have to attend to the little tasks of helping a family start their day that Margaret performed. She had nowhere to go or meetings to attend. If a little extra time was required of her to run an errand for Karen in between her kitchen tasks, the additional work wouldn't alter her morning's schedule. She not only helped Karen care for the twins, but she helped Logan's day go smoother.

They had no maid or cook like Henry and Fran did.

Margaret's presence in their home gave both of the new parents respite in the midst of their sudden changes.

Karen entered the kitchen carrying Simon while Margaret tied on an apron. "Logan says his family is arriving today on the four o'clock train. Do you know when our family will arrive? We have rooms for everyone tonight at the hotel."

"The train from Chicago arrives at two o'clock." Margaret measured out flour for pancakes as she spoke.

"That will give us plenty of time to get everyone settled. Let's plan on going to the hotel dining room for our evening meal. That will be much easier than crowding everyone in here." Karen wiped a cloth over Simon's face.

Margaret nodded. She preferred that plan over preparing a meal for so many guests. Preparations for Sunday's dinner following the church service added to her busyness, providing her with more than enough work to fill her day. She may not get it all completed before family arrived in town. Her chest tightened as she thought ahead to the list of tasks that somehow must get crammed into the short hours.

Logan entered the kitchen and sipped the coffee Margaret made. He held an infant until Karen returned with another one and made a trade. Margaret set pancakes and sausage on the table. She and Logan ate together while Karen fed a baby.

They finished their breakfast before Karen had a chance to eat, so Margaret put some food on a plate for her and set it on the back of the stove to keep warm. Logan left for work at the church with promises to return by noon. Margaret settled in to wash the dishes and restore order in the kitchen.

Questions about the family's laundry teased her mind. Margaret had not seen Karen do any wash since her arrival. That meant her daughter and son-in-law had more clothes than she thought, or there were heaps of laundry piled somewhere that needed immediate attention. Margaret paused in her work, dried her hands, and went on an investigation.

A search through a closet in the bathroom revealed a mound

of clothing that had been worn. She went to Karen's bedroom. Karen sat in the chair by the window with a baby in her arms.

"Would you like to have any clothes washed?" Margaret asked.

"Yes, thank you, Mother. I haven't wanted to trouble you with it. Caring for babies and cooking meals seems to take all of our time. But Logan's white shirt should get washed for him to wear tomorrow, and my Sunday dress also should get washed. John spit up on it last week."

"We definitely want you looking your best tomorrow." Margaret stooped to gather the pile of clothes Karen indicated, pulled her Sunday dress from the closet, and left the room.

Years had passed since Margaret had washed clothes on her own. The Millersons' household servants supervised washday with the tubs of water, the drying on lines, and the ironing. She dumped the clothes onto the table and searched for Karen's supplies.

For the sake of this new family and the guests arriving later in the day, she'd relearn the process of coaxing dirt out of fabric. Her attempt may not guarantee perfect success, but it would at least provide Karen and her family with the proper clothing for a church service.

An hour later, Margaret managed a kitchen bursting with energy. A collection of baby clothing hung from a line near the open window. Water heated on the stove for another batch, sending out a cloud of steam. The ironing board stood next to the stove.

A white baby gown was spread over it, and Margaret worked with great care to make sure every tuck and gather lay just right. Canned vegetables lined the cupboard ready to prepare for Sunday's celebration meal. Baking ingredients clustered next to the vegetables waiting for Margaret or Karen to mix them into a cake.

Margaret glanced at the clock. She had thirty minutes until she must pause in the laundry tasks and fix their lunch. How she'd love to hurry through the ironing, but the details on each little gown required her full attention. They must turn out right for the two infants who would be the stars of their special day.

The water reached its proper temperature, so she poured it into the large wooden basin and scrubbed a set of towels. She wrung them out and hung them on the clothesline in the yard. She returned to the kitchen as Logan came home.

He rolled up his sleeves. "Don't worry about our lunch, Mother. I'll whip up some fried potatoes from my bachelor days and have them ready in no time."

Margaret watched with her mouth hanging open as Logan found the skillet and peeled potatoes.

A baby cried. Karen called from the parlor for someone from the kitchen to change a diaper so she could settle the other baby down for a nap. Since Logan appeared so pleased with his occupation at the stove, Margaret paused in her work and went to help Karen.

By twelve o'clock, Logan had his potatoes cooked, leftover sausage from breakfast heated, and the table set. Karen had John asleep in the crib and Margaret had Simon changed. But her ironing wasn't done, the laundry lay around in an uncompleted state, and all that food still lined the counter. The same fear she'd felt on the day of the Library Charity Ball rose on her insides as she shared the meal with Karen and Logan.

"We won't get the laundry and the cooking finished before our guests arrive." Margaret's thoughts slipped out as she glanced at the clock once again.

"I'll put the other baby down for a nap. That will free you up to help Mother," Logan said to Karen.

"The cake shouldn't take too long to mix up. I'll do that and bake it." Karen pointed to the oven.

"What about the vegetables? Someone must take time to get those ready. And the meat. Has anyone thought about the meat? When will we prepare it? Maybe I should just stay home from the train station and supper at the hotel." Margaret's shoulders slumped. She'd mourn the loss of time spent with her Chicago family.

An evening out with them fit her style much better than the isolation of a lonely kitchen. But Karen couldn't get ready for Sunday and for entertaining guests on her own. Simon and John demanded too much of her time and energy. Margaret would tolerate her removal from the party if it helped someone else.

"No, Mother. You don't need to do that." Karen covered Margaret's hand with her own.

A new thought stung her when she heard Karen's response. "But what will we wear to the train station and to the hotel? I must dress for dinner. I can't go out for a social engagement in this dress. Think of how much time I'll take to get ready."

Logan and Karen exchanged a discreet glance. A moment later, Logan cleared his throat. "Mother, no one in Oswell City dresses for dinner. Not even the Ellenbroeks. You would actually look perfectly acceptable going out in what you have on."

Margaret's brow puckered and her mouth dropped open. "But I've spent all day in the kitchen. I couldn't think of wearing the same dress to a dinner."

Karen leaned forward. "Then go ahead and change your clothes if that makes you feel better. All Logan meant was that you don't have to feel pressure to impress anyone here. Formalities don't matter as much in our small town as they do in the city. You won't lose any respect by wearing a simple gown out in public. I do it quite often."

Margaret stiffened in her seat. Karen's speech irritated her. She shouldn't have so strong of a reaction, but Karen's implications chafed in places where Margaret experienced the most sensitivity. Of course she wasn't trying to impress anyone. Neither was she attempting to impose her standards of formality on others. Why, that would classify her as a snob. Surely she wasn't leaving that impression with the people she'd met downtown or at the church picnic.

Maybe she'd led the doctor to believe this of her. Did he

think she was a snob? Is that why she hadn't wanted him to see her sprawled in the grass or wearing her nightgown when he made his house calls? Her cheeks burned. This small town exposed her weak points and made her ashamed of what she saw in herself.

Her gaze traveled from Karen's face to Logan's. Could they see it too? Logan studied her with a solemn gravity clouding his eyes as if he felt he'd hurt her feelings. She must let him know that wasn't the case. She was more disappointed in herself than in him.

"Well then. I'll look after the laundry while Karen does the baking. That should give me enough time to make a quick change of my dress and slip on a hat." Margaret attempted a smile. It wobbled.

A brief glimmer of humor flickered in Logan's eyes, but he pushed back from the table before Margaret could detect any more of his thoughts.

After the meal ended and the dishes washed, the hands on the clock raced toward two o'clock. Margaret had barely finished her ironing when the time arrived to prepare for her trip to the train station.

Karen poured batter into a pan and set it on the table. "I'll have to bake it when I come home," she announced with an ease that would lead anyone to believe it had been her plan all along.

Margaret looked at the wet wash basin on a chair and the tiny garments hanging by the window. The full cake pan occupied the table near a stack of laundry. Dirty utensils filled the sink. A blanket hung over the back of a chair. Pans and dishes lay on the counter alongside the jars of food waiting to be prepared. The place was a mess. So different from the impeccable order the household staff maintained in the Millerson mansion. But she could do nothing about the incomplete work and the resulting disorder. She spun away from the scene and went to her room.

AT THE STATION, Margaret welcomed Fran with a hug. She didn't even want to imagine what her wealthy and proper sister-in-law would think if she could see the state of disarray left behind at Karen's house.

Julia bounced into her arms with a cheery greeting. A time of happy fellowship followed as the two grandsons from Chicago met their infant cousins. Margaret glowed on the inside as she watched her family reunite. The party migrated to the hotel where Margaret helped Julia unpack suitcases for herself, her husband Arthur, and her two little boys, Ben and Sam. They finished just in time to return to the station to meet Logan's family.

His mother kissed each baby with awe in her motions and her expressions. Once his sister and her husband and little boy, along with his mother, had their belongings settled in their rooms, the entire party met in the dining room for a large, boisterous meal.

"Congratulations." Henry approached Logan and shook his hand.

"Thank you, sir." Logan smiled at him.

"Let me see these new babies." Henry looked over at Karen and the baby carriage beside her.

Karen picked up one of the twins. "This is John. Meet your uncle, John."

The baby waved a tiny fist in the air, and everyone laughed.

Karen handed him to Margaret and picked up the other baby. "This is Simon. You've probably heard that he's named after Father." Karen's voice trembled.

"Yes, I know. Your mother told me." Henry wore a tender expression as he studied the infant. "I'm pleased to meet you, Simon. You will be someone your family can be proud of."

Karen blinked away tears. "He'll prove you right someday."

Henry rested his hand on Karen's shoulder. "The past is in

the past. As a family, we've moved on. You are married to this fine young man and have two new sons. The time has come for us Millersons to write a new story."

Margaret wiped away some of her own tears. Henry had come a long way in his attitudes toward her late husband. Karen's marriage and her choice to name one of her sons after her father had helped to heal the damage of Simon's wrongs. Her husband Logan and new baby Simon strengthened their family and made straight the path into a future of love and forgiveness.

LATER THAT EVENING, Karen rebuilt the fire in the stove and put the cake in the oven before sitting to feed the twins. Logan joined her in the parlor. Margaret overheard their cozy chat in the glow of the lamp while she hustled around the kitchen working on the laundry. Everything had dried during her absence for which she was thankful, but Karen's dress and Logan's shirt still needed ironed. The vegetables still waited to get put into dishes and the meat must be seasoned. Margaret stayed in the kitchen working by lamplight long after the twins fell asleep.

In the quiet hours, a disturbing thought pounded in her mind. Karen would never be ready for her to leave tomorrow afternoon. John and Simon required her constant attention. The laundry would have to be washed again. Then there were the breakfasts, the ironing, and the midnight tasks of changing diapers and rocking babies to sleep. How could two people do it all? Logan would have to quit his job to offer Karen proper assistance. That wouldn't help anyone.

The question of how long Margaret should stay haunted her. A day? Another week? A month? She couldn't answer it, and it hung on her mind.

AT THE CONCLUSION of his sermon during the Sunday morning service, Logan made an announcement, "Today we have the privilege of celebrating the birth of my twin sons. Karen, could you join me, please?" He glanced at her and reached his hands out to accept Simon. He laid his hand on the tiny head, quoted a scripture passage, and then asked Karen questions about her promises of commitment to God and his teaching.

After she answered them, she turned to Logan and asked him the same questions.

They must have practiced at a time when Margaret had not been present. Karen and Logan recited the liturgy, not as pastor and church member, but as husband and wife making promises to each other before the Lord in regard to their children. The scene struck Margaret as sweet and tender. She nearly forgot to join in the declaration of the Apostle's Creed when Logan and Karen faced the congregation and led them in it.

They gathered with their newborn sons around the font near the pulpit, continued with more liturgy, and then looked out at the congregation. Logan held John who emitted a squeaky fuss and batted the air with his hands. Logan gathered him close to his robed chest to settle him down. He prayed and then led the congregation in the last hymn. Karen went with him to stand at the back so everyone could see John and Simon up close when they shook hands with their pastor.

"Picture time!" Jake Harmsen, the editor of the local newspaper, called out. "Gather your family over here please, Pastor Logan. I'd like to get a photo of you all together."

"Is this going in the paper?" Logan frowned at the man.

"Not if you don't want it to." Jake motioned to the group as he spoke, helping them get into position.

"I'd rather not—"

"Oh, Logan. What does it hurt? He can put one picture of you in the paper. I'm sure the town would love to see this memory of the twins' special day." His mother Sandy breezed by him waving her hand in the air as if to shoo away his ridiculous notions about staying out of the newspaper.

He sighed and turned to follow Karen, resignation written on his face.

Margaret stifled a laugh. Logan was humble and honest. He handled authority well. But occasionally, it was healthy for him to get overruled. She followed Jake's guidance and found her place in the arrangement.

Jake backed away and stood near his tripod. "Everyone look here." He studied the group. "Sir, step closer to Mrs. Millerson."

Henry pressed in at Margaret's side.

"There we go. That looks nice." Jake stepped behind the camera and lifted a hand in the air. "On the count of three. One. Two. Three."

The camera clicked and a bright flash blinded Margaret.

"Let me take another." Jake stepped behind the camera again and counted down. Another flash captured the moment.

The group relaxed and chattered to one another.

"Thank you, folks. I'll be sure to send a print over to the parsonage for the pastor and his wife to share." Jake folded up his tripod and went home.

Margaret left the group and hastened across the lawn to put the finishing touches on the meal. Logan's mother, his sister Tillie, and Julia helped her transport the food dishes to the church where plenty of room gave the families space to sit at tables and enjoy each other's company while they ate.

"Do you need any help packing and preparing to leave this afternoon?" Julia asked as Margaret shared a table with her, Arthur, Henry, and Fran.

Margaret paused in cutting her meat. "I've decided not to return to Chicago today."

Julia frowned. "Why?"

Margaret shrugged. "Karen still needs me. I don't know how to explain, but the twins require so much care, and then there's the cooking and the laundry. I don't know how Karen will manage it all."

"How much longer do you plan to stay?" This question came from Arthur.

"I'm not sure." Margaret resisted the temptation to believe she'd reverted to the age of a five-year-old. This conversation, along with the disdainful expressions of her family, had the power to make it happen.

"What about the tea for the philharmonic society on Tuesday? Surely you don't want to miss it." Fran took a turn at frowning at her.

"No, I don't, but I may have to." The one disadvantage to prolonging her stay in Oswell City was the fact that she'd miss out on time spent with her friends at social engagements. She hated to cancel, but the well-being of Karen and her family imposed greater importance.

She looked around the table and drew in a deep breath. "Give me another week. One more with week Karen, and then I will feel ready to return home."

"We need you in Chicago. My children miss you." Julia's statements spoke volumes of the group's disapproval of her decision.

Margaret gulped in some air. "I'll miss them too. I love spending time with your family. But Karen still needs my help. If you could have seen the state of her house yesterday afternoon when your train arrived, you'd understand."

"We do understand. Karen didn't expect twins. Two newborns are a lot of work. But does that mean you'd give up your life in Chicago to stay here?" Julia's voice held a pronounced note of impatience.

The question pounded Margaret's brain. Would she have to give up her life in Chicago to stay here? The answer had better be a resounding *no*. But it stayed with her, haunting her with the possibility that the arrival of these new grandsons might somehow change her life.

She cleared her throat. "I'm not planning on giving up anything. All I want to do is stay a little longer until Karen is better able to handle the work on her own. Like I said, it's just one more week."

Julia peered at her but resumed eating. Fran still frowned. The men stayed silent. Margaret failed to interpret the meaning in their indifference. Would her decision to stay with Karen upset Henry? Maybe he would refuse to accept her choices and withdraw his generosity toward her. Would he go so far as to no longer welcome her into his home?

The idea stole her breath. But that was silly. Henry loved Karen and her new sons. He would want to see Margaret involved in Karen's life. For now, she'd stay. She and Henry would have to work out at a later time any tensions that developed.

She ate her meal in silence while Henry and Arthur ventured into a new topic of conversation. As soon as she finished eating, she'd find Karen and Logan and tell them of her decision. She could believe they would welcome the assistance her extended stay offered them.

7

Margaret followed the hallway to the pastor's study. Voices floated through the open door. She entered and discovered Karen and Logan standing behind his desk deep in conversation. Their words broke off and they both turned to look at her.

"Are you ready to go, Mother?" Karen asked as she backed away from Logan.

"That's what I came to talk to you about." Margaret heaved in a deep breath.

"What's wrong?" Logan studied her.

"Nothing is wrong. I've decided to stay in Oswell City another week. You still need help, and I don't feel I can leave you with so much work. Margaret smoothed the sides of her skirt and held her breath. "If you don't mind, I'd like to occupy your guest room for a few more days."

Karen exchanged a meaningful look with her husband. A grin pulled at his mouth, and he winked at her. She turned back to Margaret with a flush on her cheeks and a smile on her lips.

"Logan and I were just now discussing this very issue. Logan received another invitation to speak about the outreach at the orchard, and I'd like to go with him to talk about my classroom.

We'd only be gone overnight, but we would leave the twins at home. Your decision to stay is the perfect solution."

Margaret grew short of breath and her eyes widened. Karen wanted to leave her alone with two babies for a whole day and night. She couldn't possibly take over their full care alone.

She gulped in some air. "Ah, when would you leave?"

"Tomorrow afternoon. We'd return home on Tuesday." Logan rounded the corner of his desk.

"What will John and Simon eat?" Margaret glanced at Karen while she failed to keep the alarm out of her voice.

"I will leave bottles for you. Dr. Kaldenberg has been working with the twins on sucking from a bottle. You shouldn't have any problems getting them to eat." Karen's voice held excitement over this, her first excursion out of town since the arrival of the twins.

Her announcement made the situation a little more attractive, but Margaret couldn't think what she would do if something went wrong, or she ran out of milk for Simon and John to eat. "How long will you be gone on Tuesday?"

"We should easily return by noon." Logan gathered up his Bible and pages of notes.

Karen's arrival midday meant Margaret would only have the morning feeding to complete alone. Two in the night and one the evening before should make the proposition quite manageable. She'd have no one but herself to fix breakfast for on Tuesday, and the laundry could wait until later in the week. That cleared her schedule and left her with hours and hours to spend holding babies. She could do that.

"I'd love to take care of Simon and John while you are gone."

"Oh, thank you, Mother. I'll have everything ready. You won't have any reason to worry one bit." Karen hugged her.

THAT AFTERNOON, Margaret went with Logan and Karen to the hotel. In her room on the second floor, Julia packed suitcases. Ben pulled articles of clothing back out again causing more work and strain for Julia. She scolded him, which only brought tears from both of her children. Margaret took the boys downstairs and soothed them with a storybook she found in the lobby.

Logan's family descended the stairs ready for travel. He drove them to the train station while Arthur carried luggage and stacked it near the sofa where Margaret sat. The family was ready and waiting when Logan returned. He loaded them up, along with Margaret, and drove to the train station.

"Are you sure you don't want to come with us?" Julia asked after they entered the building. Arthur's furrowed brow reinforced the question.

Margaret drew in a breath. "I'm sure. You may expect me at home next Sunday."

Julia sobered for a moment but her cheery disposition soon took over. "Good-bye, Mother. Enjoy those new babies."

Margaret hugged her as the train arrived with its shrill whistle piercing the air. She followed them as they hustled out to the platform. They found their car and boarded. Margaret stood at Logan's side and waved when the train moved. In minutes, her Chicago family was speeding eastward. The empty tracks stretched far to the horizon. People scattered. Silence fell.

Logan wrapped his arm around her. "Do you wish you were with them?"

"A little." She must give an honest answer, but she wanted to stay here with Karen too. Her life might always feel this way now that she had grandchildren in two different states.

She looked up at Logan. "I'm not sorry I stayed behind. Thanks for keeping me around."

Logan chuckled. "We should be thanking you. Karen felt pretty overwhelmed. She didn't know what she was going to do without you."

Margaret went with him to the buggy. She loved knowing

Karen needed her, but one more week might not be long enough. Margaret might find leaving as difficult next Sunday as it would have been today. She tried to ignore the knot forming in her stomach as she rode back to the parsonage with Logan.

MONDAY AFTERNOON, Karen hustled around the house as she gathered items for the suitcase, set out supplies for baby care, and gave Margaret instructions.

Margaret's confidence had risen overnight and now she was convinced she could take on anything. "I'll be fine, my dear. You go with Logan and enjoy yourself. Don't even think about me or the babies."

Karen gave her a brief, humored glance, offered a hug, and raced out the door with her husband. Margaret turned back to the room where two infants lay on a quilt on the floor. Peace would reign for another hour until one of them got hungry. She'd better get her own meal now. Margaret hastened to the kitchen and fixed a plate of food.

Darkness descended on the house when she finished her meal, so Margaret experimented with lighting a fire in the fireplace. The entire evening stretched before her in which to enjoy the cozy parlor on a chilly spring evening, and a fire would provide the perfect touch. Just like on those evenings in Chicago when Henry read the paper, Fran read books, and Margaret worked on her needlepoint. She'd brought some along. She should get it out and stitch after the twins were fed.

One of them fussed when she returned from the bedroom, right on time for the evening feeding. She picked him up. The baby who cried was Simon. She'd learned to know which baby she held because his chin had a different shape from John's. John had a bit more hair and straighter eyebrows.

She made her way to the kitchen to heat a bottle. John started fussing before Simon had begun to eat, and he cried all the way through his brother's meal. Margaret could do nothing but let him cry.

A knock came on the door. Margaret rolled her eyes. Of all the times to entertain a caller. They would have to show up right when she was busy feeding a baby and the other twin demanded attention.

"Come in!" she yelled as loud as she could. Simon startled at Grandma's sharp voice and John cried harder.

The knock came again.

"Come in." Her invitation probably didn't travel to the ears of the person outside any better than it did the first time. She gave up. The caller would just have to make their own decision if they wanted to risk entry or not.

The person must have decided a visit was worth the effort because the doorknob turned, the door opened, and Matthew Kaldenberg entered the house.

Margaret's heart stopped and her eyes grew wide. "Why, Dr. Kaldenberg! Good evening."

A smile crossed his face. Such a pleasant, reassuring smile. She wouldn't mind making it appear again sometime.

"Good evening, Mrs. Millerson. I want to check on the babies. This was the soonest I could get here, and I'm sorry to have missed Mrs. De Witt."

"She and Logan left a couple of hours ago, but if you'd like to start your examination with John, he's ready for some attention."

The doctor picked John up and went to the kitchen. From the sounds that filtered into the parlor, Margaret guessed he heated a bottle of milk like she had done. Minutes later, he came to the parlor and took a seat in a chair on the other side of the fireplace. They sat together in the cozy firelight feeding babies as if they had done so for years.

Once John settled down, the doctor glanced at Margaret. "I'm surprised to find you still in town. I thought I remember hearing at the picnic that you were planning to leave yesterday."

Margaret smiled. "I was. But Karen still needs so much help. I decided to stay another week."

The doctor nodded. "Fine idea. I'm sure your daughter appreciates your extended stay. She's blessed to have a mother like you."

His praise brought a flush to Margaret's cheeks. "Thank you. I wonder if one more week is long enough. Karen's whole life has changed. She needs more assistance than what a few more days can give her. I wish she and Logan were wealthy enough to afford a nurse and a maid."

"Hmm. Help like that would certainly make life easier. You must be used to servants in the home." He gave her a thoughtful glance.

"Not always. I've had them ever since I moved in with my brother and his wife. But before that, I lived a life similar to Karen's." She paused and looked around the homey parlor. The furniture in Logan's former bachelor pad he and Karen now called home appeared more elegant than the furnishings of the parsonage she had made into a home. The women of Oswell City possessed good taste and beautifully decorated Logan's home when he came to town five years ago.

"You were a minister's wife?" The question carried a tone of deep interest.

Margaret nodded. "I was, but not anymore."

"What happened?" her visitor asked in a low voice.

She drew in a deep breath. Reliving the past was not an activity she looked for reasons to engage in. "My husband committed a crime. The offering stayed in the church building overnight until he could take it to the bank on Monday morning. A local gang attempted to rob the church, but my husband was able to prevent it." Margaret glanced at Matthew, "Over time, they grew more dangerous in their attempts to get the church's money. I'm glad that Simon didn't want to put me and our two daughters in danger by bringing the money home with him, but at times I wondered if he should have, because then I could have helped him stay out of trouble."

Matthew still looked interested so Margaret continued. "The gang threatened Simon's life. He gave them a percentage of the offering each week so they would leave him alone. He fell into gambling to make up the difference. I didn't know anything about it until a man he owed visited our house. Simon couldn't pay him, so the man had him investigated."

The doctor watched her with a sympathetic look on his face. How uncanny that she could sit here with this man and spill to him her life story. Maybe it was due to the effect of the firelight dancing on their faces and warming the room. Or maybe the fact that they both fed newborns brought them closer together.

"Simon lost his ministry and went to jail. My brother paid his bail and gave him a sales job in his steel company. But Simon got sick and lingered in suffering for several years. He died when Karen was in high school. Julia got married. Her husband is a lawyer in Chicago."

"I'm sorry you've had a difficult time, Mrs. Millerson." The doctor lifted John to his shoulder to pat the baby's back.

"Please call me Margaret." This man had heard too much of her pain to stay on formal terms.

"Then you may call me Matthew." His smile came out again.

Getting him to smile might prove easier than she expected. Maybe using his name would bring it out more often.

"I lost my spouse too." His simple comment solidified their camaraderie.

"I'm sorry to hear that."

"She died twenty years ago in childbirth. I lost her and our child." His voice held a tremor.

"Such a tragedy." Margaret couldn't imagine how she would have continued to live if Julia or Karen had died with their father.

"It was. Her death prompted my decision to become a

doctor. Now I can help others avoid the loss of their loved ones." He settled John on his lap looking him over as he talked.

"I commend you." Simon had finished his bottle and dozed in Margaret's arms as she rocked.

"Thanks. But you know what kept me going?"

She shook her head.

"I've always wanted to fly. I learned about flight in college and I enjoy reading about the inventors of flying machines." Matthew laid John down on the blanket and came to Margaret's chair.

She looked up at him. "Flying machines!" The idea of anyone leaving the ground and putting themselves at the mercy of one of those flimsy flying contraptions made her nauseous. And here the respected and dignified town doctor wanted one. She didn't dare to express her thoughts on the matter. He might tuck his smile away and never allow her to see it again.

"I've been saving money, and I saw the model I want to buy at an exhibition I attended last week." He reached to take John from her arms.

"An exhibition?" His seriousness on the subject and his nearness flustered her. He must go back to his chair and give her space to breathe and to think.

He straightened and looked down at her. A hint of insecurity hung on his face, sort of like a small boy in search of his mother's approval. "Do you think I'm crazy?"

Her reflex response pressed her to tell him he was out of his mind. But she couldn't blame him for wanting to pursue a death-defying hobby after enduring the losses in his life. This dream of flying had probably kept the poor man sane all these years. Why, in those months after Simon's arrest, Margaret would have taken to jumping off cliffs if it would have anchored her world in sanity.

She stood and faced him. Her hand rested on his shoulder, and she imagined she looked like Logan did whenever he pronounced a benediction over his congregation. "Matthew, you are not crazy. Rather, I think you are quite brave. It makes perfect sense to me that anyone who fights death in their chosen profession on earth would want to face it down in the sky. Buy your flying machine but promise me one thing."

Matthew frowned. "What's that?"

"Take me for a ride." Margaret couldn't believe those words had come out of her mouth. But in the next instant, she knew why she said them. A beautiful smile blossomed on Matthew's face. It wiped away the creases of concern and grief, making him look happy and at ease.

"Margaret, you have a deal." He reached out his free hand and shook one of hers.

Her stomach fluttered. Someday she would leave the ground and put herself at the mercy of a flimsy flying machine. Oh, dear. What had she done?

She'd made Matthew smile, that's what she'd done. Any daredevil feats she must survive made that one accomplishment worthwhile.

8

Margaret paused her ironing and checked the meat Karen had cooking for the evening meal. Logan was due home from the church at any minute, so Karen worked at setting the table.

The past few days had passed at a swift pace in an uninterrupted pattern of morning breakfasts, trips to the market, naps and feedings for babies, meal preparation, and laundry. Margaret wanted to finish the wash and the ironing so Karen would not have to think about them for several days. Her official departure date to Chicago lay only three days away, and she did not want to leave any incomplete work behind.

Logan entered the house and shrugged out of his coat. He went to Karen and placed a kiss on her mouth. Margaret moved far enough away she could no longer see them through the doorway, but she still caught pieces of their conversation as they talked about Logan's day. Margaret filled a serving bowl with vegetables and dished up the meat. They gathered at the table, and Logan prayed to begin the meal.

"I had a meeting this afternoon with Gretta Barnaveldt," Logan announced as he cut his meat. "You know she organizes the summer Bible school program."

Karen nodded.

"Her committee would like to move classes over to the orchard this year."

"Why?" Karen asked.

"They think a location in the country would provide the children with more space for their outdoor activities."

Karen considered the information. "They've used the church yard in the past. Sometimes the games spilled over onto our lawn."

"Right," Logan said around a bite of food. "Gretta said the committee feels the orchard's larger lawn would be better suited, and you already have a classroom out there."

"But don't they need more than one classroom? Where will they put the various age groups?" Karen spoke while she cut her meat.

"Gretta wants to keep everyone in the same group, sort of like the country school you taught." Logan grinned at her.

"Does that mean she needs fewer teachers?" Karen asked.

"No, I don't think so. She said the children will still meet with teachers for the lesson time, but they might use the porch and the large dining room. Maybe she will even take them outside for their lessons if the weather stays dry."

"Is she still planning on the same schedule as last year?" Karen asked.

"I believe so. Three weeks in June, meeting Monday through Thursday in the morning. She asked me to check with you to see if you wanted the fourth-grade class again." Logan glanced up at Karen.

"I enjoyed teaching Bible School last summer, but now that the twins have been born, I'm not sure I can this year." Disappointment edged Karen's voice.

"Think it over. You might feel ready to get involved again by that time, and I'd like to see you do it if you can find someone to care for Simon and John on those mornings." Logan took his second helping of mashed potatoes as he talked.

Margaret ate the rest of her meal and helped clean up the kitchen. The information Logan shared ran through her mind. She agreed with him. Karen should get involved again, not just in the Bible school, but in the singing on Sunday mornings and the various events of the Ladies Mission Society. But Karen couldn't leave the twins and the housework for her teaching and leadership roles. Everyone in the house knew the frequency of the infants' demands and the unending load of work she carried to run the household.

An idea took shape. She excused herself from the house and took a walk down the street in order to analyze this new thought and determine if it was any good.

Margaret could stay another month and help Karen through the weeks of the Bible school. By the end of June, the twins would be two months old. Sleeping and eating should go smoother for Karen by that time so she could take on more of the additional work.

But Margaret would miss so much in Chicago. Fran relied on her to co-host the fundraisers for the art center during June. Her sister-in-law would have to find another helper if Margaret stayed in Oswell City. And then there was Julia's family. They spent so many evenings at the Millersons' for dinner or went out with them on afternoon excursions to the lake or the park. Margaret was constantly in the company of her daughter's family during the summer months.

And what about Henry? Would her decision upset him? Maybe she should go home.

She sat on a park bench. She must think this through. Julia had a cook, a housekeeper, and a maid. Her family could keep going without Margaret's presence. Margaret would miss seeing them and spending time with them, but they could get along without her.

So could Fran. Her household staff was even larger than Julia's. Plus, Fran had many acquaintances in her social circle to choose from for assistance at the art center.

Karen's situation was completely different. No housekeeper or cook. No maid. Only her mother. Karen and Logan could not keep going without her. For as much as that fact meant to her, Margaret would still love to see Karen live up to her social class. Sure, her furniture was stylish, and the parsonage well maintained, but sometimes Margaret believed Karen and Logan lived just one step away from poverty.

Simon had ministered in the city, where resources and affluence abounded. He'd nurtured the connections that assured him comfort and stability were never far away. But Logan ministered here on the Iowa prairie in a tiny town dependent on the profits of the farming community. Not even the Ellenbroeks or the Koelmans, whom citizens considered the wealthiest families in town, possessed the riches of some who had belonged to Simon's congregation.

Margaret had never been in a situation like this before. She'd helped Logan plant the garden last week, and in her mind the project was entertainment. It had been for fun, like an evening at the theater or the pillows she embroidered for decoration.

As she sat thinking, she realized the haunting truth that for Logan and Karen, the garden was their survival. Without it, they would not eat those foods. This was the situation for everyone here. The people out in the country lived on their own ability to plant and harvest. But, the people in town relied on them, more vulnerable in a way, than those who farmed.

Margaret shuddered as she stood and paced the sidewalk. This small-town life loomed harsh and cruel. She struggled with a moment of hatred. Her daughter should not have to battle these forces. Neither should Logan. But they were happy, and from what Margaret could see, doing quite well together.

Her heart swelled. She was proud of them, earning the respect of the town and adjusting with such grace to the changes a multiple birth thrust upon them. They had each other, and that relationship was probably what strengthened them for the struggle.

She paced one more lap from the bench to the street corner and back again. Her own struggles and hates solved the problem for her. She may not favor Karen's circumstances, but neither did she want to abandon her daughter in them. Margaret pulled her coat tighter around her and returned to the house.

Karen sat on the sofa in the parlor with Simon lying on his back on her lap. Logan sat next to her with his arm around her. They both made silly faces at the baby while he waved his arms around in the air. The worries of survival did not threaten here, not in this space or at this time. Joy reigned and lured her to stay within its shelter.

Both of them looked up. Logan made a silly face at her until his laugh broke through.

"Come on, Logan, knock it off," Karen teased him as she landed a playful punch on his arm. "Mother, you look like you've been traumatized. What's wrong?"

Margaret sucked in a deep breath and claimed a chair. "I've made a decision."

Logan sobered and studied her.

"I'd like to see you get out again, Karen, as Logan encouraged at supper. So, I would like to stay another month and help so you can teach Bible School. Maybe you'll even be freed up enough to start helping Logan again on Sunday mornings."

The faces of both Karen and Logan brightened.

"Do you mind me staying longer and occupying the guest room?" The plan sounded brilliant out on the street, but maybe these young people had grown tired of her.

"You are always welcome, Mother," Logan said in a solemn voice.

"Yes. We would love to have you stay." Karen smiled.

"All right, then. I think I will go to the hotel and call long distance to Chicago." Margaret stood and mustered the best words to convince Fran and Henry that another extension of her stay was a good idea.

Her feet weighed a hundred pounds as they bore her down

the street. She'd learned on her previous visit to Oswell City that the village's sole operating telephone resided at the hotel. Not even the law firm or the church or City Hall had one. Her brother would fail to understand how on earth any decent business could get transacted under such circumstances.

Margaret shook her head. Progress had yet to make its way into these Iowa farmlands. And yet, maybe it had. The one telephone might represent Oswell City's interpretation of progress. At least the tiny burg had a telephone. The town could have denied its need for modern communication altogether and never installed one.

On this dubious thought, Margaret swung open the door of the hotel and approached the desk to ask for the telephone. George Brinks, the hotel owner, led her to a little room behind the desk and picked up the receiver.

"Yes, hello. Could you please connect me to Mr. Henry Millerson in Chicago? Thank you." George handed the receiver over to Margaret.

Her stomach tightened as she waited for a voice to speak on the other end. If only she didn't have to call and explain. Her change of plans changed everyone else's plans. No one from her Chicago family would welcome the abrupt halt to Margaret's involvement in their lives.

"Hello?" The housekeeper's voice answered.

"Ida. Good afternoon. It's me, Margaret." She licked her lips trying to discern how best to proceed.

"I'm so glad to hear from you. Are you still in Oswell City?"

"Yes. Could you put Fran on, please?" The tightness from Margaret's middle spread to her throat and into her voice.

"One moment." The line went silent except for scuffling in the background. Footsteps from the kitchen staff nearby likely made the noise.

"Hello. This is Fran." The smooth, cultured voice carried over the line.

"Hi, Fran. This is Margaret. I call with ... ah, another change of plans." She sucked in a breath.

"Really?" A hint of worry entered Fran's voice.

"Karen needs me until the end of June, so I've decided to stay." There. The news was out. No taking it back.

A moment of silence proceeded Fran's response. "Are you sure that is a good idea, Margaret? You do realize the art center is relying on us to plan the bazaars for their annual fundraiser. You can't possibly back out now."

"I'm afraid I'll have to." A deflated balloon couldn't feel more wilted than Margaret did at this moment.

"But who will help me?" Fran sounded nervous.

"Ask Julia or Isabel. I'm sure they would do just as good of a job as I could." Margaret glanced out the door of her semi-private quarters. A boisterous couple had just arrived at the hotel and employed a great deal of volume in securing their room. The noise distracted her and drowned out Fran's voice.

"What did you say?" Margaret frowned at the wooden box on the wall.

"I said I suppose I could check with Isabel." Fran's voice took on a defeated tone.

"Yes, start with her." Margaret nodded but then remembered Fran couldn't see her, so quit nodding. Talking into a telephone really was such a silly activity, but it did save her the time of sending a letter and waiting for the response. She could tolerate appearing foolish for the sake of this wonderful convenience.

"We'll miss you," Fran said in a soft voice.

"I know. I'll miss you too. I already do, but Karen needs me, and I don't feel right leaving her yet. You'll tell Julia, won't you?" Memories of the past summer spent in the company of Julia's young family made her eyes burn.

"I'll tell her."

"Thanks. Is Henry there? I'd like to visit with him about my decision." Margaret held her breath in anticipation of the conversation with her brother.

"He is. I'll get him." The line on Fran's end went silent for a few moments.

"Hello. This is Henry."

"Ah. Henry. Hello. It's Margaret. I wanted to talk with you because ... well, because I ah, I've decided to stay longer in Oswell City with Karen. She needs me and well, I ... um..." Margaret's words dwindled to a halt. How could she explain in a way that wouldn't alter Henry's world?

"For how long?" The words came distinct and demanding over the line.

"A month."

"That's a long time, Margaret. Are you sure?"

"Yes, I am. Karen and Logan really do have a lot of work caring for two newborns. They have no servants in the way of a maid or a nurse, you know. Only me. I'm sorry I won't be coming home for a while. I hope you aren't upset with me." Margaret drew in another deep breath.

"Upset? Why would I be upset?" Henry's bewildered voice carried over the line bringing her a measure of relief. At least he wasn't angry.

"Well, because of the change. My absence affects you and Fran. I wish there was something I could do about it, but there isn't." Margaret fought a slump in her shoulders.

"Things will be much different here without you. Fran and I will miss you dreadfully. But I'm more concerned about you making a good decision. If you are sure Oswell City is where you need to be, then Fran and I will accept it."

"Really?"

"Of course, Margaret. Did you think I wouldn't allow it?"

"No. I just ... well ... I thought maybe ... I mean you have been so accommodating of me by sharing your home with me that I thought, well, that you would change your mind if I didn't come back." Margaret's chest heaved. Confessing her worst fears to her brother required much effort.

"You thought I'd go back on my offer of providing a home for you?" Henry sounded offended.

"I did."

"Oh, Margaret. You'll always have a home with me for as long as you want it. That is one thing that will never change."

"Thank you. I didn't mean to hurt you."

"It's all right. Just promise you'll keep in touch."

"I will. Good-bye, Henry."

"Good-bye." He hung up.

Margaret returned the black receiver to its place on the side of the wooden box and stood staring at the wall. That was that. One phone call, and she'd committed herself to spend the loveliest month of the summer in a tiny town separated from her home and the majority of her family.

She turned, thanked the man at the desk for the use of the telephone, and trudged to the parsonage. Even though Karen's hospitality awaited, a heavy cloak of loneliness settled over her. Maybe this was how Simon had felt on that long-ago day when the city police escorted him away to prison.

9

Matthew sat to the right of his friend Artie at the monthly meeting of the consistory. He looked forward to these times of planning and decision-making for the congregation of Oswell City Community Church with Pastor Logan and businessmen from town. In his medical practice, he treated the physical conditions of Oswell City residents. As a member of this group of leaders, he had the chance to address their spiritual health too.

Tonight's meeting had already covered the topics of the financial status of the orchard, maintenance of the church yard through the summer, and the plans for the upcoming Bible school session. Those topics out of the way, Logan turned the conversation to the approaching weekend.

"The next item on our agenda is the start of the summer city band schedule." Logan wrote on the paper in front of him and glanced at the group. "Paul, can you tell us more?"

The mayor straightened. "I'd be happy to. As you've seen in the paper, the city council has voted to build a new bandstand in the downtown square."

Murmurs of acknowledgement ran around the group. Brief

glances at Jake, the newspaper's editor, accompanied the recognition of the familiar topic.

Paul cleared his throat. "Until then, the band must perform on the small stage the school lets us borrow. These summer months are a good time to generate excitement for the project since it is still in need of some funding.

"The city council wants to promote the Oswell City band with weekly concerts in the square. The first concert is scheduled for Friday night. Alex is planning to supply doughnuts and pastries for the event. I am going to give a short speech as introduction to the concert. The city council would like to borrow the hymn books out of the sanctuary for the band to use. I'd like to request permission from all of you for use of this music. The books will get returned promptly after the concert. I already confirmed this with the director."

Logan tapped his pencil on the table as he looked at the group. "What do you think?"

George shrugged. "I don't see why not."

The others at the table responded in favor of Paul's request. Logan made more notes on his paper.

Paul smiled. "Thank you. I'll let the band director know. There's one more thing I'd like to ask."

Some of the men frowned in curiosity. Others leaned forward.

"Several of you have played in the marching band for the Fourth of July parade, and I'd like to invite you to join the city band for their summer concerts. If you could at least be on hand for the first concert, that would give the group strong support. I understand why you'd rather put a group together for an occasional parade instead of committing to a weekly performance, but the town could use you on Friday night."

"When will you rehearse?" Logan asked.

"Wednesday evening for two hours," Paul said.

The men turned to their neighbors and discussed the invitation all over again. Matthew listened to Artie declare how he hadn't picked up a sheet of instrumental music since last summer. Like the others, he'd be a little out of practice.

The conversation died down, but James Koelman eyed Matthew from across the table. "Hey, Dr. Kaldenberg. You play an instrument, too, don't you?"

Matthew shrugged. "I play the trombone a bit. I picked it up in college, but I fear I'm not very good. Like Artie, I haven't read the notes to a Sousa march for at least a year."

James waved his hand to dismiss the comments. "We're all rusty. You should join us Friday night."

His suggestion received immediate and anonymous approval.

Matthew's chest threatened to puff up. How nice that his friends wanted him to join them in this community event. But he had a conflict in his schedule.

"Thanks for the invite, James, but I'm afraid I'm going to have to turn you down." The calm tone of his voice barely covered the excitement rolling around inside him.

"You expecting some sort of emergency on Friday?" George asked.

"No, I'm actually headed to Dayton." Matthew leaned back in his chair.

George's eyebrows rose. "As in the Ohio Dayton?"

Matthew nodded.

"You must have to attend some sort of medical conference or listen to lectures out there." Alex gestured in a general eastward direction.

Matthew drew in a deep breath. "No. I'm actually paying a visit to the Wright Brothers' factory. I've decided to purchase a biplane." He failed to keep the smile from stretching across his face.

"A what?"

"You can't be serious."

"You'll kill yourself."

The exclamations of disbelief were spoken simultaneously.

Matthew stole a glance at Logan. An expression of worry tainted with disapproval hung on his features.

Matthew's stomach pricked. The pursuit of his dream shouldn't have to come at the high price of Logan's disappointment. His good opinion meant too much to Matthew.

In a special, secret way, he looked upon Logan as a son. If his wife had lived and they'd had more children, the younger ones would have been close to Logan's age. Matthew liked to observe him and imagine a son of his own in service to the town, satisfied in his marriage, and starting a family.

The look in Logan's eyes told him much persuasion must take place before the local minister believed the purchase of a biplane was a good plan.

Matthew opened his mouth to get to work on the persuading, but questions were fired at him and cut him off.

"How did you ever come up with the idea of buying an airplane?" Alex's voice held a tone of disgust.

"Yeah. Don't you read the paper? Don't you know of the smash-ups, the crashes, the deaths?" Jake grew more dramatic with each word as though his newspaper served as the ultimate authority on the subject of flying.

"How are you gonna afford it?" This came from George.

"Where are you going to store it?" Paul fired off that question.

"No one else I know has an airplane." James's tone of voice matched the others. Together they told him, under all their questions, that he was a fool to consider such a purchase.

Matthew inhaled a long slow stream of air. This surely must be how Noah felt on the day he broke the news to his friends and neighbors of the ark taking shape in his dreams. He hardly knew where to begin in defense against the skeptics. Facts were his best ally. Like in those moments when he had to deliver sad news of chronic illness to families, he let the facts speak for him. The others in the room were free to respond as they pleased.

"Earlier this month I attended an exhibition at the Clear

Brook Fairgrounds. The Wright Model B was one of the planes that flew in the show. I'm going to purchase one. It is the first of their airplanes being built in quantity. I'm leaving town on Thursday to enroll in flying school. I'll take lessons while the plane is getting built. I've arranged for a doctor from Clear Brook to be available to you in my absence." Matthew caught his breath after the lengthy explanation. He had run out of facts, so folded his hands on the table and fell silent.

For a moment, silence penetrated the entire room. Then George broke it with a low whistle. "You'll spend a powerful lot of money on that thing. Are you sure you want to go through with it?"

Silence reigned for a few more moments.

"When can we expect you to come home?" Logan asked in a quiet voice.

"I'll be gone for about a month," Matthew said.

Logan's mouth scrunched off to the side of his face as he shifted in his chair. "Is there any other business for tonight?"

No one responded. The invasion of an airplane and the associated risk of flight had removed everyone's minds far from financial statements, Bible school schedules, and the task of filling up the band.

"All right then, let's pray to close this meeting." Logan bowed his head to talk to the Lord.

Matthew and the others followed his lead.

THE NEXT AFTERNOON, Matthew called on an older woman who had suffered a stroke. The right side of her body had forgotten how to move. Her speech came in spurts with much effort. The woman's mouth drooped, and she lounged on her bed, propped against pillows. She winced when Matthew bent the knee of her right leg with tender movements.

"You're doing well, Mrs. Van Kley. See if you can get that leg to bend a little farther." Matthew spoke as he kept pressure on the limb.

The woman closed her eyes as if all her concentration channeled into the dormant leg.

Logan sat on the other side of the bed. The Van Kley family had called him to come regularly during the week for visits. He and Matthew crossed paths often in the homes of the sick and the elderly. They worked in partnership bringing wholeness and healing to those who suffered.

Matthew continued his treatment on Mrs. Van Kley for fifteen more minutes and then packed away his supplies. Logan prayed with the woman while Matthew slipped out of the house and untied his horse.

Logan caught him in the yard just as he was ready to mount the first step into his buggy. "Doctor," he called and hastened across the lawn.

Matthew brought his foot down to join his other one in the grassy yard.

Logan reached the place where he stood. "I've been hoping to talk to you."

"Yes?" Matthew tossed his bag onto the buggy seat.

"This trip you are planning to take and the purchase you intend to make. Are you sure it is wise?" Logan crossed his arms and studied Matthew like a father expressing concern over a wayward son.

Matthew might as well have been a child in that moment. He gulped in some air to fight the sense of utter foolishness settling over him. "Wise? No, probably not. Necessary? Definitely."

Logan frowned. "I don't understand."

Matthew lifted his gaze to the blue spring sky overhead. A formation of geese flying north sailed above him. The freedom and grace with which they moved tickled his heart. Someday he would join those soaring geese in his own freedom of flight.

"Twenty years has passed since I lost my wife and child. For many years, I have been saving and dreaming and trying to hang on to my sanity. I never turned into a drinking man, although at times, it would have been a comfort. The goal of flying kept me alive. It's kept me sober, and it's given me the heart to be the doctor to this town. I have to do it, Logan." He whispered the last words and ventured a glimpse of the younger man's face.

Logan's eyes took on a layer of moisture. He was sympathetic enough to understand the devastating loss of a wife and baby. He was also in love enough to feel the pain of such a loss right along with Matthew.

"Then go. Buy your plane. Take the lessons. Come back to us and show us what buoyancy looks like." Logan spoke in a quiet voice weighted with the solemnity that came with a formal occasion.

The words trickled way down into a deep crevice of his stiff heart. This is exactly what he wanted to do. He wanted to rise above the pains and struggles that had dragged him down for so long. This young man's belief that Matthew could achieve this floating state brought a layer of moisture to his own eyes.

Logan still gazed at him as if the lightness and cheer of rising above stood a chance of penetrating Matthew's spirit too. A great rush of air left his lungs. Marvel of marvels if buoyancy, lightness, and cheer could someday describe the soul of Doctor Matthew Kaldenberg.

"Be careful." Logan switched out of his solemn mood and into his good-natured one. He rewarded Matthew with a grin and went to his buggy.

Matthew watched him leave. Logan's words struck him as a sort of commission. Matthew would take them seriously. He would buy that plane, and he would excel at the lessons. Then he would come back and demonstrate with his plane and in his life exactly what rising above could do for a man.

On his last night in town, Matthew took a break from packing his suitcase. He'd thought of everything to prepare the town for his absence, but there was one more call he must make. A stroll down Main Street and a turn onto Fifth Street brought him to the De Witt home.

He knocked.

Karen answered.

"Good evening. Is your mother home?"

"She is. Please come in." Karen gestured to the parlor as indication that he should follow her.

"No, thank you. I'll wait here." The dusky shadows of the entryway provided the perfect haven in which to share his travel plans.

"Matthew?" Margaret approached him with concern in her eyes.

"Nothing is wrong. I've been packing, and I wanted you to know my plans."

Her brows rose. "Packing? You're leaving?"

"Only for a month." He grasped her arm and brought her near.

"But why? Where?"

"Remember that flying machine I told you about? I'm going to Huffman Prairie in Dayton, Ohio, to learn how to fly it." A smile tugged at his mouth.

Margaret's hands shot to her cheeks. "You are?"

"Yes, but I regret that this is the last time I'll see you. I won't be home again until long after you are gone to the city." He gazed at her until he had every feature of her face memorized.

"Oh." Margaret pressed her fingers to her lips. "No, Matthew, there's been a change in my plans. I'm extending my stay so I can care for the twins while Karen teaches a Bible school class."

"So, you'll still be here when I return." His chest expanded.

"I should." A tremulous smile settled on her lips.

"You've promised me a ride." He spoke in a quiet voice.

"I'll look forward to it." Her smile grew wider.

"Good-bye, Margaret." Matthew nodded to her and left the house.

A mix of emotions churned on his insides as he walked home. Margaret wasn't leaving town at the end of the week. He'd have a chance to take her for a ride in his new biplane. But he'd miss out on all that time he could have spent with her. Where might their relationship go if he didn't have to travel to Dayton?

Matthew couldn't think about that now. He'd already committed to flying school. But how he hated leaving Margaret behind. If only he could pursue two interests at once. Maybe after he'd achieved success in the world of flight, he'd have the chance to do the same with Margaret.

10

Thursday morning, Matthew boarded the train and headed east to Ohio. Thoughts of those he'd left behind filled his mind as the sprouted cornfields rolled away from the speeding coach. Four weeks was a long time for him to be gone. Mrs. Van Kley may not keep up on her exercise regimen. The Haverkamp baby might decide to come early, or some disease may sweep through town before his return.

Matthew shook his head to clear it of worries. Dr. Hayes from Clear Brook had agreed to provide medical care in Matthew's absence. Millie, his housekeeper, had the contact information for the Clear Brook doctor. If anyone came to his home looking for a doctor, Millie could give them immediate directions. Dr. Hayes could also check in on Mrs. Van Kley regularly. The thought of the elderly woman having this careful attention eased Matthew's mind.

The town was in good hands, and the spring of the year with its warm weather was a good time to travel. This stretch of weeks was as good of a time as any for him to be gone. He settled into his seat and dozed until lunch time.

Later that afternoon, the train pulled into the station at Dayton. Matthew left the coach and followed the directions he'd received in a letter from the Wright Company. After making arrangements for his belongings to get delivered to the hotel where he'd reserved a room, he walked downtown and checked in. Just enough time remained in the day for him to catch his evening meal and unpack, so he spent the evening hours settling into his room.

The next morning, he followed West Third Street to the site of the Wright Company. Once inside, he discovered a man at a desk bent over a stack of papers. The man looked up at the sound of the door clicking shut.

"Good morning. I'm Matthew Kaldenberg from Iowa. I've come to confirm the order of my Model B biplane, and to register for flying school."

The man behind the desk smiled as he stood up and held out his hand for a shake. "Welcome to Dayton, Mr. Kaldenberg. I'm Grover Loening, the manager of this factory."

Matthew nodded and accepted the handshake.

Mr. Loening shifted his concentration onto the stack of papers on the desk. "I believe I saw your paperwork come through earlier this week. Ah, yes. Here it is." He shuffled through the stack and then held a lone sheet in the air. "Please sign on this line right here." Mr. Loening indicated the place where Matthew should sign and handed him a pen.

Matthew skimmed through the document and wrote his name in the designated line.

Mr. Loening watched him. "Wonderful. I'll file it away here for Orville to take a look at. Now, if you will come this way, we'll begin with a tour of the factory. It is important for all aviators of Wright Brothers airplanes to possess the most thorough knowledge of their machines as possible. That begins with an understanding of the assembly process."

Matthew followed the confident manager into the first room. Men worked with torches welding various metal pieces together. Next, Mr. Loening showed him where the propellers were made. From there, they moved on through the woodworking shop, the assembly areas, and finally to the noisy motor testing room.

"I see more students are here," Mr. Loening said when they returned to the main corridor.

Matthew glanced at two official-looking men in military uniforms. A chill broke out over his skin. He should have known he'd attend flying school with officers from the army. Articles on the military's growing interest in flight appeared regularly in the newspaper Jake printed each week for Oswell City.

Mr. Loening stepped behind the desk and asked for signatures like he'd done with Matthew. "Fine." Mr. Loening glanced over the signatures and added the papers to his file. "We will take a tour of the factory now. All of you should be ready for a bus to pick you up at the hotel at 1:30 to catch a ride out to Huffman Prairie for your first flying lesson."

Matthew nodded and left the building. His pulse raced and his steps hurried down the street. To think he would finally learn how to fly! A life's worth of dreams was about to transpire right before his eyes.

THREE HOURS LATER, he shared a bus with the two army officers, a banker from New England, and a rancher from California. All of them had traveled great distances to enter into the dazzling new world of flight.

At the flying field, Orville Wright himself met the group. "Good afternoon, men. I'm glad you are here. Training is required for all buyers of our airplanes, so I will do my best to give you as thorough of an education as I possibly can. The secret to flying is confidence. Believe in yourself, your skills, and your abilities. If you use common sense and rely on what you learn here at Huffman Prairie, you will enjoy many years as a successful and safe aviator."

A murmur of agreement ran through the students.

"Anyone can go up in the air, but true skill is necessary for coming back down. We will spend significant amounts of time practicing the landing of the biplane." Orville went on in an explanation of aerodynamics, the importance of the angle of the wings, and how curves affected speed.

Orville pointed to a Model B parked nearby and drew the group's attention to the rudders used for steering. "It is much like riding a bicycle. The machine must have balance. Watch as I hold myself upright while I steer this bicycle." Orville pulled a bicycle from a small, weathered shed behind them and demonstrated balance while he rode in circles around the students.

The bicycle had probably been built by Orville and his brother in their shop before transferring their interests over to flight.

"The winds at Kitty Hawk are much stronger than here in Dayton, so I'll show you a few tricks for a steady takeoff." Orville parked his bike and faced the group.

Matthew's heart raced. How he loved that word, *takeoff*. It rang with adventure and defiance. He couldn't wait for the day when he would feel for himself the exhilaration of leaving the ground.

The remainder of the day was spent learning about the motor. Orville insisted that the best aviators knew everything about their machines, including each detail concerning the motor. The descriptions of the moving parts appealed to Matthew's doctor mind.

A motor appeared so similar to a human body. So many moving parts that ran on a source of fuel and produced energy and power of its own. Nothing Matthew owned possessed a motor. He'd enjoy hearing its explosive noises and gliding through the sky on its power.

The next week Orville spent allowing his students to drive the biplane around on the ground at half-throttle. Matthew smiled to himself as he drove the machine through the field. Not only was he learning how to fly a plane, he was also discovering the basics of how to drive. Maybe if Martin had a good deal on a model in his showroom, Matthew might consider the possibility of owning a car.

When the week was over, Orville increased the throttle on the motor and added another propeller to the back of the biplane. Now the machine could leave the ground. Matthew spent the next several days practicing his ability to jump into the air at a height of twenty or fifty feet above the ground and coming back to earth again. Day after day, he and the other students practiced their jumps.

Then the day came when Matthew got to fly, but he went up as a passenger. Orville manned the controls and explained the function of each one while Matthew watched. He wore only a brown leather helmet on his head and tried his best to store away the information his teacher shared.

But the view and the flying sensation distracted him. The wind rushed by. Buildings, rivers, and trees appeared so tiny as they seemed to dance beneath him. His feet dangled high and free from his seat in the summer sky. He turned his face to the sun for the sheer pleasure of rising so much closer to it.

"What did you say your profession was?" Orville spoke again arresting his thoughts with a question.

"I'm a doctor." Matthew leaned in so that his answer would carry to the other man's ear above the roar of the motor.

A look of pleasure claimed Orville's face. "A doctor! Good for you. You'll do well flying. We're discovering that men with a deep sense of feeling are the most successful with their machines in the air. It's something about a sensitive touch, which is useful for managing the biplane in the atmosphere. You'll have the ability to anticipate what must be done in conditions that are always changing."

Matthew's eyebrows rose at this level of confidence his instructor placed in him. His own confidence increased. Deep feeling and a sensitive touch came natural for him. Maybe he'd do better than he expected steering a plane and using his intuition to keep it on a straight course through clouds and winds and open sky.

For a week he flew as a passenger with Orville Wright. Their group went out in the early mornings when conditions were most favorable and took turns in the passenger seat. Rain moved through, detaining the eager students on the ground for three days. Matthew borrowed a bicycle from Orville Wright and mastered his ability to maintain his balance. He rode all over town practicing his new skill. In addition to a car and a biplane, he could add the bicycle to the list of vehicles he'd learned to drive while in Dayton.

When the weather cleared, a gusty wind blew in from the north, so Orville used that time to teach the students how to set up and take apart a biplane. Matthew's mouth hung open in wonder. He'd never expected the airplane to come apart. The question of how to get the plane home to Oswell City had bothered him. He didn't know if he should try to fly it home. Finding fuel for such a long journey would cause a problem. Now he could fold his biplane up in a nifty crate and ship it home on the railroad. Such a simple solution.

Two days later, the wind died down. Orville announced the point in their training had come for them to take over the pilot's seat and fly the biplane. Matthew's turn came after both officers and the rancher. Nothing had better happen to the biplane while any of them drove it. A repair or a crash would delay his chance to put his new skills to the test.

Only a minor tune-up to the motor required attention before Matthew's turn came. He pressed his mouth shut to suppress his excitement. A debut flight required absolute and complete calm, like performing surgery or delivering a breech baby. Following Orville's instructions, he listened to the regular pops coming from the motor after the propeller had been cranked. The motor sounded strong and steady, so he waved as a signal to the fellow student to release his hold on the wing of the biplane.

The machine coasted forward. Matthew maneuvered a control and the biplane roared even louder. He covered a little more distance. The biplane bounced over the ground and lifted into the air.

Matthew held his breath as moisture gathered in the corners of his eyes. He was flying. After all these years of saving and dreaming, he was flying. An image of Margaret in her burgundy dress flashed into his mind. She'd told him he wasn't crazy. She'd asked for a ride and made him feel the happiest he'd felt in a long time. This first flight was for her. He couldn't wait to satisfy her request for a ride. If she was here in Dayton, he'd share this moment with her.

Orville complimented Matthew's abilities and directed him through a landing. Five more days of practice passed until Matthew was allowed to take the test for his Aero Club of America license. He could see the course mapped out in his mind. He must fly two series of figure eights around two pylons fifteen hundred feet apart and land each time. These two flights must exceed an altitude of two hundred feet.

He could do this. Orville handed him his helmet but stayed on the ground. Matthew must complete this mission alone with no assistance and no support if something went wrong. He claimed the seat while Orville cranked a propeller. Matthew went through the checks on the motor he'd practiced, all the while trying his best to remain calm. The plane left the ground sooner than he wanted, but he quickly applied his sensitive touch and had the biplane fully under control.

A gust of wind caught one wing as he made his first turn. After leaning to the side and maneuvering the controls, he compensated for the disturbance. Matthew took a deep breath and focused. Flying had become a part of him. All movements and use of the controls were second nature. He completed both figure eights and landings flawlessly. Orville cheered and the other students clapped. Matthew had become a competent pilot, ready to fly his own plane.

At the factory, Grover Loening handed him his license and the papers proving his ownership of a brand-new biplane. Matthew gave him the last payment due on the biplane which included the expenses he'd accumulated in flying school.

"Congratulations, Dr. Kaldenberg," he said with a broad smile on his face as he handed Matthew his papers.

The broad smile transferred to Matthew's own face. He shook hands all around with Mr. Loening and Orville Wright. Orville accompanied him to the train station and made arrangements for the biplane parts to travel safe and sound on a freight car. Matthew shook his hand once more and boarded the train.

He leaned back and thought over the past few weeks. He'd succeeded in flying school. A new plane with his address on it was going home with him. What a lot of work and what a lot of patience he'd given to this endeavor. But the freedom and sense of weightlessness far outshone the sacrifices.

The train began to move. Before long, Matthew would be at home where he could assemble his plane and fly.

11

The gown displayed in the window of Eva Synderhof's dress shop caught Margaret's attention. She'd intended to pay this boutique a visit ever since her first day in town, but the chores and baby care at Karen's house over the past weeks had kept her too busy. This morning the twins were both down for their naps, allowing Margaret a chance to shop. Since the dress shop was on her way, she could spare some extra minutes to peek inside.

After one more admiring glance at the quality work in the window, Margaret went inside. Women crowded the shop browsing the articles on the racks. Another woman visited with Eva over pattern pieces spread on the counter. A cluster of women studied bolts of material on a shelf near the window. Margaret had become acquainted with these women during her weeks in Oswell City through the weekly church services and the various groups or clubs she had joined.

Their faces brightened when they recognized her. Joanna Barnaveldt motioned for her to join in. "We are talking of the garden club meeting planned for Cornelia's house this afternoon. You should come."

The others nodded and voiced their support of Joanna's invitation.

"The garden club?" Margaret's eyebrows rose. After her experience of helping Logan plant the garden and her involvement in weeding it and tending it over the past month, any mention of the word "garden" brought to mind hours of hard work in an attempt to survive on the upcoming harvest. Margaret did not want to open her life up to any more such stresses. "I don't know, ladies. I thank you for your invitation, but I've been helping Logan tend the garden, and I don't enjoy it very much."

Grace Koelman laughed. "Oh my, Margaret. You've misunderstood. None of us wants to sit around and talk about raising vegetables. The garden club is about flowers."

"She's right," Mildred Zahn cut in. "We discuss growing them, arranging them, and planning events to display them."

Margaret loved flowers. Creating floral arrangements was one of her favorite hobbies. "I guess I could give it a try."

Joanna smiled. "I'm so glad. We meet at the Goud's this afternoon at two o'clock."

Margaret stored the information away and moved farther into the store. Her reading group at the library also planned to meet today but not until evening. She should be able to give Karen plenty of assistance during the late afternoon and supper hour.

A FEW MINUTES before two o'clock, Margaret located the Goud home a block off Main Street. Cornelia and her husband owned the jewelry store, so the short distance between the house and the business made her involvement at the store quite convenient.

Margaret knocked on the door and was admitted into a

parlor full of women. What a large club. All of the women in this town must be as fond of flowers as Margaret.

She accepted a seat near a small table with rich carvings on the legs. A crocheted doily covered the top. Margaret studied that table. She'd seen it before on past visits to the Goud home. Cornelia's Victrola usually occupied that table. She'd even played it on occasion when the other groups Margaret participated in came for an evening of recreation.

But the Victrola was gone today. Surely it hadn't broken or gotten damaged. Maybe Cornelia had loaned it to someone. Her reputation of generosity in this way supported the possibility. Even the mayor knew he could count on Cornelia to offer her Victrola for town gatherings.

Margaret dismissed the mystery and joined in the group's discussion. The current topic centered on the hydrangea display at the Fourth of July celebration.

"Again this year, we will have all vases set up on tables in a tent on the square," Clara Hesslinga announced. "If you have hydrangeas you would like to enter, add your name to the list after the meeting."

Gretta Barnaveldt held up a clipboard with a sheet of lined paper attached to it.

Fran had a row of lovely hydrangeas in the garden. Most of the shrubs bloomed white, but her gardener had discovered a solution to add to the soil to make one of the plants bloom blue petals. She'd look forward to enjoying Fran's blooms. They would be at their prime when she returned home. But it was too bad she'd no longer be here in Oswell City over the Fourth.

She'd love to see the arrangements of flowers these new friends would create straight from their own gardens. That familiar sense of feeling torn between two places crept in again. The first time she'd felt that way was due to her grandchildren living so far apart, but now she felt torn because she was making friends in this town. She had grandchildren and groups of friends in two places. She didn't know how she would ever decide where she truly belonged.

"Cornelia is also asking for a bouquet to give to the winner of the Miss Independence Day pageant. Would anyone like to contribute?" Clara scanned the group.

Lillian Ellenbroek raised her hand. Margaret had seen the beautiful rose garden behind the Ellenbroek home. If any of those lovely roses lasted until July, Miss Independence would have a gorgeous bouquet. The meeting continued with discussion of the details for both subjects that had been brought up. When the meeting drew to a close, Cornelia served tea.

Cakes, fruit, and pastries accompanied the tea, and was served with floral napkins in the colors of a spring day. The meeting and refreshment time afterward held elegance and decorum. If she were to stay any longer in Oswell City, Margaret would definitely join the garden club.

Late afternoon, she left Cornelia's house for the parsonage to help Karen with babies and the evening meal. By seven o'clock, the meal was finished, the kitchen clean, and the twins were content in the arms of their mother and father. With the household so well under control, Margaret's conscience eased about yet another club meeting in the same day.

"I'm headed to the library for my reading group. See you in a couple of hours." Margaret made her announcement to the other two adults while she positioned her hat on her head.

"Have a nice time," Karen said with her attention on the dozing baby in her arms.

Margaret left the house and strolled downtown. Hints of summer surrounded her. A rosebush rambled on a picket fence. The scent of the blossoms wafted on the warm breeze. Birds pecked at insects in the grass. A group of children laughed and called to one another as they pulled a red wagon along the sidewalk. All appeared peaceful and wholesome in this tiny town.

Funny it had the word *city* in its name. The village looked

Coming Home to Mercy

nothing like a city. The town should have the word *berg* or *crossing* in its name. Those terms better fit the size of this miniscule place.

Maybe the founders of the town hoped it would one day grow to the size of a city. Or maybe the use of a word like *city* reminded residents they could live independent, self-sufficient lives just like the people in a metropolis, even though they must also contend with the isolation characteristic of life in so vast a land.

These musings on her mind, Margaret pushed open the door of the library.

"Good evening, Mrs. Millerson." A young lady by the name of Joy Haverkamp greeted her. "I've been watching for you. I was told to stay at my desk until you arrived so I could give you the message that the reader's group is cancelled for tonight."

"Oh. I'm sorry to hear that." Margaret had managed to get her chapter read in between meal preparation and rocking babies to sleep. It was fresh in her mind, and she'd looked forward to discussing her ideas with the other group members.

"Lorraine has a sick child, so couldn't lead the group tonight. She wants to reschedule for the end of the week."

Margaret planned to travel to Chicago at the end of the week. She'd miss any more meetings of her enjoyable reader's group. She nodded to the girl and turned to retrace her path back to Karen's house. Both babies had looked ready to sleep for the night when she left, so Margaret avoided the front door and crept in through the back door in her attempt to make the least amount of noise possible.

She held the door as it swung to meet the latch in order to slow it down and muffle the sound of a slam. She paused and listened. No babies cried which meant her return home hadn't disturbed them.

Instead of baby cries filling the air, a waltz lilted through the rooms. With care, Margaret removed her hat and coat and approached the doorway to the rest of the house. Her eyes widened at the scene that gripped her attention.

Firelight flickered on the furnishings and the couple in the parlor. Logan held Karen in a tender embrace. She rested her head on his shoulder as if she found all the solace that she could ever ask for right there in his arms. They swayed together to a dance rhythm, but it didn't match the spirited strains in the air. Their rhythm flowed much slower.

Logan whispered in Karen's ear and then he kissed her forehead. Their rhythm came to a stop as Logan's kisses found the way to her mouth. The music played on. Logan led Karen back into their slow rhythm when he rested his chin on her hair.

Something in Margaret wanted to weep as she watched. She really shouldn't be watching at all, but Logan's tender care of his wife and Karen's utter trust in him arrested her. How at home they looked. How at peace and free from struggle they appeared. If only their life together could remain right here in this moment, forever.

As much as she wanted a life of ease for Karen, these sentiments didn't get to the bottom of her feelings. Margaret wanted more. This truth hadn't found her until this moment of unintended spying. Karen had something with Logan that Margaret had never had with Simon. He wouldn't have ever thought to do anything romantic for her, or to make himself so available to her as his wife that she could fully lean on him.

If only Margaret could have found that with someone who made her feel so comforted and so safe. Her marriage had brought her more loneliness than satisfaction.

Logan picked up his pace a bit and led Karen in a simple box step. Then he gave her a gentle spin but brought her right back to him. They shared a low, intimate laugh before their rhythm slowed again.

Memories of the engagement party Fran had hosted for them filled Margaret's mind. Logan had learned to waltz especially for that party. Now that Margaret thought about it, this very song was one that the orchestra played for them that evening.

Karen and her husband would have few reasons to dance in this tiny town, unless the mayor hosted a formal party. But even then, no one would expect or want their minister and his wife to know how to glide across a room to the strains of a Strauss waltz. Evenings like this one must be when Logan kept his skills in practice.

The thought sent heat burning through Margaret's cheeks. Facts and fears linked themselves together like a chain fence enclosing her. Before she could control the humiliation settling in, an entire story was locked in place telling her how life really unfolded in a town of this size. The story mocked her in her place as an outsider. If she had any question where she belonged before now, it had been cleared up with this story her mind chose to believe.

That Victrola belonged to Cornelia Goud. Logan would have had to ask to borrow it from her, and she had obviously loaned it to him. Margaret had never seen Logan and Karen dancing in the whole time she'd lived with them. This must mean they waited until she was gone to one of her social events before they felt the leisure to spend this kind of an evening together.

They knew her schedule and had help from Cornelia in planning ahead for a quiet, romantic evening together safe from any intrusion in the form of herself, the mother-in-law. This sort of thing had probably been going on ever since Margaret's first day in town, and she just happened to find out because of her premature return home due to a cancelled meeting.

If Cornelia was in on this conspiracy, then how many of the other women in town knew? Why, she'd even been to Cornelia's house that afternoon. Those other women were probably secretly laughing at her as she sat in the same room as the table with the missing Victrola. They would have known where that Victrola went. Everyone would have known except Margaret.

Heat surged through her entire body. She staggered over to

the table and claimed a chair in the shadows while the waltz lilted in its alluring call for all who heard to yield to its entertaining strains. Margaret rested her hand on her forehead. The women in that church adored her son-in-law. They would do anything to offer him assistance, right down to helping him get his wife and his home all to himself, even if just for two hours in the evening.

Maybe she really didn't have any friends in this town at all. Chicago was where she belonged. At least her hometown was a large enough place that not everyone knew everyone else's business. She'd have to step very carefully from now on. Oswell City had become a closed room to her, and for the first time in her life, she found herself locked away on the outside.

Margaret sat stiff and straight in the shadows of the kitchen as the music faded. The house went dark. All fell quiet. Only one other time in her life had utter and complete loneliness saturated her existence. It happened in the days following Simon's arrest when the truth settled in that she had two daughters to care for and no home or income.

Now it swallowed her again. Well, she would return to Chicago where she was wanted, and where she belonged. She'd make sure and let the others in this house know as soon as possible. She crept to her room and made preparations for sleep with the words she intended to say running around and around in her head.

12

The next morning, the clinking of dishes called Margaret to start her day. She frowned as she left her room. Cooking the breakfast was her job. Karen must have gotten up early, or maybe a baby had lingered awake in the wee hours of the morning and kept her from sleep.

Margaret hastened to the kitchen. Karen stood at the stove stirring a pot of oatmeal. She turned when she noticed Margaret. A note of cheer lifted her voice.

"Good morning, Mother. I sat up early this morning with Simon. He has a bit of a runny nose and couldn't fall back to sleep. I thought I would go ahead and take care of breakfast to give you a break."

Margaret should smile at the news. Karen could just as easily have gone back to bed, but instead she chose to think of her mother. Forcing a smile, she did her best to lay her hurt feelings aside and reply.

"Thank you, my dear."

A glance at Logan seated at the table and sipping coffee told her he felt no inconvenience over the substitute cook at the stove. He was dressed in his crisp shirt and tie with his hair in perfect order and his spectacles resting studiously on the bridge of his nose. Nothing in his appearance betrayed him as the romantic waltzer Margaret had spied the evening before. The fact didn't deserve another surge of heat through her veins, but she failed to control it. She marched stiff and straight to the table and claimed her usual chair.

Logan grinned at her in his winsome, adorable way.

No wonder Cornelia let him have her Victrola. He'd probably used that same grin on her when he'd asked to borrow from her. No woman could resist it.

But she could this morning. Logan's smile failed to produce any happiness on her face.

The slightest bit of a question entered his gaze before he stood to refill his cup.

Karen came to the table with the oatmeal as Logan took his seat.

As soon as the prayer was over and their bowls were filled, Margaret released the speech she'd stored away the evening before. "I'm leaving Thursday afternoon. It's time you started learning to get along without me. The twins are two months old and sleeping longer through the night. You don't need me as much as you did at first, so I will return to Chicago where I belong."

If words could be seen as well as heard, a blast of red flame had accompanied Margaret's announcement in a swirl across the room.

Logan's movements halted with his spoonful of oatmeal suspended in the air halfway between his bowl and his mouth. He blinked and glanced at Karen who winced as if she'd been burned.

"You seem upset, Mother. What happened? Did we offend you in any way?" Karen frowned at her.

Karen's words carried only peace and goodwill, but they poked Margaret in places tender with hurt. "I'm not offended. I've just learned that my place is not here in Oswell City anymore. I'm sorry I suggested staying as long as I did. You shouldn't have had to endure my presence for so long."

"But we've needed you. We've loved having you here with us. I don't know what I would have done without you. I still don't. Just because the twins are a little older doesn't mean the responsibility is any less." Karen laid her hand on Margaret's arm.

Margaret ate her breakfast in silence.

"Won't you stay a little longer? I'd hate for you to leave so upset. The change would be too abrupt." Karen watched Margaret eat as she spoke.

Tears gathered in the corners of her eyes as Margaret shook her head.

Karen leaned back with a sigh. "I'm sorry you feel that way. Logan has received another invitation to speak in chapel at a nearby college. I would like to go with him, and I was hoping you would be willing to take care of the twins again."

"I wish I could." The idea of all those women she thought were her friends kept her from cooperating.

"But, Mother. What's wrong? This is so unlike you. I don't understand." Karen watched her for a moment before stirring her oatmeal around with her spoon.

She'd rather eat in silence and then do what she had to do to get out of this town as soon as possible, but Karen's plea for understanding wrenched Margaret's heart. None of this was Karen's fault. Margaret sat straight and made her best effort to keep her voice even.

"All right. I'll tell you. I've gotten to know many of the women in town during my stay. I thought they were my friends, but yesterday when I went to the garden club meeting at Cornelia Goud's, I noticed her Victrola was missing."

Karen frowned at her. "What does that have to do with anything?"

Margaret looked Logan in the eye. "I saw you dancing last night. I came home early from the library because the meeting got cancelled. I didn't mean to spy, but what I saw convinced me that you need your house and your family back."

A hint of red stained Logan's neck above his collar but he held her gaze.

"Those women probably all think I've interfered here with your home life. I'm truly sorry about that, and I am hurt that no one said anything to me. Instead, everyone has gone around behind my back when I wish someone, you or my friends, anyone, would have just told me." A tear slipped loose as she spoke, but it didn't stop her from telling Logan what he needed to hear.

"Mother, you misunderstand completely." Logan's voice held a solemn tone.

Margaret glanced away. She must have a second opinion before she believed him. She looked at Karen who sat nodding her head.

Logan cleared his throat. "Let me tell you something. It may come as a surprise, but I think it will help you get a sense of what is going on."

Margaret frowned at him. Surely a larger conspiracy than what she'd uncovered wasn't spun around her and trapping her.

"Cornelia's husband brought their Victrola to our house yesterday while you were at the store. We've kept it in the bedroom because the rest of the house is full of supplies for the twins. We aren't trying to keep any secrets from you. Our use of the Gouds' Victrola is a business transaction, really.

"You see, Karen wants to use it at the orchard on the last day of Bible school. Since it was in the house last night, we thought we might as well put it to good use discovering if I still know how to dance. Turns out that I do." With a shrug and a grin at his wife, Logan fell silent.

His speech penetrated her brain. Logan's possession of the Victrola was about the children in Karen's Bible school, not about his mother-in-law's invasion of his home. "So, the Gouds are the only ones who know you have it."

Logan nodded.

"And this is the first time you've borrowed it from them." She peered at him ready for any answer.

"Yes, and probably the last." Logan picked up his coffee cup and sipped from it.

Margaret's eyelids fluttered shut. Oh, goodness. She and Logan had experienced misunderstandings in the past, but this one by far exposed her own miscalculations. Maybe she did have friends here. They might grow into the sort of friends that meant more to her than surface acquaintances. What if this tiny town on the Iowa prairie became a place of warmth and belonging where the loneliness and fears left over from her disappointing marriage were eradicated once and for all?

The faces of the women she'd met in the dress shop yesterday appeared in her memory. Good, kind women who knew how to stand by others through difficult times. Maybe they would lend her a little of their support too. Her questions deserved answers.

But she couldn't find those answers while also staying as a guest in her daughter's home any longer. She glanced at Logan with yet another message he should hear, one that she did her best to fill with words he would find encouraging.

"Thank you for clearing that up. I'm happy to know I'll always have a place here with you, but if I'm going to continue helping you with the twins, I think it would be best if I found another place to stay."

Logan frowned and Karen shook her head. "Oh, but Mother."

A tiny smile tugged at Margaret's mouth. "I'm flattered by your wish to keep me here, my dear, but you and Logan need your home to yourselves again. You haven't had the chance yet without anyone else around to adjust to life as a family. I want to give that to you now."

Karen looked from her mother to her husband with a hint of bewilderment hanging on her features. Logan reached out and clasp her hand as if to say she should welcome her mother's unexpected news.

Karen drew in a deep breath. "All right. I see what you are saying, and it makes sense."

"I'll stay in your guest room until the end of the week so you still have my help through the end of Bible school, but then I will make plans to leave. If nothing comes available in town for me to use as another home, I will return to Chicago. Then you and Logan will be on your own without any help. I'm not sure you are quite ready for that.

"But if I do find a place to live, then I think the arrangement would work out really well. I could come over during the day and help you with whatever work you have or care for the twins. And at night, I would go home again to my own house. What do you think?" Margaret studied Karen as she waited for her daughter's answer.

Karen glanced at Logan. He gave her the slightest nod, but it was enough to cause a smile to bloom on her face. "That sounds like a wonderful arrangement. Thank you, Mother. I will pray that just the right home for you comes available."

The words pricked Margaret in her tender and hurting places. She wanted the perfect home too. Not just a place to stay to fulfill an obligation or to force herself on another as an intruder, but a home where she knew without any doubt that she was welcomed, loved, and could go on enjoying it forever.

13

Mid-afternoon, the train stopped in Oswell City. Matthew studied the crowd for his brother-in-law, Tim Van Kley. Several letters had passed between them making arrangements for Matthew's new plane to be stored in a barn on the Van Kley farm. Tim was even willing to create a runway along one side of his pasture for Matthew's new mode of transportation. The offer filled him with delight. He certainly had to have a runway. The Van Kley farm spread over such a large number of acres Tim shouldn't miss the strip of land designated for biplane use.

Matthew's new aircraft required only one hundred yards for gaining enough speed to leave the ground. Even a man with a much smaller farm than Tim's wouldn't notice the reduced space available to him for grazing his cattle. Matthew allowed a smile to peek out as he emerged from the train.

Tim waved at him from farther down the platform near the freight cars. Matthew hastened in that direction so he might be on hand for the unloading of the crate containing biplane parts.

"Welcome back." Tim slapped him on the shoulder.

"Thanks. Glad to be home."

"Got your license?"

"Right here." Matthew patted the satchel he carried.

Tim clicked his tongue. "That sure is some accomplishment. Never dreamed anyone in my own family would learn how to fly a plane."

Matthew smiled again while his insides glowed with the pleasure he found in Tim's words.

A crew of railroad men gathered and worked to remove Matthew's freight from the train. Tim maneuvered his hayrack as close as possible to the car and helped the men secure the crate for travel.

"Fits pretty well," Tim said with a hint of surprise in his voice as he studied the load.

"Orville said a crated biplane could fit in the back of a truck." Matthew hadn't yet decided if he should believe those words.

Tim chuckled. "I wouldn't try to cram all those parts into a truck bed, but maybe city people have to settle for that. Come on. Let's get you out to the farm and unload this thing. I'm dying to take a look at it."

"I'm afraid you'll have to wait for that. I must put it together first." Matthew jumped onto the front of the rack.

"Shouldn't take too long. I'll help you." Tim picked up the reins and glanced at Matthew.

"Sure!" Cheer and lightness found a crack in his soul and made themselves at home there.

Tim guided the horses around the depot and onto Main Street.

"Stop here, Tim. I want to check in with Millie." Matthew pointed to his house, next door to the trim little medical clinic. He jumped down and went to the door.

Millie must have seen him coming because she opened the door before he had the chance to turn the knob. A bright expression claimed her face. "Welcome home, Doctor. Good to have you back."

"How are things?" He gazed into her eyes in an effort to detect any trouble.

"Fine. The Haverkamp baby came last night. Dr. Hayes drove

Coming Home to Mercy

over and delivered it. A girl. She's healthy, but the family wants you to come. They prefer attention from their regular doctor, I suppose."

"How about Mrs. Van Kley? Any improvement?" The woman suffering from a stroke was Tim's aunt. Matthew didn't want the family worried about her if her condition grew worse.

"Yes, a small one, I believe. You'll want to call out there as soon as you can."

"Of course. Anything else?" Matthew held his breath against the news of any sicknesses or deaths.

"No. Everyone's getting along pretty well. You picked a good time to leave." Millie slipped a dish towel from the rack near the stove and dried a plate.

Matthew exhaled. "Glad to hear that. I'm going with Tim out to the farm and will come home around dark."

"You really did buy a biplane?" She craned her neck for a glance at the street.

"I did, but it is in a crate right now. I have to put it together."

Her eyebrows rose. "Can't wait to see it."

Matthew nodded and left the house. By the time he claimed his spot next to Tim on the rack, Main Street was flooded with people. Curious people who knew he'd been in Dayton and now waited to catch a glimpse of a real, working flying machine. Like Tim and Millie, the town would have to wait a little longer. His biplane had arrived in pieces. Not until it was assembled would he be ready to put it on display.

People congregated along the street and waved. George Brinks stood on the steps of his hotel calling out to him a welcome home.

Matthew nodded and waved back at him.

"Hey, Doctor, is that your new plane?" A youth called out. Others in his cluster of onlookers pointed at the hayrack and shouted with excitement.

People came out of stores and watched him ride by. Paul Ellenbroek and some councilmen waved. James Koelman leaned out the second story window of his law firm with a hearty welcome home. The banker and some tellers stood in front of the bank waving and smiling. Pastor Logan sprinted out the church door in time to call out and wave at him.

Matthew might as well have been his own parade for as much attention as the crate behind him received. He even noticed Jake Harmsen hovering around back there somewhere near City Hall flashing photos with his camera. Matthew wouldn't be a bit surprised if an oversized article appeared in this week's newspaper.

"Turn in here. I want to let my parents know I'm home." Matthew pointed as Tim guided the horses onto a quiet street near the edge of town.

At the home of Abraham and Mina Kaldenberg, Matthew strode across the lawn. The elderly couple sat in rockers on their porch. Abe lifted his hand in a wave. "Welcome home, my boy. How was your trip?"

"Fine. I've got my license." He took it out of his bag and showed his father.

"Is that your flying machine?" Matthew's mother pointed at the crate on the rack.

"Sure is. Maybe you'd like to go for a ride when I get it put together." Matthew flashed a smile at his mother.

The couple laughed before Abe spoke. "I'm just fine with both my feet planted right here on the ground. Got by this long without leaving it, so I suppose I'll make out all right staying put."

"You can watch me fly." Matthew might as well have been a child on Christmas morning with a new toy.

"Wouldn't miss it." Abe waved at him as he jumped on the hayrack next to Tim.

Tim guided the horses down the road north of town for two miles until arriving at his farm. Matthew's sister, Rebecca, came out of the house and met them in the yard. After a brief hug and welcome home, she joined the men on the rack and rode with them to the barn. They drove far out into the pasture until arriving at the weathered building Tim used to store hay. He flung the doors wide open revealing a large, empty space.

Matthew's mouth fell open at the absence of the usual piles of hay. "Where did you put it all?"

Tim grinned. "Moved it. This barn is all yours. What are those sheds called where planes are stored? Hangars?"

Matthew nodded. He'd learned about hangars, even saw a few, while in Dayton.

"Well then, this barn is your very own hangar. Probably the first one ever in Oswell City. Rebecca, I do believe we are making history today." Tim went over to her and took the box she held. He turned and handed it to Matthew.

"A gift from us." Rebecca smiled as she stood at Tim's side.

Matthew frowned. First the whole town watches him drive down Main Street. Then Tim mentions the notion of Matthew's contribution to local history. Now his family presents him with a gift. All because he'd been gone for a month learning a new skill and spending a large amount of money. He really didn't need this sort of treatment, as if he was some important celebrity. He was just a man with a new hobby, nothing more.

He shook his head. "You didn't have to get me a gift."

Rebecca's face lit up. "Oh, but we wanted to. This is a big day."

"Go on." Tim thrust the box at him.

For their sake he would tolerate being the celebrity. He accepted the box and opened it. Inside he found a fabric cone-shaped article. He held it up. "A windsock!" He'd seen one of those on the peak of the roof of one of the buildings at the Wright Company. He'd mount it on the peak of his new barn-hangar to watch the wind.

He smiled his thanks. Tim found a ladder and hung the windsock. The wind was light, so the sock didn't respond much to the breeze and hung limp. These sorts of conditions made for ideal flying. If only he had his plane assembled, he'd take it up right now.

Tim stayed in the barn and helped him unload the plane from the rack, piece by piece. Rebecca walked to the house to prepare the evening meal. Matthew found the instructions, so he and Tim worked together for the next hour. Rebecca returned with a full hamper of delicious-smelling food. They ate quickly, for which Matthew was glad.

He wanted to get as much of his plane assembled yet today as he possibly could. The demands of his medical practice would close in on him in the days to come, pressing any spare minutes to the outer fringes of each day. He'd have to stay up quite late in the evenings to get his plane ready to fly. At least the summer evenings provided light long into the evening. That would help him complete the project sooner.

After the picnic in the barn, he and Tim worked for another two hours. The framework for the wings and the motor were in working order, but so much more still must get done on the plane. As he rode in Tim's buggy on the way back to town, Matthew's mind spun with all the small details of building a biplane. He could hardly wait to take it out on the first flight. But first he must let Margaret know he was back in town.

Maybe tomorrow he could find the time to make a call at the parsonage to check on the twins. Then if Margaret happened to be at home, he'd tell her all about his trip and set a date for her to take that promised ride with him. He smiled to himself. He had it all planned out.

Tim let him off at his door and waved goodnight. When he got inside, Millie met him with a message.

"What's this?" His brow furrowed as he accepted the note from her.

"Dr. Hayes called over the telephone while you were at the farm. Walter brought this for you from the hotel. There's a fever outbreak at the children's home in Clear Brook. They are asking every available physician to come and assist."

Matthew read the note, but Millie had already told him everything it said. "I'll go tonight."

"But aren't you tired from your trip?" Concern edged his housekeeper's voice.

I'll rest later," he called out over his shoulder as he headed to the clinic for supplies. This was the doctor's life, putting health and the fight with death above all else, including sleep, assembly of new biplanes, and enjoyable visits at the parsonage.

None of that could be helped now. He raced around his examination room collecting instruments and supplies he knew would be helpful in contending with fever. Those residents of the Clear Brook children's home already faced so many challenges. He'd do his best to protect them. Matthew leaped into his buggy and followed the road to Clear Brook, ready to give all of his energy to the night's battle with suffering and pain.

14

Matthew entered the children's home, hushed with the distress of death fought but not yet defeated. There was no other place he'd rather be. Death loomed as the ultimate enemy. One he'd spent his career fighting. He'd won more times than he'd lost, and he had every intention of continuing his successful record through the hours of this night. A nurse led him to the hall that had been converted into a ward for the diseased children. Beds lined both sides of the room. Little pale faces lay on the pillows. Clean white blankets covered the suffering forms.

"Your patients are the last three beds at the end of this row." The nurse pointed to the line of beds on his right.

He nodded and followed her past other doctors and nurses working among the beds. When he reached his assigned patients, he rested his hand on the forehead of each one. Two of the children were little girls he didn't recognize. The third patient was Albert, the boy who had suffered so many setbacks already. He did not need the stress on his health a fever caused.

"The children showed signs of sickness two days ago. The fever is reaching its climax in many of the patients. We need more help now caring for them." The nurse talked in a quiet voice.

"I'm glad I could come." Matthew pulled back the bedclothes on Albert's bed and raised a corner of the boy's shirt. Red spots covered his chest. Just as Matthew suspected. "These children are sick with typhoid fever."

"Yes, Doctor." The docile manner of the nurse told him she was well aware of the diagnosis.

"Your water must be contaminated. Isn't something being done?" Matthew pulled his stethoscope from his bag.

"Clear Brook is looking into it. Until a solution is found, we are using water transported to us from across town." The nurse moved closer to Albert's bed ready to offer her assistance.

"Good idea." Matthew gave directions to the nurse and together they offered care to the three children.

The night wore on as Matthew watched the conditions of the little girls worsen. He did everything he knew to do, but by morning the fever had formed an alliance with death and snatched their lives away. The nurse rolled their beds to a different area of the children's home while Matthew focused all of his energy on saving Albert.

The great destroyer had no right to enter this place and claim for itself the lives of these innocent children. From the interactions he'd had with the other doctors and nurses during the night hours, Matthew learned he wasn't the only one losing patients to the fever. Other children had succumbed to the complications resulting from the disease.

The facts didn't alleviate his own distress. If he could have his own way, everyone he treated would live. They would go on to recover and enjoy healthy, happy lives. He'd do as much as he could while he worked here, but he also had his own practice that demanded his time and energy.

Restlessness overtook him and left him with the strong desire to pound something, to roam all through the building slamming doors and groaning. He struggled in this way every time he lost a patient. It didn't happen often, but when it did, Matthew sank into a pit of agitation. Only thoughts of flying free pulled him out of it. He dwelled on those thoughts now to push the grim sense of defeat far from him.

A real biplane sat in the barn on his sister's farm. He'd come closer than he ever had before to rising, to ascending, to lifting beyond the place where loss and death's defeat could hold him down. He'd win. Someday, he would win. He might still lose the occasional patient like he did last night, but peace would belong to him. Death would lose its power to unsettle him and turn its mocking scorn on him.

He was a doctor with the skill to save lives. He knew how to defy the most determined of foes. Compassion brimmed in his heart leaving no room for insensitivity or laziness. He got to work applying every last bit of his compassion and skill to Albert. The boy must not die. He must not.

Matthew had cared for him through the years and the recent eye condition. Albert had overcome so much. He couldn't lose now. This pointless fever couldn't mean the end of Albert's existence. Matthew must work to prevent it.

MID-AFTERNOON, Matthew transferred Albert's care to another doctor. The pressure of responsibility for a life lifted, Matthew's eyes drooped as he drove to Oswell City. He hadn't slept since the last night he'd spent in the Dayton hotel. Unless an emergency arose or a baby needed delivered, Matthew would rest in his own bed at his quiet house.

Several hours stretched ahead of him before he could enjoy the close of the day, so he drove to Mrs. Van Kley's home east of town. Tim was there. So was Logan. The two men gave Matthew an update on the woman's condition. Their report included a slight improvement in her speech. Matthew chose to believe the news indicated a degree of healing had taken place over the past weeks.

He approached the woman's bed and smiled down at her. "Good afternoon, Mrs. Van Kley."

She looked at him. One corner of her mouth, the one unaffected by the stroke, smiled back at him. "Hi, Doctor." The speech was still quite slurred but sounded a bit clearer.

"How have your exercises been going?" He pulled a chair up next to the bed.

"Fine. Watch." Her attention rested on her leg. It twitched before her foot slid along the bedsheet with a slow, creeping movement.

"Very good. Keep working. Someday the movement will get easier. I'm hoping for a full recovery for you." He felt along the side of the leg she'd moved.

"I want that too, Doctor." The words came out slurred, but they carried eons of meaning.

Matthew smiled then spent the next hour examining her. He also received a full display of the work she'd accomplished with her exercises during his absence.

When he finished at the Van Kleys', he drove on to the Haverkamp farm. The family had been in Oswell City for nearly two years. The group of two brothers by the names of Dirk and Joost, their wives, and their children had immigrated to Iowa from a province in Holland. Matthew recalled their experiences well. Dirk and Joost had started farming together in the autumn season. Shortly after Christmas, Joost had fallen through the ice of the pond. Dirk broke his arm trying to save Joost from the freezing waters.

Matthew's services were required for both men to recover. The broken arm had healed nicely allowing Dirk full use of it again. Joost was the father to the baby born earlier in the week. Matthew turned his buggy into their drive and searched the yard to see who of the large family was at home.

Laundry fluttered on the line next to the house. Smoke

curled from the pipe in the kitchen roof. The house appeared as if the new mother had assistance. Matthew parked his buggy and went inside.

A neighbor woman stood at the stove. She welcomed him in.

"I heard Mrs. Haverkamp has had her baby, so I wanted to stop in for an examination," he said as he removed his hat and laid it on the table.

"She sure did. A nice baby girl. That's five girls now in addition to their three boys." The woman led the way up the stairs and knocked on the door. "Adrianna. The doctor is here to see you."

Matthew entered and smiled at the new mother. He visited with her about the birth and then gave her a full examination. Pleased with his findings on the progress of her recovery, Matthew went to the crib and reached for the baby. The little girl also received an examination from the doctor. He found nothing to cause him alarm. The newborn appeared perfectly healthy and was maintaining a satisfactory weight.

He visited a bit more with Mrs. Haverkamp before heading downstairs. The neighbor insisted on sending several slices of a freshly baked cake along with him. He couldn't refuse. He'd hardly eaten a thing since his return from Dayton. The cake would supply him with a nice snack as he drove home.

On the way, storm clouds gathered. The wind picked up and rain poured down. It hammered the buggy top and ran along the sides of the road. Matthew hastened the horse into town and worked with swift movements to bed the horse down in his small stable. He sprinted across the lawn to his clinic and found two people waiting there for treatment. One person had come from the lumberyard and was in need of stitches. The second person asked for salve for a burn. Matthew helped them both and then locked the door for the night.

The rain still fell. The dark unbroken clouds alerted him that rain would fall most of the night and perhaps some of the next day. Matthew winced. The spring and summer had been wet months. Their area had already received so much rain. Creeks ran full to their banks, and rivers flooded the lowlands. Tonight's rain would add to the surplus and might even cause rivers to overflow. His mind reeled back to the children's home so near the river. Any more rain may put them in serious danger. He'd investigate the situation when he returned to care for Albert.

Matthew entered his house and sat down to Millie's good food. He could survive as a bachelor the rest of his life if he had Millie around to provide the simple comforts for him of clean linens, good food, and relaxing quiet. His hunger satisfied, Matthew's eyes drooped. He should go to Tim's farm and work on his biplane, but the project wouldn't hold as much pleasure in the rain.

Seeking out his favorite chair in the parlor, Matthew settled in with a book. The steady tap of rain on the windows and the cozy glow of the lamp held him in their power. In minutes, deep, bone-weary fatigue claimed him.

"Excuse me, Doctor. Do you have a minute?" Mayor Ellenbroek entered the clinic during the noon hour.

"I certainly do. Let me get these papers filed, and then I can see you." Matthew slipped the folders among other files in the drawer.

"What can I do for you?" He looked at the clock. His appointments had run late that morning, and now his lunch break had shrunk.

"I don't need to make an appointment for a health issue. There is a matter I'd like to discuss with you, and since I had some time over my lunch hour, I thought I'd run across the street to the clinic." Paul removed his hat.

"Have a seat. What's on your mind?" Matthew pointed to one of the empty chairs for Paul to use while he claimed another one.

"The Fourth of July festivities are getting planned. This is a big year for us as a town, you know. We are celebrating sixty-five years since the day of our founding."

"I heard about that. Jake ran an article in the paper a couple of weeks ago."

"I believe he did. The city council met last night and finalized plans. They decided ... well, actually, I mentioned to them that it would be a good idea to ask you to participate."

"In what way?"

"We have a banner that we'd like to have flown over the downtown square while the band plays. It's important for the citizens of Oswell City to understand that we are a town of innovation and progress. I can't think of a better way to prove that than to have the owner of a brand new flying machine take part in the celebration."

Matthew's eyes widened. "I'd be honored. I'm in the process of assembling the plane. So far the work has gone smoothly. If I don't run into any troubles, the plane should be ready in plenty of time."

"Fine." Paul smiled. "I'll look forward to it." He stood and shook Matthew's hand. "I'd better be getting back to the office."

Matthew watched him leave the clinic and cross the street to City Hall. The mayor wanted him to fly his biplane as part of the town's festivities to celebrate their historic anniversary. He recalled the conversation that took place with the town leaders and businessmen before he left town to purchase the plane and take lessons. Some of those same men were on the city council. The mayor must have convinced them that the purchase of a biplane was a good idea or they would not have agreed to ask for Matthew to fly this banner.

But what other means did they have to get it in the air? Unless the city council would have decided to display it somewhere on the side of a building. Maybe that was their original plan.

Matthew shrugged and turned away from the window.

Whatever had transpired in last night's city council meeting had been to Matthew's advantage. He'd prove to the town that a biplane wasn't dangerous, and, like the mayor said, it was an important proof of progress and innovation. A surge of pride swelled within him. He was a leader in his own right, exercising the foresight to purchase a modern machine like a biplane.

The town would see that he knew what he was doing. And as Logan encouraged, Matthew would display what rising above and being a success looked like.

15

Margaret's search for a new place to live proved unsuccessful. One house she considered sat on the edge of town, requiring a long walk back and forth to Karen's each day. Another possibility was an apartment above one of the businesses on Main Street. The location would grow warm and stuffy during the summer months. Noise from the street would also make the location undesirable even if it was within easy walking distance of the parsonage.

The third house she looked at sat directly across the street from Karen's. Although an ideal location, the price of rent was high. Margaret had some money of her own from a fund that had belonged to Simon, but she didn't want to drain her resources on rent payments.

No other homes were available to a single woman like Margaret in Oswell City. The fact decided the matter for her. She would return to Chicago, leaving the two precious grandsons and her budding friendships behind.

"Are you sure, Mother?" Karen asked one afternoon as she leaned her head against the door frame of the room Margaret had been using and gazed at her with sad eyes. "Stay here until you find a place."

Margaret inhaled as she secured her hat on her hair. How she'd love to just keep on going as a member of the De Witt household. But she couldn't. Beyond her desire for Karen and Logan to make a good adjustment to their new life as parents of twins, a deep restlessness had taken hold of her.

The marriage Karen shared with Logan caused it. Margaret could no longer stay here witnessing the love the two young people had for each other. It chafed on her heart much like rough clothing irritated the skin. A rash had broken out in her tenderest places. If she didn't get away and find relief from the affection, the mutual respect, and the devotion, then an incurable case of discontentment and perhaps even a little jealousy would eat away at Margaret's sense of wellbeing.

She couldn't comprehend why the love in this home bothered her so much. Maybe it served as an unending friction between her dreams and the realities of her younger years. Or maybe it scratched those places that still waited for fulfillment.

The reason dared not matter to her. She'd lived that part of her life, raised her children, and laid her husband to rest. The devoted, affectionate kind of love had never been hers. She must not waste time mourning over it or exhausting her energy searching for it. She must face life as it really was and accept whatever loneliness the years ahead held.

Margaret turned from the mirror and looked at Karen. "You know I can't do that, my dear. Logan deserves to have his home to himself, and you both are still adjusting to life with twins. I wish I could stay in town and help you. I'm going to miss you so much. But nowhere is available here for me to live. I must go."

Karen wiped a tear from her face. "I can't believe this is for the best. You have friends here. We still want your assistance with the twins. Maybe Logan can ask around among the people in the congregation. I'm sure someone could give you a room."

Margaret shook her head. "I don't want to impose on anyone. I'm quite capable of looking out for myself. Now, I'm going to

Coming Home to Mercy

buy my ticket for tomorrow's morning train. I should return in plenty of time to help you with the evening meal."

Karen bit her trembling lip as Margaret passed by into the hall.

She slipped on her gloves, gathered up her handbag, and with one more smile at Karen, left the house.

The afternoon had grown overcast. A light mist of rain fell from the clouds. She'd heard enough talk around town during the past weeks to know that Oswell City and the surrounding area needed no more rain. Rivers flowed as high as their banks. Creeks swelled. Low-lying ground covered in mini lakes still waited for the year's planting of crops. Any more water could create a crisis. Life here was difficult enough. As she walked, Margaret prayed the sun would shine and dry the sodden fields.

At the train station, Margaret approached the window and made arrangements for travel the next day. Satisfied with the price and the departure time, she left the building and returned to the street. After passing the doctor's office, a man fell in step with her. She knew someone walked at her side because of the shadow his frame cast on the brick fronts of the Main Street stores.

"Good afternoon, Margaret." The voice of Matthew Kaldenberg carried smooth and sincere to her ears.

She glanced at him. "Good afternoon. I'm glad to see you back in town. Are you on your way to a house call?"

"No. Actually, I just returned from the children's home in Clear Brook. I have nowhere to go at the moment except wherever you are headed."

She paused and turned to him. Matthew stayed so busy every minute of the day. She couldn't imagine why he would find interest in her afternoon plans.

"When I saw you pass the office, I rushed out to extend an invitation to you." He stood straight and tall with his hands clasped in front of him and a hopeful light in his eyes.

She searched his face as questions multiplied in her mind.

"I plan to have the biplane assembled this weekend. If the weather is favorable, I would like to take you with me on the first flight." Matthew's smile stretched across his face.

Margaret's eyes widened. A host of emotions assaulted her heart. The first sensation came about from the glimpse of the smile on Matthew's face. Such a lovely smile. It didn't come out in the open without a good reason. A sober and dignified person like Matthew would never waste smiles on shallow, trivial matters. The invitation meant a great deal to him for it to come accompanied by his smile. Margaret would have no complaints of a life with the task of making that thoughtful, intentional smile appear as its highest priority.

The meaning of the invitation brought on her next reaction. Her legs weakened and her head went dizzy. Accepting his request meant leaving the ground and entrusting her life to a flimsy frame of fabric and sticks. She surely couldn't keep her end of the promise. Gliding above the trees at the mercy of the wind would break her neck.

Her shoulders threatened to slump. Even if she admired his smile and dared to accept his invitation, she couldn't go with him. The ticket for tomorrow's one-way trip to Chicago was tucked in her handbag. The break had been made. She was leaving town.

"Oh, Matthew, I so appreciate you asking me, but I can't. I'm leaving for Chicago tomorrow." The disappointment saturated her voice. She didn't try to hide it.

His eyebrows raised. "Leaving for Chicago?"

How she disliked the look of horrified surprise on his face. It deserved the words "I'm sorry," but all she could do was nod in affirmation of the truth.

"But ... how?" He inhaled and shifted his attention to the leafy branches above. "I thought ... why?"

She shivered when his gaze returned to her. "The twins are older now. I'd just be in the way if I stayed. My family in Chicago needs me too."

Pain entered his eyes. His distress was too awful. She looked away. "I'm sorry, Matthew. Truly. Enjoy your new plane. Think of me when you fly." She patted his arm and walked away.

The memory of those stricken eyes stayed with her. Even if she lived through another century never seeing the man again, those eyes would stay with her, haunting her, following her. But she could do nothing. The ticket was bought. The decision had been made.

"Don't go." The words shot through the air with as much force as if they were ammunition from a rifle.

Margaret jerked to a stop like she'd taken a bullet in her back.

A warm hand rested on her shoulder. "Don't go. Please."

Another hand rested on her other shoulder and turned her around in a gentle motion. Those pain-filled eyes leveled with hers. The light of hope had returned. Its dim glow softened the tragedy she read in his gaze.

"Stay here, Margaret. Stay with us. Stay with me."

The last words were whispered, urgent in their attempt to convey feeling that reached into cavernous regions below the surface. Here was a man who knew what it meant to love. His wife had probably known, like Karen did, the respect and affection of a devoted husband. Some women truly did have all the luck.

Margaret ventured a glimpse deep into those eyes, windows into a soul refined in suffering and courageous in hope. Matthew's invitation might hold more than just the request for one day's worth of adventure. Maybe he wanted her to understand his heart. What if devotion and affection still resided there? What if he was trying to tell her of his willingness to show these hidden chambers to her?

Margaret blinked and drew in a deep breath as the lessons of the moment enlightened her. "I ... I have nowhere to live." The words escaped on a sigh like her mind had emitted an apparition in the form of an audible thought.

Matthew straightened and studied the buildings on Main Street. His gaze paused on his own house and office before moving across the street to the houses that occupied shaded lots of cool green grass.

"I wonder if Clara has any room." He spoke the words much like Margaret had done, in a vapor of transparency.

He turned to look at her. Hints of respect and affection glowed in his expression, turning the lines of concern to creases of happiness. "Would you be willing to share a home with an elderly woman?"

"I suppose."

"Clara Hesslinga lives alone. Her niece stayed with her for a while but married and moved away. I'd like to see her have a companion. Clara is in very good health, but if something happened to her, no one would know, perhaps for a very long time. If you lived with her, I could see the arrangement solving both of your problems."

"I can give it a try if she wants me. I certainly do not wish to impose on anyone."

Matthew's smile peeked out while affection continued to glow in his eyes. "Come with me."

Margaret followed him across the street and up a trim little sidewalk through a gap in a picket fence to a tidy front door. Matthew knocked. After a moment, Clara opened the door and greeted him.

"Good afternoon, Clara. I apologize for calling on you unannounced. I'm hoping you might help us out with something."

"Why, of course, Doctor. Anything." Clara watched him with eagerness in her gaze.

"Mrs. Millerson is wishing to move out of the parsonage so she doesn't overstay her welcome. I wondered if perhaps you could offer her the rooms your niece Florence used when she lived with you." Matthew fell silent. A look of patience mixed with a bit of anticipation claimed his features.

"I'd be delighted. That is if Margaret would be happy with my accommodations after living at the parsonage. But I have two extra rooms, a bedroom and small parlor, she might use as her own. We'd have to share the kitchen and bathroom you know, but I wouldn't find that inconvenient at all. And, Margaret, I wouldn't charge you a thing."

Margaret's jaw dropped. "Oh, but, Clara. I couldn't allow you to share your home with me for nothing."

Clara crossed her arms and nodded her head. "Sure, you can. I'd want you to. We'll just live together as good friends helping each other out."

Silence fell. Margaret looked from Clara to Matthew and back again to Clara. Both of them watched her with satisfied expressions on their faces. She took a deep breath. The perfect solution had dropped right into her lap. She couldn't possibly turn it down. Oswell City might be where she belonged after all.

"I'll take it. Thank you, Clara. This is very kind of you."

Clara waved a hand in dismissal. "Don't mention it. You just get your bags or your trunks or whatever you have and bring them on over here. Tell Pastor Logan to bring his wife and those dear babies along, and we'll all have supper together tonight."

Laughter bubbled in Margaret's throat. "Well, all right then. I'll let them know."

Clara turned to Matthew. "You come, too, Doctor. Give Millie the night off."

With a fond glance at Margaret, Matthew gave his answer. "I'll do that."

Heat warmed Margaret's cheeks. She shouldn't blush like a teen, but no man had ever given her a look like that before. She left Clara's house entertaining the thought that a whole new life was about to open up before her.

Matthew went with her down the street. "I'll help you carry your belongings to Clara's."

She answered him with a smile.

They arrived at the parsonage at the same time as Logan.

The men greeted each other warmly as Karen joined them in the parlor. Margaret inhaled in preparation of making her big announcement.

"Karen. Logan. I've decided to stay in Oswell City."

Logan gave a little cheer.

"But not with you." Margaret held her hand up. She and Logan should avoid another misunderstanding.

He frowned.

"I'm going to live with Clara. She has offered, and I accepted. It sounds like the perfect arrangement. I'll come here to help Karen during the day and return to my room at Clara's in the evenings." Margaret released the rest of her breath unsure what to expect as a response. But she had no reason to worry.

Karen hugged her. "I'm so glad. I feel so much better about this plan than the one that involved you leaving town."

Logan kissed her cheek. "Good for you, Mother. I'm happy for you, and for all of us."

Everyone laughed. Logan's sentiments described best the feelings of everyone in the room.

"Clara has invited all of us for supper, even John and Simon. Dr. Kaldenberg came to help me carry my things to her house. We'll get started and meet you there." Happiness rang in Margaret's words as she led Matthew down the hall.

That train ticket was still tucked in her handbag, evidence of a move she'd thought irreversible. Matthew had changed all of that. A look, a touch, a moment of honesty had altered her course. If Oswell City was truly the place for her, then with the help of people like Clara, Matthew, Karen and Logan she looked forward to discovering what her purpose here would be.

16

"Albert is improved." Matthew made the announcement to his housekeeper when he entered the kitchen.

"Good to hear. You've been worried about that boy." Millie talked while she stood at the sink with her hands busy swishing a plate in the water.

"I have. It turns out the abundance of rain over the past weeks had saturated the ground, causing a leakage of impurities into the well that supplies water for the children's home. Serious situation. I'm glad they discovered the cause for their sickness. They shouldn't lose any more children now." Matthew worked at the stove boiling water and using it to clean his instruments.

Dishes clinked as Millie dried them and put them in the cupboard.

"You are welcome to take another night off when you get those dishes put away." Matthew watched her in her work.

Millie glanced at him over her shoulder. "Two nights in a row? You wouldn't be planning to spend the evening with Mrs. Millerson again, would you?"

Matthew relied on no words for an answer. The pleasure in his eyes would speak for him.

Millie smiled. "I knew it. You are seeing her again. Is Clara fixing supper for you like she did last night?"

"No. As a matter of fact, I'm taking Margaret on a picnic. I want to show her the progress I've made assembling my biplane." His heart thumped. This simple conversation should not have that much of an effect on his blood pressure.

"Ah. I see how it will go. You'll fall for her and ask her to move in here. Then you won't have need of me anymore." A grin tugged at Millie's mouth.

He made the attempt to tease her back, but his voice wouldn't cooperate. His usual solemn tone took over. "I'll always have need of you, Millie. Even if I should choose a wife and marry again, I'd still want you to stay."

Her grin grew. "Well, well. Here's the doctor talking about getting married. Never thought I'd live to see the day. But thank you for the assurance that I'll still have a job. I think Mrs. Millerson and I would get along quite well together."

Matthew could think of nothing to say to her cheeky speech. All he could do was laugh at her and shake his head.

Millie disappeared into the pantry for a moment and emerged with a basket." What would you like for me to prepare for your picnic?"

She stood at the table in eager anticipation of his suggestions. The sight of his housekeeper with her graying head and spotless white apron made his throat ache. He couldn't imagine what these long years would have been like without her. She looked after his comforts so well, almost to the point of mothering him at times. Her careful attention to his meals and housework had pushed the loneliness far enough away to prevent him from turning into a hard and bitter skeptic of the world.

"You won't need to make a thing. I bought the food in Clear Brook and have it packed away in a shady corner of my buggy. Go ahead and take some time off. I'll see you in the morning." He dried his instruments and placed them in his bag.

Millie gave him a suspicious glance. "I don't know about you, Doctor."

He raised a brow. "Oh, really?"

"If you were any other man, I'd say you'd already lost your heart to her. But you've gone for twenty years without so much as a glance at a woman. And yet, you've got the signs. Yes, you've definitely got the signs." Millie studied him as she backed into the pantry with her unused basket.

Matthew shook his head. Little did Millie know how accurate her intuitions were. Matthew had lost his heart to Margaret. He probably shouldn't have allowed it to slip away so easily. Like Millie said, he'd endured twenty years. If he would have lasted a little longer and survived Logan's wedding reception, he could boast of an unbroken record.

But Margaret had been there. Her grace, her elegance, and her interest in him blasted to pieces any accolades he'd managed to secure in his status as a bachelor. His days were numbered. He was starting over. Millie may very well have to accustom herself to cooking for two.

She emerged from the pantry, untied her apron, and hung it on a peg.

"Have a good evening, Millie." Matthew waved at her on his way out the door. He made a quick stop in the clinic to put his bag on a shelf before hopping into his buggy and driving to Clara's.

Less than a block away from his office, Matthew passed the spot where he'd conversed with Margaret the day before. His stomach clenched. Maybe he shouldn't have been so willing to spill his heart right there in the street. He should have worked harder to hold it in, to contain that steady burn to his insides. But it wouldn't tolerate concealment.

When he'd learned of Margaret's plan to leave town for good, the flame of his strongest feelings had burst from him and kindled a wildfire. It had leapt beyond the confines of his own heart and threatened to char a path of destruction through his profession, his relationships, and most of all, through his own ability to maintain a world in which he might always stand strong and victorious in the face of loss or pain.

In the moment when Margaret admitted her need of a place to live, he'd wanted nothing more than to take her home with him, to have her there always in the beautiful commitment of marriage. If anyone had done a thorough examination on him, that is what they would have found. The desire to get married again prowled deep within his being. The quiet and unfettered bachelor years had lost their appeal. The time had come to run that awful, ecstatic risk on love.

Matthew parked his horse and buggy in front of Clara's house with these thoughts on his mind. His head swam and his knees trembled as he fought with the sidewalk in his mission of walking a straight line to the door. Clara answered and welcomed him inside before his strength returned. Margaret appeared and smiled at him, making his symptoms worse. He leaned on the door frame under the ruse of appearing casual, but only he knew how close he really was to falling over.

In her smile he read a story of uncertainties similar to his. Maybe she felt a love for him that caused her to call into question her own lonely existence. The fact that she might have feelings for him made his pulse pound in his veins. This was knowledge worth discovering.

"Ready to go?" His voice shook the slightest bit.

Margaret nodded and put on her hat.

"Have a nice time," Clara called after them.

On his trip back to the buggy, Matthew did better at following the straight sidewalk. He helped Margaret over the wheel and then claimed the space next to her. He couldn't remember the last time he'd shared his narrow buggy seat with a woman. As far as he could recall, it had never happened. He settled back and enjoyed the drive made pleasant by the summer evening and by Margaret's presence so near at his side.

"Where are you taking me?" She asked when the buildings of the town fell away and rolling countryside surrounded them.

"I know of a peaceful spot on my brother-in-law's farm where the creek flows among the trees."

Margaret held onto her hat with one hand and grasped his arm with another hand when the buggy wheels hit a hole in the road. More holes made the way rough enough for Margaret to keep her hold on him until they reached their destination. He regretted leaving the seat and breaking the contact. Who would have thought that the wildfire he'd started would burn in this way of wanting to stay near to her supporting her and protecting her?

His knees shook again as he came to her side and helped her down. He reached for the large hamper from the store in Clear Brook and led Margaret to a clump of birch trees on the bank of the creek. She spread the quilt she'd brought along. When they were settled, Matthew brought out from the box the item that lay on top. It was a group of pink roses he'd bought special for her.

"These are for you, Margaret." He passed them to her and watched the pleasure of his gift enter her eyes.

"They are lovely. Thank you." She held the bouquet to her face and sniffed the petals.

He tore his attention away from the gracious picture she made and laid out the items for their meal. The Clear Brook clerk had supplied him well. His hamper contained a loaf of bread, dried beef, a round of cheese, a cluster of grapes, and two delectable-looking cherry turnovers.

Margaret laid her roses aside and filled her plate with food. They talked of his trip to Dayton as they ate. Margaret asked him questions and he supplied her with stories of the flying lessons, the other students, and of bringing the biplane home. According to her responses, Matthew's exploits were most impressive and deserved the celebrity status Tim and Rebecca had tried so hard to bestow on him.

"Oh, I don't know." His face flushed. "I'm just a lonely man in pursuit of a new hobby. Nothing too heroic about that."

"A brave man." Margaret corrected him in a quiet voice. Admiration shone on her face.

Margaret, along with Tim, Rebecca, and the rest of the town were getting the wrong idea about him. He must make her understand. The whole truth of his years of saving and dreaming would take hours to explain, but maybe he could allow her a small glimpse of one of his struggles.

He cleared his throat. His voice slipped into his earnest, professional tone. Margaret deserved more passionate expression than what his doctor voice could give, but he couldn't risk altering it now. The truth sitting on his heart asked of him every bit of courage just to get it spoken.

"Margaret, I have something I must tell you. I've kept it to myself for a very long time, but I can no longer conceal it. You see, I've fallen in love with you. It began on the evening of your daughter's wedding and has grown ever since. I loved you the moment I first saw you. Now that you are back in town, I find my feelings to be even stronger than when we first met all those months ago." His chest collapsed. What a long speech for a man who rarely shared anything but the facts if he could absolutely help it.

A pink glow stained Margaret's cheeks. "Oh, Matthew. Can you believe, I've felt the same way?"

"You have?" The thought had flitted through his mind, but he hadn't dared to take it seriously.

She nodded. "Yes. I've loved you ever since the time we spent together at Karen's reception. I went home to Chicago with you in my heart. Not a day has gone by when I don't think of you or wish for another evening with you."

"And now I've given it to you." He reached for her hand and held it.

"Not only did I get to spend this evening with you, but I

have you all to myself." She glanced at him like a child might who'd confessed an act of wrongdoing.

She had no reason to feel guilty with him. He'd wanted time alone with her too. "Do you think, would it be possible? I mean, I tell you these things because I would like to begin to court you."

A hint of sadness entered her gaze. "I don't know that I'm ready."

"I'm sorry if I've rushed you."

Margaret shook her head. "I enjoy not being married, and I don't expect to ever marry again. My circles of friends and my family mean too much to me. I wish there was a way for us to go on loving each other and spending time together without it leading to a courtship that ends in marriage."

Her words should deflate him. They should puncture him with disappointment. Instead, they fueled the burning flame inside of him. She knew who she was and what she wanted. He admired her strength and her honesty. A pursuit that should sink him in defeat brought on a surge of victory. He'd found the right woman to share the rest of his life with. He'd wait for her and he would win her. Love would melt her aversions. Her heart was on his side.

Matthew stood and assisted Margaret to her feet. As soon as she'd gained solid footing, he eased her into his embrace. "I'll wait." He whispered the words while searching the depths of her eyes.

Margaret's arm slid over his shoulder and around his neck as if it followed its own pleasures without any effort from her at all. She returned the serious gaze while an unseen bond drew them together.

Her lips didn't resist when his own rested on them. The sweet contact lasted for just a few brief moments, but it was long enough to convince him that only a woman willing to consider marrying him would share a kiss like that one.

She pulled away first and stared at him with large, startled eyes. Questions and fear lurked on her face. If she was afraid of him or of her own readiness to yield to him, her silence didn't say. Matthew smiled at her with a large, satisfied grin that stretched across his whole face, the first one of its kind in a very long time.

Margaret relaxed and even gave him a small smile of her own. "Isn't it time now to take a look at that biplane?"

How he'd love to keep on standing here holding her and reveling in the release her love gave to his soul, but he'd probably asked enough of her for one evening. At lease she hadn't demanded he take her back to Clara's and cut the outing short. He'd return to the pragmatic world of machinery for the sake of spending more time with her.

"Yes, of course. Let me gather up the remains of our supper, and I will drive you to the barn." He made quick work of cleaning up the picnic area and helped Margaret into the buggy.

17

"Karen, my dear, this next batch of laundry is finished. I'm going out to hang it on the line." Margaret called to Karen, who was seated in the rocking chair with John.

"Thanks, Mother."

Margaret lifted the basket from the table and left the kitchen. The clothes hanging on the line from earlier in the day were dry in spite of the humid summer weather. She took those clothes down and replaced them with her batch of damp sheets and towels.

While she worked, her mind reviewed the Saturday and Sunday that had passed since her last conversation with Matthew. She hadn't been home to Clara's for very long before she sensed that some portion of her world had shifted. Habits and expectations that had fit her with perfect comfort no longer eased into place.

The sensation made her feel as though she stood in Miss Rose's Chicago boutique fitting on a waistband of a skirt with a twist in it. This new rumple in her life didn't lay right. It bulked up refusing to smooth down. She couldn't find the beginning, nor could she see where the disruption ended.

Maybe the shift had started many months ago during Karen's

wedding. Far below the surface, her heart may have already been moving, searching for this beautiful gift that had come to her. Unaware, she may have strayed into a tangle that held her bound and crumpled.

Her chest tightened at the possibility as she moved along the strand of wire, pinning up the clothes. Perhaps she couldn't wrest her way free from Matthew's love. And yet, her heart reminded her constantly that she wanted it. Oh, what a mess. Why did she have to go and fall in love with the doctor of this town? Her plan had been to visit Karen's household for two short weeks, help her get established as a new mother, and return home to her predictable life.

Now she couldn't even say with honesty where home was. Yes, she had family in Chicago, and yes, she was welcome in her brother's home for as long as she wanted to stay. But Karen and her family were here. So were Clara and Lillian, Eva and Gretta, and so many other women she'd grown close to over the summer. And then there was Matthew. She could search the whole of Chicago and find no one like him. The scales had tipped. Oswell City had begun to hold more beloved relationships than her hometown.

She frowned at the baby blanket she pinned to the clothesline. When had that happened? Surely one night on a picnic with the esteemed doctor hadn't influenced her opinion of the rest of the town. She shook her head. The shift had begun long before Friday night. She wouldn't have gone on a picnic with him in the first place if she didn't already love this town and feel at home in it.

Margaret actually loved Oswell City. The behind-the-times dinky rural village had captured her heart. Not because of the lack of modern conveniences or the daily struggle to survive, but because of the people. The faces of members of Logan's congregation, the Ladies Mission Society, town leaders, and businessmen filed across her memory. She cared about them.

Sighing, Margaret reached for a towel. If only she could mesh her life farther into the community she'd discovered without the pressure of making a decision about Matthew's request for a courtship. What a way to complicate matters. She shouldn't have kissed him so willingly.

How wishy washy she'd acted to declare to him one minute she didn't want to marry again, and then lean into him the next. Oh, dear. If she couldn't find a way to understand her own mind, how could she ever expect him to figure it out? Margaret bit her lip in concentration as she hung up the last of the towels. The effort might distract her enough to stop the memory of Matthew's kiss from filling every minute of her day.

"I won't marry him. I can't marry him." Margaret declared to the eye-level row of towels as she clipped the last clothespins in place.

A flapping sheet a short distance away caught her attention. The next second a tall, professional man stood between the rows of clean laundry calling her name. "Margaret."

She stared at him while her heart threatened to succumb to a stroke. Surely he hadn't heard her talking to herself a moment ago. "Matthew! Where ... ah, where did you come from?"

He strode forward. "I was over at Conrad Van Drunen's place. When I saw you outdoors, I cut across the neighbors' lawns to reach you." He picked up her hands and held them in his. "The biplane is assembled. I finished it Saturday. Come take a ride with me."

"Now?" Her eyes grew wide and her heart forgot how to beat. Soon she'd collapse at his feet, providing him with a medical emergency.

"The wind is calm. Not sure how long it will last, and I don't want to fly in the dark." He glanced at the sky and back at her.

"Uh, well, all right. Let me, um, take this basket back inside and tell Karen." Margaret smoothed her skirt and looked around at the laundry, the basket in the grass, and the house.

"Sure. I'll wait."

Margaret's heart throbbed back to life once more. There

were those words again. They held the same steadfast promise from the first time he'd said them. Her gaze flickered to his face. The tenderness in his eyes assured her that he, too, noticed the deeper meaning in his response.

She rushed to the house.

Karen emerged from the bedroom with a finger held to her lips. "Shh. Both boys are asleep."

Margaret nodded and inhaled to catch her breath. "I must leave early. Dr. Kaldenberg caught me in the yard. He ... ah, he wants me to accompany him to his sister's farm this afternoon. I'm not sure how long this errand will take. You'd better not plan on me returning any more today." The words spilled from her mouth in a rush of energy even though she'd tried her best to honor Karen's request for quiet speech.

She flashed a skittish glance out the parlor window. Would Matthew wait for her in the back yard or out front by the street? Karen really should not discover the doctor mulling about the yard with no house call scheduled. Margaret might as well have been a youth trying to sneak out of her parents' home. How tangled her life had become in such a short time.

Karen's brow wrinkled. "Mother? What is it? Why do you have to go with the doctor? Is someone sick at the Van Kleys' and he's asking for your help?"

Margaret shook her head. "Nothing like that. Everyone is well. He only wants to show me his biplane. He got it put together last week." She couldn't bring herself to mention her promise to fly with him. That would lead to questions about their relationship, and Margaret couldn't talk about that. She didn't know how. There were no words to explain.

Karen still frowned at her as if none of her questions had been answered.

"I have to go. I'll see you tomorrow." Margaret reached for her hat and went out the same way she came in.

Matthew met her at the clothesline and led her to his buggy parked in the street near Conrad's home. He helped her to the seat, hopped in, and followed the road out of town. At the farm, he parked beside a weathered barn and helped her out. Then he opened the doors and led her inside.

"Here it is. Finished and ready to fly." A smile nearly as wide as the one he wore when he'd kissed her stretched across his face.

Margaret's heart gave her problems again as an undisputed truth ironed out one of her rumples. This was why she would find the courage to fly with him. The man needed to smile more. She'd helped him accomplish it the night she asked for a ride and again the night she'd let him kiss her. Whatever she must do to bring light to his darkness and joy to his sadness, she'd accept as her own exclusive assignment.

"It looks marvelous, Matthew. I'm quite impressed." Margaret clasped her hands as a smile bloomed on her own face.

"Thanks. Look here. I got the cloth stretched properly over the frame." He smoothed his hand along the bottom wing.

"I remember you were having difficulties with that on Friday." Margaret's gaze took in the motor, the controls, and the two seats on the lower wing. Her stomach flipped. One of them belonged to her as soon as she was ready to entrust her life to the skill of the pilot, the strength of the biplane's frame, and the whims of the breeze. Oh, dear. She couldn't go through with this.

But her willingness to fly with him made Matthew smile. Margaret drew in a breath. She must go through with this.

"How about if I take it up for a test flight before inviting my special passenger to go with me?" Matthew asked as he slipped on a leather helmet and a pair of goggles.

"That sounds like a good idea." Her breathing grew ragged. The extra time alone on the ground might end up giving her one more chance to back out. She couldn't do that. Matthew might see her flee. She'd chain herself to a tree in order to wait for her ride if her desperation came to that.

Matthew climbed into the seat. "Now I need you to spin the propeller."

Propellers! She didn't know a thing about that piece of equipment. Margaret held her breath. She may have gotten herself into something larger and more dangerous than she first expected.

Margaret looked at the wooden blade stretching above her head. This task couldn't be too different from the work of cranking a car. She'd watched Henry's chauffeur do it several times. Margaret reached up and pulled the blade down.

"Again!" Matthew called out.

She followed his direction.

"One more time," he said again.

After her push on the blade, the propeller spun on its own, with the second propeller joining in. The plane lurched forward. Margaret leaped backwards as the propeller blade nearly clipped her hat. She held it on her head as the engine started. It puttered like a happy child ready to seek out an adventure.

Matthew drove the biplane to the edge of the pasture and paused at the start of a long dirt path. She followed behind and watched Matthew race down the path. Before long, the wheels left the ground. He rose above the trees and sailed in the summer sky.

Margaret squinted against the sun to watch him. Like a bird or a large insect, the plane glided and swooped through the air. He flew farther to the horizon and turned back again. The biplane lowered and skimmed over the path until coming to a stop beside her.

"Flies perfectly! Come get on." Matthew patted the empty seat next to him. "Don't wear your hat. The wind will catch it. Another helmet and a pair of goggles are in the barn."

Margaret hastened to find the items and soon returned with them in place. Matthew helped her into the seat, gave her his most brilliant smile yet, and put the biplane in motion.

She allowed the force of the wind to push her against the back of her seat while Matthew gained speed. Near the end of the path, the wheels left the ground. A floating feeling like the one she got when riding in the elevator of Henry's office building overpowered her stomach. She swallowed against the sensation and scrunched her eyes shut.

The biplane tilted to one side as if they were about to turn upside down. Her eyes shot open. Matthew brought the biplane back to a level position and sped through the air high above the trees.

Margaret dared to look down. Houses and barns appeared as little toys. Creeks ran like blue ribbons through the fields. Cattle were but dots on the green carpets of pasture. Amazing. Margaret shifted her attention to her feet dangling in the air far above the solid ground. A sense of calm settled over her.

Flying wasn't so scary after all. At least not when a person flew with a skilled and capable pilot. She stole a glance at Matthew. A sense of calm had settled over him as well. She saw it on his face and read it in his eyes behind the goggles.

A sudden lightness overtook her until Margaret believed she might lift right out of her seat and soar higher than the biplane. Matthew had something in his life that brought him peace and a sense of pleasure. Sharing in it with him was her great honor. She settled back and found enjoyment in the rest of the flight.

Eventually, Matthew brought the biplane in for a landing. He brushed over the tree tops and descended to the path. Slowing his speed, he came to a complete stop only feet away from where he had started.

"How do you like it?" He turned to her and asked.

"I loved it. Flying is so much fun. I never expected to enjoy it as much as I did. But what I liked most was seeing you happy and relaxed. You need to do that more often." She looked into his eyes as she spoke, and her voice took on a sincere tone.

"Good advice. But it won't be the same unless you come with me." His tone was as sincere as hers.

"Anytime."

He put the plane away in the barn and took her back to Clara's in time for the evening meal. Clara asked him to stay and eat with them, but he wanted to go back to Conrad's. The young father and his two small children lived alone. Matthew liked to check up on him at regular intervals to assess his outlook. The man had experienced the same losses in his life that Matthew had.

Margaret admired his understanding and his willingness to care for more than just the physical ailments of the town. She didn't press him to stay. Rather, she told him good-bye with promises to fly again soon. Turning back to the kitchen, she prepared to satisfy Clara's curiosity about her afternoon's adventures. First Karen, and now Clara. Margaret might as well get used to questioning.

18

Karen and Logan accepted another speaking engagement, leaving Margaret in charge of the twins. On the last day of their absence, she took John and Simon out for a stroll.

The morning sun cast light over the homes and yards along the street. It reflected in the windows and warmed the summer air. A light breeze rustled the leaves and wafted the scent of flowers into the street. Dogs barked. Birds chirped. Horses pulling carts or buggies passed by. Cars shared the street with them, the whir of the motors growing closer, then farther away as the vehicles sped along.

Margaret strolled down the sidewalk pushing the carriage in which her grandsons rode. One of the babies waved his hand in the air and gurgled with contentment. His brother watched every object that came into view with large, marveling eyes. Margaret glanced down at John and Simon. They were healthy, well-dressed little men.

A surge of pride filled her chest. Karen and Logan were good parents. Their children would be a credit to them as the years passed. The two small boys were already favorites among Margaret's circle of friends. She couldn't wait to show them off today as she did her shopping in the various stores.

She started with the bakery. Once inside, she stepped up to the counter and presented her list.

Mr. Zahn leaned over the counter for a look at the infants. "Good morning, Mrs. Millerson. The minister and his wife are still gone on their trip I see."

"They'll return this evening." Margaret's mind jumped ahead to the short afternoon in which she must finish the ironing and cook the evening meal before Logan and Karen arrived.

Mr. Zahn nodded. "Just in time for the big sixty-fifth anniversary celebration of the settling of Oswell City. I'm on the planning committee, and we have some questions for the minister."

"He'll be home in plenty of time to answer them, I'm sure." Margaret gave him a reassuring smile.

Mr. Zahn looked over her list. He took it with him and collected the items she'd written down.

After paying him, Margaret left the store and went to the dress shop. As soon as she'd decided to stay in town, Margaret made up for lost time in developing her summer wardrobe. She had arranged with Eva to sew two new blouses and one lightweight Sunday dress. This visit would provide Margaret with an update on Eva's progress.

Many of her friends were already in the shop lined up at the counter or gathered around dress forms. Grace and Joanna turned to greet her. They chatted of the garden club's final plans for their floral display during the celebration that was scheduled on July Fourth, less than a week away.

Margaret and Clara were working together on designs for a generous floral arrangement filled with blooms from Clara's garden. She cultivated a colorful, thriving yard behind her house. They spent many hours in the evenings tending the flowers or sitting on Clara's small back porch enjoying them. The garden club counted on Clara for showy entries. She had a knack for flower arranging along with a dependable supply of blooms to fulfill the requests of the garden club. Margaret was eager to see the final product of their partnership.

Grace reached to pick up John and Joanna held Simon, freeing Margaret to visit with Eva about her orders.

"Your blouses are done. I can send them home with you today if you like." Eva slipped a tape measure around her neck.

"Please. I would appreciate that."

Eva nodded. "Let me go get those for you." She left the counter for the rear of her store and soon returned with two boxes.

Margaret opened one and unfolded the contents. Holding the garment in the air, she examined it.

"How does it look?" Eva asked.

"Lovely. You are every bit as talented as my dressmaker in Chicago." Margaret folded the blouse up and returned it to the box.

"Thank you." Eva beamed.

"How much do I owe you?"

Eva named the price. Margaret paid her, collected her goods and her babies, and returned to the street.

"Margaret!"

She stopped. Margaret would know that voice anywhere. It stayed in her memory as the last sound she heard at night and the first one of the morning. Turning around, she came face to face with Matthew.

"Would you care to come to the house for some coffee? I have something I need to ask you." Matthew shielded his eyes from the bright sun as he stood looking down at her.

She nodded. "Do you mind having the babies along?"

"Not at all. They seem to be in good spirits this morning." He reached to pick up Simon and held the little boy against his shoulder as he guided her to his house.

They made quite a homey picture walking along the bustling downtown street on this summer day. Matthew held Simon safely in his arms while Margaret walked at his side with the carriage. Sometimes, in the quiet of her room at Clara's, she pondered if perhaps she and Matthew had somehow always known the other was out there in the world, and if the bond they shared hadn't been in place years before they met on the night of Karen's wedding. Moments like this one led her to believe it might be true.

They sauntered along together talking about the twins and celebrating each little step of growth as if Simon and John were their own children, and they were the ones responsible for bringing the twins into the world.

People turned and stared at them. Others smiled and waved, calling out, "Hi, Doc!" in a greeting. The journey brought them to Matthew's front step.

He opened the door. "Millie?" he called into the spacious kitchen.

An older woman hastened into view. "Yes, Doctor. What is it?"

"Don't get alarmed. There is no emergency. I've brought home some guests and I wonder if you might fix us up some coffee." Matthew opened the door wider.

Margaret picked John up from the carriage, and, leaving it in the yard, entered the house.

The woman's gaze traveled over Margaret as a grin stretched her mouth. "Well, well, Doctor. You've brought her home at last. Better introduce me."

Matthew's neck turned red as he cleared his throat and gestured to Margaret. "Millie, this is Margaret Millerson and her grandsons Simon," he said while pointing to the baby on his shoulder, "and John. Margaret, please meet Millie, my housekeeper."

Margaret nodded to the smiling woman and echoed her "pleased to meet you."

"Now about coffee." Millie snapped into action. "You folks go on out to the parlor and I'll be along shortly."

"I'm glad I caught you in town this morning. With my

schedule of appointments at the office, I wasn't sure when I'd have the chance to see you again." Matthew spoke as he brought Margaret into the parlor and offered her a chair.

She sat and adjusted John on her lap so he could look around.

Matthew claimed the end of the sofa, folded a blanket, and laid Simon on it next to him. "The mayor has asked me to fly a banner behind my biplane over the downtown square during next week's celebration. I wanted to ask if you would go with me."

Margaret gulped. She and Matthew weren't courting, and yet he wanted her to go with him in his plane in the sight of the whole town. All those people! But flying was so much fun. And Matthew was such a good pilot. Flying with him would make him smile. Oh, she hardly knew what to say.

Millie arrived with a tray holding the coffeepot, cups, and a plate of cookies. The interruption gave her time to manufacture an answer.

"Do you need time to think it over?" Matthew asked as he filled a cup with coffee.

"No, um, well, maybe yes ... a little." She stammered as her honesty caught up with her surprise.

"Fine. I understand. The celebration is still five days away. I don't need an answer right away." He reached for a cookie and ate it without looking at her. A hint of resignation threaded through his voice.

Margaret didn't want to be the cause of any more sadness in his life. She must say something to cheer him up. "My hesitation isn't because I don't want to go with you. It's just that, well, I like flying out in the country, but this flight will go over the town. Everyone will be watching. They will think ... they will think that you and I are ..." Margaret exhaled. She didn't know how to finish in a way that wouldn't make him sad.

"Courting? Is that it? You don't want to fly over town because you fear it will give the impression that we are courting." Matthew's full attention stayed on her as he sipped from his cup.

If she were a child, she'd give in to the urge to squirm under his gaze. Again, she felt the need to apologize but instead gave a silent nod in agreement.

"Aren't we?" He reached for a second cookie.

She frowned. "Aren't we what?"

A tiny smile tugged at his mouth. His voice flowed deep and convincing as he spoke. "The night of your daughter's wedding is forever seared onto my heart. I can't forget."

The quiet words drove a dagger through her tender, injured places. He wanted to court her, to wait for her, to never finish loving her. Nothing she could think of to say could match the meaning that simmered in his earnest words. She filled her cup with coffee and drank it so she wouldn't have to give a reply.

"I will fly over downtown at two o'clock in the afternoon. The flight will begin at the Ellenbroeks' where I'll take off in a nearby field. If you want to come, meet me there at one forty-five. I won't make you give me an answer. Take your time to decide." Pain shadowed the blue of his eyes telling her what the relinquishment cost him.

Margaret turned back to her coffee cup. Everything in her screamed at her to stay away. He could fly alone. The town asked him to perform the feat, not her.

They struggled through a jolted conversation about the babies and Karen's and Logan's trip. Her coffee gone, Margaret gathered the twins and returned to the parsonage with Matthew's pain-filled eyes haunting her.

The rest of the week, Margaret did her best staying focused on her work at Karen's, but Matthew's invitation snagged her thoughts infusing them with fear and unrest. As she sat in church on Sunday listening to Logan preach, the matter found resolution in Margaret's heart. She would not go with him. Her consent to fly would send Matthew the message that she wanted a courtship.

It would send the town the message that she and the doctor were going in the direction of marriage. Neither of those statements were true. Messages carried meaning, as Logan was demonstrating so well right now. Margaret didn't want to proclaim any sort of message that was inconsistent with her desires or that she'd come to regret later. She'd made friends here. Now was not the time to start burning bridges.

ON THE DAY of the festivities, Logan and Karen brought the twins as far as Clara's. They met Margaret there since Clara had already gone to set up the garden club's displays. Margaret went with her family to the square where they sampled pastries, watched the Miss Independence Day pageant, and heard the mayor's speech.

Her eyes trailed to the sky on occasion throughout the day. Matthew would fly his plane up there. Maybe she should go. Each time she considered the idea she dismissed it. She would not go. They were not courting. Matthew must fly alone.

She didn't see him among the crowd of townspeople. Maybe he had been called on an emergency or was busy at the farm preparing to fly. Margaret pushed the question of his whereabouts from her mind and made the effort to focus on what Paull Ellenbroek said from his place behind the podium.

At the point in the speech when he commended the businessmen, someone whispered in her ear, "Mrs. Millerson."

Margaret turned to find Millie standing near.

"Do you know where the doctor is?" she asked with a worried expression on her face.

"No, I do not."

Millie bit her lip. Margaret must not have given her the answer she wanted.

"What's wrong?" Is there anything I can do to help?"

"Two people are at the office with heat exhaustion. I made them as comfortable as I can, but they really need to see the doctor. I don't know where to find him. This isn't like him. He usually tells me his schedule, at least as much as he knows of it anyway since it is always changing, but I can't find him." Worry creased Millie's brow and drooped the corners of her eyes.

"I might."

"Really?" Millie brightened.

"He told me his plans for this afternoon when I came for coffee at his house last week. I can give him the message."

"Thank you, Mrs. Millerson. I'll head back to the office and take care of those folks until he comes." Millie patted Margaret's arm and then walked away.

Margaret turned to Logan who stood next to her in the crowd around the mayor's platform. "I must go find someone. I'll meet up with you later." She left the assembly without waiting for Logan's response.

Taking a deep breath, Margaret followed the street away from the center of town. The one place she didn't want to go was the very one where the uncontrollable events of the afternoon took her. This road had better not lead her into any trouble.

19

"Looks ready to go!" Tim called to Matthew as they walked around the biplane in one last inspection.

"Let me check the fuel." Matthew opened the tank and glanced in.

"You've got plenty." Tim looked over his shoulder.

"Matthew!"

His name carried from the direction of the road. He turned to find Margaret hurrying across the field.

"You came!" His chest expanded. He might have even heard the church choir breaking into song somewhere behind him.

A solemn expression stayed on her features. "Millie found me downtown and asked me to let you know that you have two visitors at your office who are in need of medical attention for heat exhaustion."

"I thought this might happen." Matthew fought the slump threatening to weigh him down, but he couldn't keep the disappointment out of his voice. Margaret hadn't come because she'd chosen to fly with him. She'd come on business, and only because Millie asked her to. And now he might not get to go up in the air at all.

He should have learned by now that getting excited about anything only led to discouragement.

Tim jogged over. "What's the matter?"

"Two patients are at the office. I may not be able to fly now." His voice gave a clue to the sorrow flooding his soul.

"Leave them to me. Just tell me what to do and I'll take care of it until you can get there." Tim slapped Matthew on the back.

"That's a good idea."

"Unless Mrs. Millerson would like to tend to the patients. She might know more about that than flying." Tim squinted against the sun and glanced at her.

Margaret shook her head. "I don't know anything about how to help a sick person. I might even make their condition worse."

Tim chuckled and pointed at Matthew. "Then you'll have to go with him so I can work at the clinic."

Margaret shot a look at him filled with questions and also with some horror mixed in.

"Uh-huh." Tim nodded. "We discovered a few minutes ago that Matt needs a passenger to go along with him. I was going to do it, but he might prefer to take you."

Margaret frowned at him. "What is the passenger supposed to do?"

"Keep watch on this banner streaming out behind the biplane so that it doesn't get caught on anything. Matt will have to keep his eyes on where he's going. He needs someone to pay attention to the banner behind him." Tim pointed to the mass of cloth spread over the field. Parts of the letters were visible between the folds.

"Please, Margaret? I could really use your help." Matthew tried to keep the pleading out of his voice but failed.

"Come on! It's two o'clock right now. I'll spin your propeller." Tim sprinted over to the plane.

Matthew ventured a glance at her face and held out a shaking hand. "Shall we?"

Margaret studied his hand for a moment and then grasped it.

He led her to the biplane and gave her a helmet while his heart praised God for divine intervention in the forms of his housekeeper and those poor people waiting for medical attention at the clinic.

"Hey, Tim!" Matthew called out.

"Yeah?" Tim looked away from the propeller he clutched.

"Come here a minute. Let me tell you what to do for those patients at the clinic."

Tim came over and listened to Matthew's instructions. He nodded and then went back to spin the propeller.

They settled in their seats as the engine started. Tim gave him a salute as if to say the engine sounded strong and capable of making this historic flight for the sake of the town.

"Ready?" He turned to Margaret and studied her solemn face.

She nodded her head.

"Thanks for coming with me." He reached over and held one of her hands for a brief moment.

The plane lurched indicating the propellers were in motion and eager to lift off the ground.

Matthew grasped the controls, and the speed of the engine increased. The plane jerked forward and ate up the ground beneath them. Soon the wind caught the wings and they were off. The cloth banner fluttered in the wind behind them, proudly displaying the words, *A Day to Remember: 65 Years.*

As soon as they rose above the trees, Matthew directed the plane toward the center of town. Soon the assembly on the square came into view. The sound of the band playing a rousing march floated to the sky. People waved and cheered with their faces lifted to the heavens. The sun shone. The engine roared. The seat next to him carried the most precious person to him in all the world. What a perfect day for flying.

They zoomed over the square and on past Main Street with its box-shaped brick buildings that looked like fragile little toys from this vantage point. On past the hotel, the train station, and the lumberyard they flew. This was too much fun to end so soon.

He made a wide turn to the left and circled the square once more. Now everyone watching the sky was sure to get a perfect view of the banner waving behind him.

Gusts of wind flapped the cloth.

"Oh no! Be careful!" Margaret turned to look at him for a moment and then shifted her attention back to the banner.

A stronger gust caught the plane and jerked it to the side. Matthew jammed the controls to correct their position, but the plane failed to respond. It twisted in a downward motion until colliding with the branches of a huge oak tree in the small forest north of the downtown square.

The sounds of ripping fabric and splintering wood reached his ears. Matthew slammed to a complete stop high in the tree where he dangled far out on the end of a limb over shaded grass that appeared miles and miles below him.

His stomach lurched into his throat and his head went dizzy. The sensation of flying at a swift speed still controlled him. His body had not yet caught on to the fact that it had come to an abrupt stop. Matthew reached for the nearest stationary object. If he didn't hang on with all his might, he could very well somersault over the front of his wrecked plane and crash on the ground.

He closed his eyes for a moment. When the world felt stable again, he looked over at Margaret. Twigs from a branch had torn her helmet off. Her hair hung tangled in the tree. A gash dripped blood from the side of her face. She looked at him with wide eyes and a white face. Even her lips had turned white.

"Your plane is ruined," she whispered.

"Never mind the plane. I'll tend to it later. You are hurt. I need to get you out of this tree." Matthew studied her neck, her hands, her blouse. No other blood appeared.

"There's nothing wrong with me. Well, maybe. My ankle is a bit twisted. It is caught in the branches." She closed her eyes and winced in pain.

The sight of pain on her face flared to life every doctor

impulse he possessed. Coupled with the love that filled his heart, Matthew believed he had enough strength to pull that entire tree down with his bare hands.

"You need examined. I must get you out of here." He squirmed every which way in search of an avenue of escape.

"Matthew, don't." Margaret laid a limp hand on his.

His activity rustled the branches which shifted the plane into a more precarious position.

He quit moving and looked at her once more. "I don't have a cloth to wipe your face."

"The bleeding will stop soon. Don't worry." She gave him a shaky smile.

Matthew's chest ached. First, she worried about his plane being wrecked. Now she told him not to worry about her. She'd been right in her hesitation to fly with him today. He shouldn't have taken her along.

"I'm sorry."

She shook her head. "None of this is your fault."

"Doctor! Hey, Doctor Kaldenberg. Where are ya? We saw your plane go down." Harley, the owner of the lumberyard, yelled through the small forest.

"Up here. We are in the oak tree, way at the top," Matthew called back.

Harley and two other men came into view.

"Look up," Matthew yelled.

The men stopped and followed directions. "Good grief, Doc. You got yourself stuck all right," Harley said.

"Help us down. Mrs. Millerson is injured." Matthew watched the men while he tried to sit very still. Any more shifting about and the plane could crash to the earth.

Harley stepped up to the trunk of the tree and rubbed a hand over its surface. "What do ya say, boys? Looks like we'll have to cut her down to get the plane out."

The others nodded and murmured in agreement with him.

Harley stepped away and looked up. "We'll come right back with some help and equipment."

"Please hurry," Matthew called out.

The men rushed away leaving Matthew and Margaret alone in the tree.

He had nothing to say. This entire misfortune was his fault even though Margaret tried to tell him otherwise. He should do something or say something, but he didn't know what. His mind strayed to the patients in the clinic. They may have to wait a long time now for medical treatment. Maybe Millie and Tim had done enough to help then through the emergency.

A gust of wind rustled through the tree. It shook the plane causing Margaret to clutch his arm. "Oh! Matthew! I'm falling." Her grasp tightened.

"I won't let you. Come here." Matthew slid out of his seat to a sturdy place on the wing undamaged by tree branches. He pulled Margaret with him so she might have his driver's seat. A big branch protruded through the frame of the biplane on his other side. He held onto it for support. If the wind should blow again and frighten Margaret, she could join him on the wing and cling to the branch too.

She didn't wait for a gust of wind. The plane shifted enough on its own to scare her. With his help, she crept onto the wing and wrapped her arms around the branch. There they sat, legs entangled and arms clinging to the tree when their rescuers arrived.

Harley had brought an army with him. Marching at the front were Logan and Karen followed by Tim and Rebecca, Matthew's parents, and the crew from the lumberyard.

Matthew drew in a deep breath. The men had also brought a horse and wagon, axes, rope, and a ladder. Before much more time passed, Matthew and his passenger would be safely on the ground.

Harley stood the ladder against the trunk. He climbed up as high as he dared and then chopped at a branch with his axe.

Coming Home to Mercy

"We're clearin' a way for ya to get down, Doc. Just hold tight. We'll get ya out of there in no time."

When the branch fell under Harley's axe, one of the men tossed a rope up to him. He tied it to a thick branch behind the biplane and hoisted himself up. Tying and hoisting, Harley worked his way to the top of the tree.

"All right, Mrs. Millerson. You're first. Hold my hand. I'll help you." He reached his muscular arm away from his stout frame in readiness to catch Margaret's hand.

With one fearful glance at Matthew, she leaned over the rickety edge of the wing and placed herself in Harley's care.

"Careful of her ankle," Matthew cautioned as he watched their progress through the gaps in the branches. The rope around her waist, Margaret limped down the tree under Harley's steady guidance. The pair finally reached the ladder.

Cheers rose from the spectators when Margaret settled her good foot on the top rung. Logan stepped forward. "Let me help you, Mother." He reached to take her in his arms before her twisted ankle sustained much strain. Logan settled her in the grass at the base of another tree.

"You're, next, Doc." Harley appeared among the branches and reached for Matthew.

With the same careful descent, Harley assisted Matthew down the tree until reaching the ladder. Matthew raced to the ground and leaned over Margaret. The firm foundation under his feet restored his sense of control.

"Bring the wagon around. We must get Margaret home so that I can tend to her gash and examine her ankle."

Harley joined him on the ground and untied the rope from his middle. Logan picked Margaret up once more and put her in the wagon. Matthew and his family, along with Logan and Karen rode with her through downtown.

At the clinic, Matthew stood. "Stop! Please. I must check on some patients and get my bag."

"The patients are all fixed up, Matt," Tim informed him.

"You won't need to worry about them any more today. Millie and I took care of them."

Matthew nodded his thanks as he leaped from the wagon. He gathered his supplies and returned in an instant. When they reached Clara's, Harley parked the wagon in the street. Logan carried Margaret into the house and set her on her bed. Matthew learned from Karen that Clara wasn't home because she had gone to the parsonage to care for the twins so Logan and Karen could go to the scene of the accident.

The doctor in him spurred him into action. He asked for a basin of water and a cloth to cleanse Margaret's face. Family members milled around between the bedroom and the parlor while Matthew worked. He wanted to tell them all to go home, but they were probably a bit shaken up, too, and one more visit with Margaret might make them feel better.

Margaret's face clean and bandaged, Matthew set to work on her ankle. He pressed in various places to detect the areas of the most pain. He and Margaret talked in low, serious tones through the exam and the treatment. At his request, his mother brought him a chunk of ice from Clara's ice box. Matthew sat on the edge of Margaret's bed for a long while moving the ice around on her foot to help the swelling go down.

"How are you feeling?" He stood and looked at her.

"A little frazzled. But good sleep will straighten me out." She gave him a wry smile.

No one else occupied the room, so Matthew applied the one ministration he believed most helpful to this exclusive patient. He bent and placed a kiss on her forehead. When he straightened, Margaret looked into his eyes with trust glowing in hers.

He left the room to address the family members in the parlor. "Mrs. Millerson is going to be fine. Her gash did not require stitches, and her ankle has a mild sprain. In a couple of days she will feel much improved. You may go in to see her now."

Tim, Rebecca, and his parents went in first. After wishing

Margaret a swift recovery, they told Matthew of their relief over his lack of injuries and left the house.

Karen and Logan remained. They followed Matthew into the bedroom. Karen rushed to her mother's bedside. A mixture of pity and frustration rang in her voice.

"Mother, what were you thinking to participate in such a stunt? I don't know where to begin telling you of my shock to discover my mother as the doctor's passenger when he flew over. My mother! You know Logan didn't approve at first of the purchase of this biplane. I'm glad it is wrecked. Now no one else in this town will take any more foolish risks."

Matthew worked about the room rolling up bandage and restoring order as he listened. His heart throbbed. He could understand a daughter's concern for her injured mother. But her impassioned feelings about his biplane revealed to him a new side of his minister's wife. She might influence Logan to return to his original opinions. Matthew's wish to repair his biplane might cause nothing but conflict among the people he cared about most. He and Logan needed to have a talk.

Karen fell to her knees at Margaret's bedside as her voice took on a pleading tone. "Why did you do it, Mother? Why?"

Matthew glanced at Margaret as curious as anyone else in the room what her answer would be.

She met his gaze as a smile broke out on her face. Turning to her daughter, Margaret spoke in a voice a mother uses to teach small children important lessons.

"Karen, my dear, there is something you must understand. The fine doctor of this town and I have discovered that we love each other. He has asked to court me and I ... well, I have accepted."

Matthew's brows rose. The circus of emotions performing on his insides pressed him to do much more, but he'd save his proper response for later when no one but Margaret would see. She looked at him with unwavering trust shining in her eyes.

He hardly knew what to do. To think he could actually win

the woman of his dreams by tangling her up in a wreck in the top of a tree. Maybe he'd gone about this courtship business all wrong. He'd have to chat with her and find out what in the world had changed her mind.

Karen's mouth hung open at the news.

A grin stretched across Logan's face. "That's good news. Congratulations." He came over and shook Matthew's hand.

Matthew nodded. At least Logan approved of this venture. Maybe convincing him of the necessity of repairs to the biplane would prove easier than he thought.

"You ... you ... and the doctor?" Karen had found her voice and now tried to comprehend the facts.

"Yes, my dear," Margaret answered with a calm confidence.

"Does this mean you are thinking of getting married again?" Karen crossed her arms as a hint of hostility crept into her voice.

Margaret smoothed the bed covers. "We haven't gotten that far yet. But if we do, I wouldn't make such a large decision without consulting you and Julia."

Karen relaxed a tiny degree.

"Come on, sweetheart. Let's go home and check on the twins." Logan went to her and settled his hands on her shoulders.

She allowed him to usher her out of the room, leaving Matthew alone with his unpredictable and enchanting patient. He settled on the edge of the bed and took her hands in his.

"What made you change your mind?"

"I feel safe with you. The truth occurred to me as we crouched together on the wing of your plane while we hung onto that tree for dear life." She laughed softly but then grew serious again. "You'd never let anything dangerous happen to me. You'd do whatever you had to do to protect me. It's enough for me." She reached up and smoothed the hair that had long ago fallen over his forehead.

His eyes threatened to mist over. "You're right, Margaret. You mean that much and more to me."

The tears on her cheeks made him want to carry her off that very minute and take her straight home with him. He wiped one of them away as celebration erupted on his insides. Today, he'd made great strides toward his goal of winning her. That knowledge would uphold him through the remaining conquest.

20

Matthew circled the hayrack. It had once been the vehicle of honor that transported his brand new biplane through town, but now it served as a hearse ready to cart the destroyed remnants of that cherished plane away from the scene of demise.

"We told the mayor in the last city council meeting that his plan held risks." Artie Goud stared at the wreckage with his hands on his hips.

"Yeah. We've known from the first time you told us you were going to Dayton to buy the thing that it would cause you nothing but trouble." George Brinks crossed his arms over his chest and shook his head.

"Not sure it's worth fixing, Doctor." James Koelman had come out of his law office to join the group gawking at the broken biplane. "Are you sure flying is worth the expense of repair and the time required to restore it?"

Matthew's throat ached. If these men only knew what the biplane meant to him. If he could just find the words to explain the thrill of flight and his deep longing for the freedom it gave him, they might see this situation differently.

"Where do you want us to take it?" Harley shifted his weight to one booted foot and wiped his brow. His crew of salvagers turned their attention from the mass of torn fabric and broken frame they tied to the rack and watched Matthew for his answer.

He shook his head. "I don't know." He paused and looked up at the disfigured flying machine. "Tim's barn is the best place, I suppose. But the plane needs too much repair for me to store it at the farm."

Harley tromped over. "Where does a fella go for fixin' up a biplane? When cars get wrecked, Martin works on 'em over at the car garage. But planes, well, no one around here has ever flown one or wrecked one. Until now. Never heard of a plane repair shop."

"They don't exist." Matthew's gaze traveled along the bent frame of the upper wing. He didn't want to think of the cost or the time involved in restoring his prized means of transportation to its original glory. Maybe James was right and he should forget about the endeavor.

"Then what's a man supposed to do when he gets in a wreck?" Annoyance tainted Harley's voice.

"The plane shouldn't get in a wreck in the first place. But if it happens, the pilot must fix the plane himself. I'll have to send away to the factory in Dayton for new parts and do the work on my own." Matthew ran his hand over a frayed end of fabric.

"That doesn't make any sense. You've gotta have some help. The plane has a motor, doesn't it? At least take the plane over to Oswell City Auto and have Martin take a look at the motor." Harley huffed as he made one last tug on a rope.

Orville had trained Matthew on everything there was to know about a biplane motor. He would be able to detect damage without any help from the car garage. But then again, the parking lot at the car garage might offer enough space for him to store his plane until new parts arrived. Martin might even let him work on his plane at Oswell City Auto, saving him the strain of hauling the broken plane across town, through the country, and then cramming it into Tim's hay barn.

Coming Home to Mercy

"Worth a try. Let's go." Matthew leaped up onto the rack along with Harley's crew and watched the road as Harley guided the team of horses to Oswell City Auto.

Martin's brother, Ezra, who was also his partner in the business, met the conclave in the parking lot. Ezra was a cheery and slightly nervous man, as indicated by his slim build and lean frame. Always on the move, this man had proven himself as a large key to the auto business's success. He was only two years settled in Oswell City after immigrating with his family from a province in Holland. He greeted the group with a wave of his hand in the air.

"Saw you coming, Doctor. What is all this, the plane you flew over town yesterday?" Ezra lowered his hand and waved it in a flourish at the hayrack.

"It is. Harley suggested that one of your men might look over the motor. I wonder if you might have room for me to store it here until replacement parts arrive." Matthew shouldn't impose in this way, but instead go to the extra work to haul his plane out to the farm and deal with his problems there.

The morning breeze caught the shredded banner that had managed to remain attached to the plane during its extraction from the tree. It flapped it in the air. The number 65 representing the years Oswell City had existed as a community were torn away, but the words *A Day to Remember* waved visible for all to see. Yesterday had certainly been a day to remember. His pride and confidence had come crashing down along with his plane. He, Matthew Kaldenberg, the doctor, defiant of death, courageous in his new hobby, had failed.

The mayor, representative of the town, had given him an important assignment. But he'd tangled the banner in a tree instead of completing the mission. Even worse, Margaret had finally agreed to go with him, but he'd exposed her to danger and injury. The few times when she'd gone in the air with him might stand as the only times he'd have the pleasure of her company on a flight.

Matthew's heart shrunk. Sure, he'd made a mistake in his service to the town and also allowed Margaret to get injured, but his most notorious failure was his desertion of the commission Logan had given him. The day of flight over the town square should have been his chance to prove his ability to rise above.

He could overcome grief and sorrow, loss and loneliness. Everyone should have had the chance to see him soar free and light. But instead, they'd watched him wreck. The ascent back among the clouds was a long one indeed. Maybe it was too high for him to ever consider reaching.

Ezra showed Harley into a lane near the rear of the building. They worked together unloading the plane and assessing the damage. Ezra put the plane on the schedule for one of his mechanics to service during the upcoming week.

Taking Harley up on his offer of a ride, Matthew jumped back onto the rack and asked to be taken to his parents' house. He must hash this all out with these important people in his life. They would help him the best of anyone to regain perspective and recover his enthusiasm.

Father met him at the door and showed him into the dining room. "Nice to see you, son. Your mother is dishing up food for our noon meal. Come join us."

Matthew washed his hands and took a seat at the table. It had been his regular one through his years of growing up in this home. It offered him a view through the wide windows of the street and the houses on the other side. Rebecca had always sat across from him with Mother to his right and Father to his left. This was how life had always been before he married and lost, went away to medical school and started his life over.

Matthew gulped to push those sad memories from him. How he treasured entering into the family circle once more and reaping the blessing of this fellowship, eating his mother's good food, and hearing his father's prayer for him.

The conversation centered on the festivities of the previous day while they ate their meal. Matthew told of the conditions that led to the tangle in the tree. He shared his feelings of failure and his concerns of repairing the plane.

"Don't let the crash get you down, Matthew. You'll get your repairs made and fly again." Mother and Father lavished encouragement on him in their quiet and supportive way.

Matthew left the house satisfied that he'd received what he'd come for, but one unanswered question hovered below the surface. He must seek out one more special person in his life in his attempt to lay it to rest.

Turning right onto Fifth Street, Matthew walked to the church and went inside. Logan might not be in his study at this early afternoon hour. If he wasn't, Matthew would go next door and ask Karen for a clue to his location. If that didn't work, Matthew might drive around town in search of him. The hope of a discussion with Logan weighed that heavy on his mind.

Matthew walked the hall and discovered an open door.

Logan sat at his desk. He glanced up at the sound of footsteps on the stone floor and smiled. "Good afternoon, Doctor. What can I do for you?"

Matthew slipped into Logan's study and sat down. "I want to talk to you about yesterday."

Logan dropped his pen and leaned back in his chair.

"I didn't realize Mrs. De Witt would be so upset about her mother flying with me. I thought she knew about us. I assumed Margaret had been keeping both of you informed of our interest in one another as well as of the enjoyment she finds in flying with me.

"But, from hearing Mrs. De Witt's conversation with her mother in the sickroom yesterday, I see now that I was mistaken." Matthew clasped his hands and settled them in his lap. He'd run out of facts. He must wait now to see how his son in the Spirit would respond.

Logan raised a brow and shook his head. "It was new to us. Yesterday was the first we knew of the flying or of the possible courtship. Karen's mother has said nothing about any of it."

Matthew frowned. "How unusual. But I suppose Margaret knows how to handle this sort of a circumstance with her daughters."

Logan nodded. "Karen resists the idea of her mother marrying again. I'm sure her dislike has nothing to do with you. She respects you very highly."

"Sure, I understand. Margaret has told me enough about her past for me to know what life must have been like for your wife in the days of her childhood." Matthew paused, glanced out the window on the summer day, and then looked back at Logan.

A smile stretched Logan's mouth and a soft expression of empathy entered his eyes, but he offered no reply.

Matthew leaned forward. "I wonder if the most appropriate next step for me to take would be to ask for your permission to court Margaret."

Logan looked amused. "Why do you need my permission?"

"For the sake of your wife and her mother. If Mrs. De Witt knows I've formally asked for a relationship with her mother, maybe it will wipe away the secrecy and confusion. It will make her feel like she has some influence over the situation. Over time, I hope she gets used to the idea of her mother remarrying and will even accept it instead of resisting so much."

Logan grinned. "Then I say 'yes.' But we should probably include one condition."

"What's that?"

"Karen will never approve of her mother going up in a biplane again." Logan's expression held a hint of apology as if he knew how much the stipulation changed Matthew's strategy.

"Agreed. The biplane is in bad enough shape that it will be quite some time before it is ready to fly again." A chuckle rumbled in his throat.

"I'll tell Karen that we've talked. Maybe you'd like to visit with her sometime yourself." Logan folded his arms over his chest.

Matthew nodded. "I'll do that. Thank you, Logan. I feel

much better about this situation now that I've talked it over with you."

Logan reached to shake his hand. "My pleasure. Stop in any time."

Matthew left the church with his heart lifted and his questions answered. The only person left to share thoughts and feelings with was Margaret. He'd go to Clara's this evening after spending the remainder of the day at the clinic. He had some hard news to deliver from his talk with Logan. Matthew made a brief detour into one of the downtown stores to purchase the perfect gift that would help him smooth the way.

21

Margaret dabbed her forehead with her handkerchief. The parlor had grown stuffy in the afternoon hours. The heat of the day contributed, but so did the steady stream of visitors she'd received. Lillian and Eva, Cornelia, Mildred, Grace, Helen, Gretta, and Joanna had come to see her. A couple of the women had even brought bouquets left over from the Garden Club's Fourth of July display.

The gesture meant so much. These women truly were her friends. Margaret had succeeded in penetrating the close ties of this small town and become one of them. The ladies had sat in the parlor with Margaret, careful not to bump her foot, resting on a stool, while Clara served sandwiches and lemonade. The afternoon had resembled a party more than a sickroom where calls were made on the suffering.

Margaret didn't suffer at all. In fact, her sprained ankle had served as the catalyst to so many blessings. The accident causing her injury deepened her trust in Matthew. It also had presented her with the perfect opportunity to tell her daughter of her true feelings. She would not have known where to begin explaining to Karen this new and unexpected interest in a man.

She'd given both of her daughters every reason to believe she had no desire for another marriage. Surely she hadn't deceived them. Memories of the conversation with Karen from the day before rushed into her mind. Karen did not want to see her mother hurt by someone again. She would need time to accept the idea. Maybe she'd allow Matthew to prove to her in some way his love for her mother.

Margaret sighed. More conversations and more tense days were ahead if she really allowed this new courtship to take its course. Thoughts of her friends resumed, replacing the dreary ones about her daughter. Because of this sprained ankle, she'd discovered the sincerity in her new friendships.

They had each come to call on her, some bringing flowers, and all of them expressing concern for her. Margaret settled back among the pillows propping her up on the sofa. Life had taken a turn, but it was a new and interesting direction. She could remain quite content in this place surrounded by friends and assured that she was wanted here.

A knock came at the door. Clara's footsteps clicked on the floor from the kitchen to the front of the house. Margaret waited. Perhaps this caller was another person come to see her.

Karen entered the room. A solemn look hung on her face as Margaret greeted her and invited her to sit down.

"I can't stay too long. Logan is at home with the twins. But I wanted to come and check on you. Has you ankle improved since yesterday?"

"Yes, my dear. The swelling has gone down. Clara expects that I should be able to walk on it by Monday, but we must wait to see what the doctor says." Margaret adjusted the lightweight afghan Clara had arranged over her leg earlier in the day.

At the mention of the doctor, Karen straightened and a flicker of pain crossed her face. "Has he been here yet today?"

Margaret shook her head. "No. I'm sure he is very busy."

Karen fingered the edge of a lace doily on the arm of her chair. "How often have you flown with him?"

The quiet firmness in Karen's voice and her refusal to meet

Margaret's gaze made her heart swell. Karen was a very good daughter. She'd rallied after her father's death and gone on to college to prepare for a teaching career. Her first position had been miles away from home in a country school.

Then she married a pastor and made the necessary sacrifices to share life and ministry with him. This saint of a girl was the last person on earth who would sanction any mistreatment in Margaret's life. She loved her mother, protected her, and stationed herself on the watch towers of Margaret's existence sounding the alarm against any foe to her mother's independence and happiness.

"The trip across town yesterday was only the second time." Margaret laid her hand on Karen's knee.

"But you intended to do it again, didn't you?" Karen spoke in the tone of a mother disciplining a small and wayward child.

"Probably." Margaret heaved in a large breath.

"Mother, how can you agree to such nonsense?" A tone of hurt entered Karen's voice as if the simple confession included a personal insult.

"Karen, my dear, flying is fun. I love it." A smile stretched Margaret's face but Karen rolled her eyes. "And, well, flying with Matthew makes him smile. When I go with him, he is relaxed. That man needs to enjoy life more."

Margaret looked out the window and caught a glimpse of the cloudless blue sky. If Matthew's plane wasn't wrecked, He'd probably find the time to fly it today. If her ankle wasn't injured, she'd find a way to go with him.

"I'm not sure it is your job to help him have fun." Karen crossed her arms.

Margaret met Karen's gaze. "He needs someone. That person might as well be me."

Karen frowned. "I wish I could tell you what to do."

Margaret patted her cheek. "Don't worry, my dear. Matthew is the most courageous man I know. He will keep me safe."

Karen's gaze trailed down to the ankle propped up between them. The expression on her face told Margaret she disagreed.

Another knock came on the door. Karen stood. "I must go. Logan will be waiting for me to feed the twins before we can have our supper."

Matthew entered the room. He carried a beautiful arrangement of white roses. "Good evening, ladies. How are you feeling, Margaret?"

"Better. The swelling is less, but I'd still like for you to take a look at it."

"I'd be happy to."

Karen bent to place a kiss on Margaret's cheek. "Take care, Mother. I'll stop in again tomorrow to see you."

Matthew reached out and grasped Karen's arm. "May I stop over at the parsonage in a little while? There is something I'd like to talk to you about."

A startled look crossed Karen's face. "Yes, of course."

Matthew nodded and Karen left the room. "These are for you." He held the bouquet out to Margaret.

She took them and admired them. "They are lovely. Thank you."

He set the flowers on a nearby table and settled on the sofa next to her. "Margaret, I'm so sorry about the accident yesterday. I wish I could have prevented it so that you weren't injured. I'm honored that you were willing to go with me. Thank you for taking the risk."

Her eyes misted. "I wanted to. I like knowing I can give you joy in that way."

His smile came out. She was becoming quite practiced lately in making it appear.

He cocked a brow. "Even though it gave everyone the impression that we are courting?"

"Yes, Matthew, even then. There are some things more important than my own silly worries about appearances." Too many times, she focused on the superficial. Living in this small town and getting to know Matthew was curing her of this weakness.

As Matthew examined her ankle, memories from her marriage to Simon flashed into Margaret's mind. Her first husband had only given her two bouquets of flowers during their life together. The first bouquet had come on their first wedding anniversary. The second one had come after a terrible argument about money. Days later, the police had arrived at the house and exposed the truth about Simon's gambling crimes.

She'd thrown those flowers out. They'd only served to remind her of the pain she suffered as the wife of a prestigious pastor of a wealthy city church reduced to scandal and shame.

But Matthew's flowers came with honor and respect. He gave them with apology and gratitude. A different kind of love radiated from his gift. Maybe it was the real quality of love, and the brand she'd experienced with Simon had only been a false template.

These comparisons had never entered her mind before now. She'd believed the kind of love her marriage offered had been the only kind available. But what if a different, deeper, and more authentic kind existed? And if it did, was Matthew the best one to show it to her?

AFTER TWILIGHT, Matthew walked over to the parsonage. He entered a home filled with evidence of cherished babies. A pile of diapers lay folded on the table. A blanket draped over the arm of a chair. The cradle stood near the sofa. Logan held a baby on his shoulder as he led Matthew to the parlor.

His heart pricked. If Matthew were to marry Margaret, Logan would really be his son. They would belong to the same family. This thought brought a glow to Matthew's insides. No longer would he carry a secret comparison of this young man to the children he never had. Marriage to Margaret would offer him children, and those children would be of a higher quality of character than he could have known to ask for.

Karen greeted him and invited him to take a seat. "We've been expecting you. What do you want to talk about? Does it have something to do with the twins?"

"No. I've come to visit with you about your mother." Matthew took a seat and looked at Karen.

"My mother?" Her posture stiffened. "What about her?"

Matthew swallowed. With a quick glance at Logan for support, he plunged in. "I'd like to ask your permission to court your mother. I'm so very sorry for how the flight through town went. I never intended for your mother to get injured.

"Neither did I know that she'd kept our growing relationship a secret from you. I don't know why she did that. I certainly did not pressure her into secrecy. I thought you supported our relationship and knew of your mother's interest in flying. My sincere apology for deceiving you."

Throughout the speech, Karen's mouth dropped open and a disbelieving expression claimed her face. The tiny word "oh" escaped from her mouth. Several moments passed in which Karen sat with her eyes closed.

Finally, she spoke. "Dr. Kaldenberg, I appreciate your honesty in telling me this. I don't know, either, why Mother didn't feel she could tell me about her feelings for you. She has never expected to remarry, so it is likely that your interest in her has caught her off guard. I wish I could with unrestraint say 'yes' to your request to court Mother. I appreciate you asking. But, I cannot.

"I don't want Mother hurt again, not from flying or from another man. She has been through so much heartache already. I can't, with a good conscience, agree to those difficulties entering her life again. I have to say 'no' to a courtship."

Matthew's pulse throbbed. In the course of her few determined words, he was cut off. Denied. Rejected. Finished. She left him with no space to negotiate. He wanted to remain in the favor of Logan and his wife, but he shouldn't have to pay so high of a price for it.

He straightened, stiff and offended. "Oh, well, I see. What if I were to tell you that your mother and I discussed the issue of flying when I examined her ankle this afternoon? What if I were to tell you that she has agreed to quit flying for the sake of respecting your wishes?"

Karen shook her head. "Mother doesn't know what she's doing. My opposition has nothing to do with you, Doctor. Please know that. Rather, my resistance is for her own good."

Matthew's hopes deserted him. With Karen's answer went the possibility of belonging to their family. He could do nothing to make it happen as long as Karen stood her ground.

He rose to his feet. "Well then. I understand. Thank you for allowing me to impose on you this evening." He replaced his hat on his head and went out the door. He didn't mean to act so abrupt, but he must leave before he said something he regretted or started an argument.

What a surprise that Margaret's own daughter should oppose him so strongly. He should have gone with Logan's response and not given Karen the chance to interfere. His conscience alerted him to the fact that ignoring Karen was not the best way to handle the situation. Maybe no good way existed to please everyone. What a sticky mess.

If only he had the nerve—or the arrogance—to push ahead according to his own agenda and not care about others. But that approach would get him into trouble as well. He must stay friends with the De Witts. They needed each other and served their community together. None of them could afford a rift.

OVER THE COURSE of the next weeks, Matthew threw himself into his work. Babies still must get delivered. Injuries and illnesses must get treated. He enjoyed his usual routine of clinic work and house calls as he doctored Oswell City through the month of July.

The replacement parts had arrived, so Matthew repaired his biplane and moved it back to the farm. He took it out for flying whenever he got some time to spare, but he always flew alone. He missed Margaret in the seat next to him enjoying the ride and sharing the experience with him. Those solo flights just weren't the same without her.

He called on her twice a week. If Karen hadn't disapproved of a courtship, he would have proposed long ago. They could be planning a wedding ceremony and working on moving Margaret's belongings to his house. The thoughts of what he was missing sank his spirit and made his heart ache. Surely he could find a way to convince Karen that remarriage for her mother was a good idea.

Or maybe Margaret should confront Karen and make her own preferences known. Margaret was the mother after all. Karen shouldn't get the full right to tell her mother how to live her life. He brought the subject up with her one Sunday evening as they strolled a side street in the summer dusk.

"Karen still needs my help with the babies," was Margaret's response. "My reason for coming to town in the first place was to help her, not to pursue my own interests. So you see she does make a point. She still views my home as being in Chicago where her aunt and uncle, sister and nephews live. Karen hasn't yet accepted the possibility of me finding a new home. But she'll come around. That's why I didn't say anything to her about us. I expected a conflict, and I didn't want to fight the battle until I was sure it was something I wanted to fight for."

"Do you want to contend for us?" Matthew reached for her hand and held it as they walked.

"Yes. But I'd feel more ready if I knew I could convince my daughters to support me."

"How much does Julia know?" Matthew asked.

"I wrote her a long letter but I haven't heard from her yet. If she is in favor of my remarrying, then maybe I should have her talk to Karen."

That train of thought sounded like a good idea. If he wasn't a stranger to Julia, he'd call her up himself and help the persuasion along. But he'd probably better stay out of the conversation. The issue was between Margaret and her daughters. They must work it out for themselves in order to arrive at a peaceful and lasting solution.

MATTHEW WORKED HARD in the days to come giving his mind something else to think about besides Margaret and their stalled courtship.

On three successive evenings, thunderstorms moved into their area and poured rain. Puddles sat everywhere. The sky remained overcast with low dark clouds. So unusual for early August weather. Farmers talked of crops under water. Bridges washed out requiring alternative routes of travel. Matthew had to drive his horse and buggy the long way around town to reach homes out in the country. The mud sucked at the buggy wheels and slowed him down. Each night's rain brought more struggles.

Wednesday morning, Walter Brinks came to the clinic. "Doc, there's a woman on the phone over at the hotel. She's waitin' to talk to ya. She says it's important."

Walter panted for a moment to catch his breath and then sprinted out the door and down the street.

The message came so unexpectedly and the messenger disappeared so quickly that Matthew doubted he really heard anything. He exchanged puzzled glances with his patient, Eva Synderhof, who'd made an appointment to get examined for a case of abdominal pain.

"You'd better go take that call, Doctor. I can reschedule." Eva gathered up her handbag.

"I'd rather get you some answers on this pain you are having.

It could be serious. Please let me give you a quick examination." Matthew lifted the stethoscope hanging around his neck.

Eva agreed so Matthew gathered enough information to prescribe the best medication. After explaining the correct dosage, he rushed out the door. He couldn't imagine who might be calling him over the telephone. All of his family lived nearby. If they wanted him, they could come to his home or the clinic to deliver news. He darted into the hotel where George Brinks, the hotel's owner, directed him to the room with the telephone. The black receiver lay on a nearby table.

He picked it up. "Hello?"

"Dr. Kaldenberg. This is Mrs. Garner, the matron of the children's home in Clear Brook. I'm calling to tell you that your monthly visit will need to be cancelled." Her voice carried tense and worried over the line.

"That's fine. I can reschedule. But why must I cancel? Are you dealing with sickness again? Is there trouble of some sort?" Matthew asked into the box on the wall.

"No sickness, thank goodness. But we are in a bit of trouble. The river around the children's home continues to rise, and is expected to overflow its banks. We must evacuate."

22

The ominous word *evacuate* rang in Matthew's ears. The faces of those children he'd treated scrolled through his memory. Each one had so many challenges. They did not need the stress of a flood endangering their home. Especially Albert. The boy could walk, but only with the aid of a crutch or a cane. Matthew didn't know how the staff would succeed in moving the children away from everything that helped them live their lives.

"What is your plan? Do you have one?" In his agitation over this new development, Matthew nearly shouted into the phone.

"We've moved as many of our children and staff to higher ground as we possibly can, but we have five children left who still need a place to go. The bridge on the main road washed out last night, so no one can get into town to help us. Water is starting to seep up around our building. We can't allow these children to stay. Our water supply is probably contaminated again. I'm not sure what to do." Mrs. Garner sighed like a woman who carried a heavy weight on her shoulders.

The matron continued. "What we really need is a vehicle of some sort that could descend from above. If only a hot air balloon or a glider could land in the pasture near our building, we'd have the children gather there and get lifted to safety. But neither of those contraptions are fast enough or strong enough to be of any help to us. I fear we are trapped."

"I own a biplane." The words shot from Matthew's mouth. "It has two seats. One for the pilot and one for a passenger. It flies faster than a car can drive. I could land it in the pasture."

"That sounds like a real possibility. Don't do anything too dangerous, but if you think it might work, we'll start moving the children outdoors." A bit of the heaviness left Mrs. Garner's voice.

"I do think it will work. In fact, we have a place south of town where I can take the children. They'll stay safe and dry. Let me ask some people to help me, and then I'll be on my way." Matthew caught a glimpse of George Brinks. The man's furrowed brow told Matthew that he knew something was wrong.

"I'm so glad I called you." Mrs. Garner's voice lightened a little more.

"Expect me in an hour."

"We will."

Matthew hung up and eased past George who kept his eye on him from his place behind the desk. "No need to worry." He held his hand up to assure George no trouble brewed anywhere in the world that he, with the Lord at his side, couldn't handle.

Gray clouds hung in the sky, still left over from yesterday's rainstorm, but at least no rain fell right now. The wind didn't even blow too much, and weak sunshine peeked out from cracks in the clouds. It was actually a nice day for flying, and would stay that way if another thunderstorm didn't develop. Getting his biplane out during wet weather meant taking a risk, but the safety of those children in Clear Brook depended on him.

Matthew sprinted onto the front step of the parsonage and banged on the door. Logan answered.

"What's wrong?" Logan studied him as if the evidence of crisis hung on him like clothing.

"I need your help." The words came out in puffs from

Matthew's tight and breathless lungs. "I'm glad I caught you at home."

"I'm here to eat the noon meal." Logan opened the door wider and welcomed him into the house.

Karen and Margaret stood around the table in the dining room, each with a combination of silverware in their hands that they lay on the partially set table. They paused in their work and stared at him.

Matthew spilled the whole frightful story. "Mrs. Garner from the children's home in Clear Brook called me on the hotel phone. They are in trouble. The children's home is in danger of flooding. Most of the children and staff were evacuated this morning, but the rest have no way of escape. I'm going down there. Could you please go out to the orchard and get the house ready for these children? Fix lots of hot food and find a pile of blankets. These children will be chilly. Watch for me in an hour."

He turned away. This errand had taken too much time. He must get in the air, and fast.

Margaret was the first to find her voice. "Oh, but, well, of course. The orchard, yes. We can do that, can't we Karen? We already have all of this food for dinner made."

"We'll have it packed up in no time." Karen's voice followed her mother's to Matthew's ears.

"I'll get the buggy. We can pack John and Simon in blankets," Logan joined in.

"Wait, Doctor. How are you getting to Clear Brook?" Karen's question stopped him short.

In his haste to communicate his plan he'd left out the most important part. He turned around. "I'm flying."

Karen's eyebrows rose.

Surprise flashed on the faces of the other two.

Matthew left the house, closing the door on three frozen, paralyzed people. He prayed that they would snap out of it in time to meet his first passenger.

He went home, hitched his horse to his buggy, and drove to

Tim's. After a brief explanation, Tim offered to shelter Matthew's horse during the expedition. Matthew thanked him and went to his barn-hangar. He shoved the doors open and lit a lantern.

The light glowed on repaired fabric. It glinted off the shiny motor inviting him, enticing him to a contest with a natural disaster. In that moment, he made up his mind. He would win. No more wrecks. No more damage. No more loss. Today was his chance to rise above. He wouldn't accomplish it alone. Clear Brook Children's Home would share the glory.

Matthew put on his leather helmet and his goggles and claimed the pilot's seat. This flight was for Margaret. For Karen. For the children. Tim came to the barn and spun the propeller to start the motor. Matthew drove the biplane out of the barn, and then Tim extinguished the lantern and closed the barn door. When the propellers raced in the wind, Matthew turned his attention to the controls and sped down the runway. A puff of wind caught his wings and lifted him into the air.

Matthew saw the swollen river below him. Water covered farm fields well beyond the confines of the banks. A road ended in the place where a bridge should have spanned the rushing waters. The children's home came into view. It stood like an upended brick as dark water swirled and foamed around its back side. When he spotted the pasture Mrs. Garner had mentioned, Matthew started his descent. He aimed for the open grass on the low hill and not the rushing river. Landing the biplane required no more than one hundred yards. He could do this.

Twice he circled around, growing lower with each orbit. He directed the plane straight for the pasture. The wheels jerked as they made contact with the grass. He maneuvered the controls and rolled the plane to a stop.

"We're so glad to see you." Miss Worley stood with a huddle of two girls and three boys.

"We brought everyone at the same time so we could get out

here before the water rose any higher. I fear my office, the dining area, the kitchen, and the classrooms will soon be flooded." Mrs. Garner clutched the sides of her head as tears glistened in her eyes.

Matthew glanced at the building behind them. A shallow pool of murky water surrounded it. "You are all very brave," he said to the children. "I'm sorry about the flooding, but we'll look after you." He looked around. "Who gets to go first? I can take one rider at a time."

"Take the girls first, starting with the youngest ones." Miss Worley squatted down. "How would you like to go now with Dr. Matt, Ruby? Remember how we told you he would come and give you a ride on his biplane?"

The little girl leaned into Mrs. Garner's skirt. Ruby's spectacles hid her eyes, but Matthew could still see the hesitation in her shy nod.

Mrs. Garner picked her up with motherly tenderness and held her in her arms. "You need to go with him now so you can be safe from the water."

"Wrap her in a blanket," Matthew called out as he claimed the pilot's seat. "Miss Worley, could you please help me with the propeller?"

She nodded while Mrs. Garner settled Ruby into the passenger seat. The little girl whimpered.

Matthew turned to her. "Shh. You're safe with me. Don't be scared."

He helped her put on the extra pair of goggles and the helmet he'd brought along. Sized for an adult, the headgear was large on a small girl like Ruby, but it would do the job of protecting her while in flight.

"Ready, Ruby?" He glanced down at his rider.

She turned large, panicked, bespectacled and be-goggled eyes up to him.

Anyone could see she wasn't ready. Not now, and probably not ever. But no one could wait around for a toddler to look forward to the ride of her life. More children waited for rides tonight. He must get going.

"Hang on, Ruby." Matthew gave Miss Worley the signal to spin the propeller.

When the propellers started up together, the biplane lurched forward. Matthew held his breath. The plane sped across the grass and zoomed into the sky. Matthew manipulated the controls, turning the plane around the corner of the building. As he'd hoped, the wind caught the wings and lifted him up. Raised him above. Safe from the water, he kept the biplane at a height far above the flood. A confirmed victor over loss, he would win. He was already well on his way.

23

Margaret stared at her daughter while Karen stared back at her. Logan stood at the end of the table with his arm extended in the direction of the slammed door. Erie light from a crevice between clouds slanted across Karen's bewildered features.

"Did he ... did he just say he planned to fly to Clear Brook?" Logan tilted his head as though listening for whispers. His stutter told Margaret the doctor's rash actions bothered him as much as they did her.

Karen shuddered as she drew in a breath. "Yes. That's what I heard him say." She glanced at her husband.

"Storms could pop up at any time. I hope he doesn't kill himself." Logan frowned and shook his head.

Margaret's attention shifted to the tree in the yard. Wide green oak leaves waved in the light breeze. She scurried to the window. A flimsy biplane could so easily lurch and twirl if a storm came up. The sensation of spiraling into a treetop filled her memory and upset her stomach. Matthew's flight might meet a dreadful end long before he reached his destination.

But he'd already left. Determination had infused his words.

Nothing would stop him. The only choice any of them had was to do as he asked. Cooperation would make his mission easier.

Margaret turned away from the window. "We must get this food packed up. Karen, get some towels. I'll prepare the babies. Logan, bring the buggy around for us."

Karen eased away from the table and moved in the direction of the bathroom. After a cautious glance at the window, Logan put his coat on and left the house.

Margaret bustled into the parlor and scooped up Simon. She fit his tiny arms into a sweater and wrapped him in a blanket. John received the same care. Soon the household, along with their meal and a stash of blankets, was headed down the wet road to the orchard.

Helen Brinks, the orchard's housekeeper, opened the door in answer to Logan's knock. Her hand fluttered to her chest and her eyes grew wide as she looked at the cluster of unexpected visitors.

"Hello, Helen. We're so sorry to impose on you unannounced in this way. But you see, Dr. Kaldenberg is on a mission with his biplane and will be arriving soon. He's bringing children with him from the children's home in Clear Brook. They need a safe place to stay since the building is in danger of flooding. He wants to bring them here. I expect his rescue mission to take the rest of the day." Logan paused and shifted the baby in his arms.

Helen turned and glanced at the room behind her. "Why yes, of course. Anything to help out the doctor. It sounds like those kids are in real trouble. Since we've only got one family living here right now, there should be plenty of room for guests. Please come in." She opened the door wider and reached for the bag Karen carried.

"Put the babies here in the parlor." Helen led the group to a crib between the windows.

Karen and Logan laid the boys down and covered them with a blanket. They were the only ones in the family with full tummies so they settled into their new surroundings with contentment.

"I was just putting our noon meal on the table. Have you folks eaten already?" Helen asked.

"No. We brought food with us." Karen gestured in the direction of the buggy parked in the yard.

"Bring it right in. We'll add it to our dinner and save the extra for the kids." Helen hastened to the dining room where she set more plates on the table.

Logan went in search of extra chairs while Karen and Margaret went to the buggy for the food.

Within minutes, everyone was seated at the table for the meal. Margaret had met the current residents at the picnic. She'd also seen the family at church and in the downtown stores, but she hadn't yet had a chance to visit with them.

Logan opened the conversation. "We've enjoyed having your family in attendance on Sunday morning, Mr. Broekhuizen. Do you plan to farm in the area?"

The father of the family shook his head. "No. I'm actually a college professor. I taught history in Amsterdam before immigrating to America."

His English was very good. Each word held careful pronunciation and even a bit of a lilt, possibly created from the mixture of a Dutch brogue and English inflection.

Margaret paid closer attention to his appearance. He wore wire-rimmed spectacles similar in style to Logan's. His hair and beard were carefully trimmed. Even his clothing, although not the suit he would typically wear in a classroom, lent to his scholarly appearance.

"What brings you to Iowa?" Logan asked as he spooned gravy over his meat.

"The college in Clear Brook has offered me a position. Many of our acquaintances from Holland are already settled in this area, so we thought we might come here too." Mr. Broekhuizen gave his wife a smile.

"Good for you. I've spoken in chapel at that college about the operation the church is running here at this orchard," Logan said.

"Will your children attend school?" Karen asked the mother.

"We hope to enroll them in Clear Brook as soon as we find a home to live in. If our search takes longer, then, well ... we aren't sure what we will do about schooling." Mrs. Broekhuizen toyed with her napkin.

"I teach a class right here at the orchard. I'd be happy to include your three children if you are still living here in September." Karen looked at each of the well-behaved children, two boys and a girl, seated across from Margaret.

"Thank you." Mrs. Broekhuizen smiled at Karen.

A whirring, puttering sound reached Margaret's ears. Her thoughts jumped to the contraption making the sounds and the man it belonged to. She left her seat and rushed to the door.

"It's Matthew! He's safe. I hear his biplane. I wonder where he'll land." She held the door open.

"A biplane? How interesting." Mr. Broekhuizen commented with his attention on the large bay window.

Logan gave a hasty explanation of the reason for the biplane's arrival as he put on his coat.

"He's landing on the road," Margaret called out. The faint silhouette of the biplane against the gray clouds told her of Matthew's location. "Logan, go help him. He probably has a passenger." Margaret patted Logan's back as though to push him out of the house.

"On my way." Logan sprinted past her.

Karen, Helen, and Mrs. Broekhuizen joined Margaret in the bay window as they watched the yard. The apple trees hid Matthew and his biplane from view, but soon they heard it take off again.

Logan rushed into sight with a bundle in his arms. Margaret opened the door as he crossed the porch and entered the house.

"This is Ruby." Logan set the bundle on the floor and

Coming Home to Mercy

unwrapped a blanket to reveal a bespectacled little girl, a toddler of three or four years old. "She's cold and probably hungry. Get her warm and give her something to eat. The doctor says she has a lung condition and should get warm as quickly as possible."

Karen picked up the little girl and took her to the parlor all the while talking to her in soothing tones about the big ride she'd had and the nice people here ready to take care of her.

Helen emerged from the kitchen with a tray of food fixed from the dishes on the table. Logan sat down and continued his conversation with Mr. Broekhuizen while they finished their meal. Margaret tried her best to eat as well, but her mind stayed distracted with thoughts of Matthew.

His first trip between the children's home and the orchard had gone well, but what about the return trip? What if a gust of wind blew him into a tree, or what if he ran out of fuel? Did he have anywhere safe to land at the children's home? A host of worries assaulted her. Matthew's mission was fraught with risk and danger.

When the meal was finished, Mrs. Broekhuizen retired to the parlor with her children and spent time holding a baby and helping Ruby become acquainted. Margaret helped Helen clear the table and had the dishes washed just as the whir and putter in the air announced Matthew's arrival. Logan and Mr. Broekhuizen went outdoors to meet Matthew's new passenger.

The afternoon continued in much the same pattern. Each hour brought Matthew on a return trip with another child. Around six-thirty in the evening, Logan brought word that the pilot left for one more round trip to rescue the last child.

"Albert is his name," Logan said. "He has a physical disability that makes walking difficult."

Margaret left her place by the sofa where she'd been feeding hot soup to their most recent delivery, a boy of about ten years old by the name of Lance. He, too, wore spectacles. His speech was quite clear, but his walking required a cane. Maybe he'd recently had surgery or struggled with a more chronic ailment.

She looked out the window with one more silent prayer that Matthew might stay safe through one last trip. Reluctantly, she turned away and went to help Karen settle Lance in for the evening meal. After the children had found chairs at the table, Karen sat down to feed the twins.

The Broekhuizens joined the children at the table, and Helen worked in the kitchen. Margaret tried to eat, but eventually she gave up and went to the windows. Where was Matthew? He should have arrived by now. A dark bank of clouds appeared in the southwest.

"Logan, look." She glanced at him as she pointed out the window.

He came to stand at her side. "Another storm is on its way."

"Matthew hasn't come yet."

Logan didn't say anything, but instead gave her a sympathetic gaze. He understood her fears.

"Come, let's try to eat supper." He applied a gentle pressure to her back and guided her to the table.

The food choked her. Matthew was out there somewhere facing the danger of a brewing storm. A gust of wind might catch the biplane and smash it to the ground. What if he nosedived into the flooded river? He may not come back to her. She'd never see him again. The thought crumpled her confidence and sank her stomach.

When the meal was finished, she sat in the parlor with the other adults and kept watch on the clock's hands as they crept along. After darkness had fallen, the household prepared for bed.

"Mother, you should get some rest." Logan stood before her with concern furrowing his brow.

"But Matthew isn't here yet. I must wait for him." She straightened in her chair.

Logan exchanged a worried glance with Karen and then went down on one knee, bringing him to eye level with Margaret.

"But there's nothing we can do if ..." He cleared his throat.

"What I mean is, Dr. Kaldenberg can handle his biplane. He'll return soon."

"Then I want to be waiting for him when he does. I couldn't sleep anyway. I'd only lie there thinking about him." Tears threatened to flood her eyes.

Logan sighed and stood to his feet. Karen stared at the scene. A sober expression straightened her brow and tightened her jaw.

Margaret left her chair. "Please go on to bed. Both of you. Tomorrow will be a busy day."

"Mother." Karen murmured with impatience in her voice.

"Come on." Logan whispered as he laid his hand on Karen's arm and guided her to the stairs.

Their footsteps faded into a room above. A lamp glowed on the low table near the window where she'd left it all evening. Now it provided her with companionship. She wasn't all alone on this dark night and frightened out of her mind. She had the comforting light of the lamp to soothe and console. Matthew would surely come at any minute. She must be ready for him, alert and attentive.

This delay in Matthew's return mirrored their relationship. Tonight she waited for him, but he'd always been the one waiting for her. He'd kissed her weeks ago and told her of his desire for a courtship. How would their relationship have grown if Margaret hadn't delayed with worries about Karen's acceptance, her friendships, and her freedoms?

She might have already become Mrs. Matthew Kaldenberg, living in his house and calling this town her home.

Is that what she wanted?

Yes. Yes, it was. The truth soaked into her heart much like rain soaked into soil. A life with Matthew sharing his home and his town was certainly what she wanted. With very little adjustment on her part, this dream could become a reality. Her wait in the night watching for Matthew, hoping for Matthew, served as her declaration saying to everyone around that she welcomed the joys and the uncertainties that a life with Matthew would give her.

A flash of lightning cut through the night. Margaret rose and faced the window. Her stomach plummeted as thunder rumbled. The wind picked up and rain began to fall. A storm. Her worst fear had happened. Matthew hadn't come. He'd been lost to a storm. A tear trickled over her cheek.

24

"Albert, use your cane. It will help you get up the hill." Matthew held onto the boy's arm and steered him toward the biplane.

The gray clouds lowered, blocking the sunset. Darkness would come quickly, bringing with it more rain. They must not waste any time getting Albert, Miss Worley, and Mrs. Garner to safety. The river had crested during Matthew's afternoon flights and now water poured over the bank. Mrs. Garner's office, the kitchen, and the other rooms on the first floor would soon be under water.

Matthew turned his attention back to Albert. The boy needed the steady support of Matthew on one side and the cane on the other.

Mrs. Garner stood at the plane ready to help Albert into the seat. Less agile than the other children, Albert required more assistance to get his stiff limbs to cooperate with the effort of climbing onto a biplane.

"My biplane is nearly out of fuel. I don't have enough for a trip to the orchard by Oswell City. Is there somewhere near Clear Brook where I could find fuel?" Matthew brought Albert to a stop and visited with the matron.

"Yes, I believe there is. It's the farm belonging to the parents of Miss Holt, my assistant. Some of our staff went there this morning. Miss Holt is there too. Her father keeps fuel on hand for his tractor." Mrs. Garner glanced at the dark clouds. "We don't have much time before more rain comes. Go ahead and take Albert to the farm and then come back for myself and Miss Worley."

Matthew knew which farmstead the matron described. It occupied a rise of ground less than two miles away. Free from flooding, this farm was the perfect place to take the remaining passengers. Round trips would go much quicker than the route to Oswell City.

But Margaret and the others would be watching for him. Logan had told him of their concern for his safety. If he didn't appear at the orchard on time, they might think he crashed. He glanced at the faces of Miss Worley and Mrs. Garner. He must deliver them to safety before dark, and before the rain began.

"Good idea. I'll fly Albert to the farm and return soon." He nodded to Mrs. Garner.

"A real live flying machine! I can't believe I get to ride in it." Albert twisted in his seat to watch Miss Worley.

"Yes, sir. You get to have a ride right now." Matthew sped across the grass, maneuvered the controls, and glided into the air.

Albert squealed. "This is fun, Dr. Matt. How'd you learn to fly?"

Matthew held his breath instead of replying. This moment after takeoff was the most crucial. He must make sure and turn the wings just right so that he didn't swoop into the river. A quick slide of the controls tilted the biplane so that it caught the breeze rushing around the side of the building.

A floating sensation lifted in Matthew's stomach. Albert must have felt it too because he squealed again.

During the flight, Albert kept trying to turn around and watch the propellers. Matthew did his best to keep the boy facing forward by explaining to him the science of flight. Albert may not understand very much of it, but the information would at least entertain him until their arrival at the farm.

The rooftops of the house and barns emerged in the twilight as Matthew veered to the left. An open field of alfalfa spread along one side of the farm.

He hated to damage the farmer's stand of healthy hay. Instead of landing in the middle of the field, Matthew aimed for the edge nearest a barn. His plan succeeded. He brought the biplane to a landing in a spot where minimal stems would get flattened.

"It's over already?" Disappointment echoed in Albert's voice when the biplane came to a halt.

"I'm afraid so, son. We need to get you inside somewhere. You are cold from the wind, and I don't want you to get sick." Matthew removed his goggles and helmet.

"Aw." More disappointment from Albert told Matthew the boy would sit for hours in the rain if it meant staying with the biplane.

"Come on. I'll help you walk." Matthew assisted Albert out of his seat and handed him his cane.

They moved together over uneven ground, through some trees, and across the farmyard to the house's front porch. Matthew's gaze traveled over the door on which he should knock. He raised his fist to the door's surface, but hesitated. Maybe he was intruding. He may have miscalculated and arrived at the wrong farm. The staff might not be in this place at all. A cantankerous, angry person might meet his knock and send him away.

Looking down at his passenger, Matthew saw the chatter in Albert's teeth. The boy looked back at him with a plea and a little fear reflected in his eyes. The bravery and adventure of the ride was gone. Matthew's heart twitched. Albert needed someone to take care of him and to comfort him.

Sucking in a deep breath, Matthew faced the door once more and pounded out a firm knock.

It opened and a young woman stood in the doorway.

"Good evening. Are you Miss Holt?"

I am."

He smiled. "I'm Dr. Kaldenberg, and I've been working with Mrs. Garner to evacuate children this afternoon. I have Albert with me. Do you have room for him to stay?"

"Oh, yes, of course. Bring him right in." Miss Holt opened the door for Matthew and Albert to enter. "We've been so worried about Mrs. Garner and the children left behind. You've found places for them?" She talked as she led him to the parlor.

"Yes. The orchard in Oswell City has room. I've taken four of the children there, but I stopped here with Albert because my biplane is nearly out of fuel."

"You came with a biplane?" Miss Holt glanced at him in awe.

"I did. It has worked well for rescuing the children."

"A ride on a biplane sounds like fun."

"Sure was." Albert answered with the sound of renewed adventure in his voice.

"I'll be bringing Mrs. Garner and Miss Worley. Do you have room for them?" Matthew helped Albert find a seat in the parlor.

"Plenty of room. I'll give them thick blankets and then we'll all have a nice big supper together." Miss Holt lifted Albert's feet onto a low stool. Her mother came to the parlor and spread a blanket over Albert.

Supper sounded good to Matthew. He'd love to join them, but he'd rather have his flights completed by that time and on his way back to Margaret.

"Do you happen to know if your father has any fuel? Mrs. Garner thought this farm might have some on hand." Matthew clasped his hands behind him. How imposing, to ask this woman for fuel. But the two women waiting for him to deliver them to safety loomed more important than his discomfort. "I'll pay him for it."

Miss Holt waved her hand as though pushing his thoughts aside. "Don't worry about that right now. My father keeps a barrel of fuel next to the door of the largest barn. He's probably doing chores outside somewhere. Have him help you."

"Thank you." Matthew turned away as Miss Holt's mother went to the kitchen to warm some milk for Albert.

In the barnyard, Matthew met Mr. Holt. "Good evening, sir. I had to park my biplane in your field, but I tried not to crush your alfalfa crop. I'm sorry if there's any damage."

The man smiled. "I saw that flying machine land here. It made me wonder what's going on."

"I'm helping Mrs. Garner evacuate children. Since several of the staff came out here this morning, she suggested that I bring one of the children here too." Matthew spied the barrel of fuel Miss Holt had mentioned.

"We're happy to help out."

Matthew cleared his throat. "I'm in need of fuel for my biplane. I must make two more trips to bring the matron and a teacher to your farm. Could I please buy some from you?"

Mr. Holt shook his head. "Don't worry about payment. We're just glad to contribute to the rescue of these kids. Take all you need."

"Thanks. Do you have a container for me to put it in? I won't be able to drive my biplane through the yard because the wingspan is too wide and I would hit the buildings."

"I do." He went in the barn and returned with a jug.

"If I could trouble you with one more request, I need someone to turn the propeller for me."

His eyes widened. "I guess I could give it a try, but I've never seen a biplane before or helped anyone operate one."

Matthew smiled. "It's easy. I'll tell you exactly what to do. Come with me to the hayfield."

He nodded, filled the jug to the brim with fuel, and followed Matthew.

At the biplane, Matthew slowly poured all of the fuel into the tank until reaching a level of half full. That should be enough to complete his trips to the farm and return him to Oswell City.

He put on his goggles and helmet and started the engine. Then he waved at Mr. Holt to spin the propeller.

"I'll be back soon." He yelled out over the noise of the engine.

Mr. Holt returned his wave, picked up the empty jug, and walked away.

Matthew zoomed along the perimeter of the field. The wind caught his wings and lifted him into the sky. Dusk had arrived during his time in the house. Night would soon come, but two more women must reach safety before dark.

He soared beneath the clouds until the children's home came into view. Water surrounded it, covering the lawn and inching up the sides of the pastured hill. Mrs. Garner and Miss Worley stood at the top. His landing required careful skill. He must stay out of the water while at the same time avoiding the women who waited for a ride.

Working the controls, he brought the biplane to the ground and coasted to a stop.

The women jogged alongside. "Take Miss Worley first. Hurry! The water is rising." Mrs. Garner yelled.

Miss Worley scrambled into the passenger seat. She put on the headgear while Matthew turned the plane around. With the propellers still spinning, he increased his speed and raced over the grass. In minutes, the biplane left the ground.

"We heard thunder while we waited for you." Miss Worley raised her voice over the sound of the engine.

Matthew checked the sky. The same low clouds blocked the light. They looked as if rain could fall from them at any minute. He must complete this mission before another storm moved in.

Mr. Holt met them in the hayfield when Matthew landed.

Miss Worley stepped off the plane as the sky continued to darken.

"Get Mrs. Garner!" Miss Worley waved to him as she followed Mr. Holt to the house.

Night would soon be upon him. Matthew raced over the field and ascended into the air. The darkness hindered his vision, so Matthew followed the path of a flooded creek back to the orphanage.

Mrs. Garner stood at the top of the hill. He landed and picked her up.

"Is everyone all right at the farm?" She asked as he soared into the sky.

"Yes, and they are watching for you." Matthew glanced at the sky as a flash of lightning illuminated the cloth on the wings.

Mrs. Garner gasped. "We shouldn't be in the air."

"I know. Hang on." Matthew increased the speed of the plane as he followed the creek back to the farm. Thunder rumbled in the clouds.

Another flash of lightning illumined the hayfield, guiding Matthew where to land. Mr. Holt stood by his barn watching. As soon as Matthew touched the ground, Mr. Holt jogged over to the biplane and stayed at Matthew's side until the biplane coasted to a stop.

"Get inside!" He reached to assist Mrs. Garner from the passenger seat.

She wasted no time in her trek across the field.

Large raindrops pelted Matthew's face. He'd landed just in time. If one more person waited for a ride, he wouldn't have been able to rescue them. Taking a deep breath, Matthew wiped the rain from his goggles.

"Bring your biplane to the barn. I've got room at one end to store it for you." Mr. Holt jogged ahead of Matthew to lead the way.

At the barn, Mr. Holt threw the double doors open and

guided Matthew inside. Lightning flashed. Thunder boomed. The wind picked up and more rain fell.

"Thank you, sir." Matthew shook Mr. Holt's hand. "I didn't want the fabric to get wet. I'm glad you have enough room for my biplane in here."

"You can see that it's a tight fit. We'll have to rearrange some things to get it out in the morning, but don't worry about that. Come to the house. My wife has a big meal fixed for everyone." Mr. Holt led the way across the barnyard to the house.

If only Matthew could get word to Margaret about his decision to spend the night at the Holt farm. But he had no way to assure her of his safety. As soon as he could in the morning, he'd fly to the orchard. For now, his greatest concern was to prevent a total soaking from the pouring rain. He stepped onto the front porch and shook out his coat as another bolt of lightning flashed.

MARGARET SHIFTED in her chair and rolled her head to the side. Birds chirped in a tree by the window. A cow lowed in the distance.

Her eyes fluttered open to the gray dawn. A mist of rain hazed over the valleys. Margaret roused to full wakefulness. She must have fallen asleep here in the parlor.

Matthew never returned. He'd either crashed or drowned. But he said he would return. A man who kept his word, Matthew had kept her safe in the past. He'd rescued her, tended her sprained ankle, and shown her his heart. She found a shawl and threw it around her shoulders. A trip outside will help her stay calm.

Closing her eyes, Margaret leaned her head against the trunk of an apple tree. Calling upon the Lord to quiet her heart, she took in deep breaths to ease her nerves. She must believe that

Matthew was safe. Somehow he'd survived the storm. This had to be true. Standing here waiting for him would make it true.

The clip of horse hooves drew nearer. Margaret opened her eyes to find a farmer directing a wagon and team of horses down the road. He nodded at her and drove on but stopped after passing her.

He turned around on the wagon's seat. "You all right, Mrs. Millerson? Why are you standing by the road this early in the morning?"

She gulped in some air. "Dr. Kaldenberg has been out all night with his biplane. Have you seen him?"

"Can't say that I have." He shook his head. "I'll keep an eye out for him. Maybe he'll show up soon." He waved and drove on.

Margaret shut her eyes again as the morning fell quiet. Cattle lowed in the distance. The breeze rustled through the leaves. And then she heard it. A whir. She held her breath. The sound might only be the windmill. She opened her eyes to check.

A distinct putter accompanied the whir. Windmills didn't have engines. These sounds came from the opposite direction of the windmill. Margaret turned and watched the sky.

25

A tiny form, like an insect, emerged from the clouds and flew in her direction. Hands clasped, Margaret held her breath and watched. A biplane and its pilot lowered to the road, drove in front of her, and came to a stop. The engine shut off and the propellers paused. The pilot left his seat and stood in the road.

Energy surged through Margaret. She ran to the pilot and threw her arms around his neck.

"Oh, Matthew," she sobbed. "I've been so worried about you."

He wrapped his arms around her and drew her close.

"I'm so glad you're here. I didn't think I'd ever see you again." She buried her face in his shoulder and choked out the words.

"I'm sorry to cause you worry." His low voice sounded tired.

She pulled back and glanced up at him. "Where were you? Why didn't you come back?"

"My fuel was nearly gone. I didn't have enough for another round trip, so I changed my route and went to a farm near Clear Brook instead. A storm moved in, so I spent the night there. Then I flew to you as soon as I could." Apology, longing, and fatigue mingled together in his eyes.

She shook her head as a fresh supply of tears coursed down her cheeks. "Don't leave me again. Please."

He studied her carefully. "I won't if that's what you really want."

"It is." She nodded. "You've been waiting on me all these months. As I spent the night waiting for you, I began to understand how much I need you."

A smile stretched across his mouth. It probably would have been a brilliant smile, but he looked too exhausted to give an accurate indication of what her words meant to him. She'd made him smile. For now, that truth was sufficient. Another time, when he was rested, she'd see his rare, happy smile.

"Oh, Margaret." He whispered and pulled her close to him once more.

"How is Albert? You told us to expect him here." She glanced up at him.

"He's fine, safe at the Holt farm and at this moment devouring his breakfast."

Margaret joined in when he chuckled. "I'll have to tell the others. They will be relieved to know."

He smiled again and pressed a kiss to her forehead. "Come on. I'm anxious to check on the children and see how they are."

Arm in arm, they walked the lane. The windmill turned, churning out a friendly welcome. The cow lowed in the pasture requesting relief from its supply of milk. Conrad, the orchard's handyman, would see to that chore when he arrived for the day's work. Chickens crowed on a neighbor's farm. Birds twittered in the tops of the apple trees.

The gray dawn lightened a shade as Margaret followed Matthew into the house. Karen sat in the rocking chair with a baby. Her eyes widened and her mouth fell open.

"Dr. Kaldenberg!" Her exclamation, too quiet to carry upstairs to awaken children, startled the baby in her arms.

"Good morning, Mrs. De Witt. My passengers are still

sleeping, I trust." Matthew removed his shoes and went to the parlor.

"They are. We gave everyone supper along with a hot broth when they arrived. We also found places for them to sleep. Everyone is upstairs." Karen's eyes returned to their normal size as she spoke. "How is Albert? We were watching for him."

"Fine. I delivered him to a farm near Clear Brook where the staff are staying. I'm glad to hear the children are taken care of. Let them sleep as long as they like. Those children had quite an adventure yesterday." Matthew settled into a chair and pulled a blanket over his knees. "Still a bit chilly and damp this morning. Feels good to get out of the wind."

"Let's get you some breakfast. It's probably been hours since you last ate." Margaret hastened to the kitchen and found an apron.

"Breakfast sounds perfect. Thank you, Margaret." Matthew's voice followed her.

She overheard him visiting with Karen while she worked with the stove. Matthew asked questions about John and Simon. Karen answered with reports of their growth. Their conversation sounded peaceful. Maybe Karen would change her mind about accepting a courtship between her mother and the doctor.

Margaret's feelings had solidified. She wanted everything that courtship would offer. And yet, the courtship must not last forever. Last night's agonized fear that she'd lost him had taught Margaret that she wanted to be with Matthew always. To marry him, and to spend the rest of her days sharing her life with him, living here in Oswell City among friends.

Margaret sighed as she broke eggs into a bowl. How could she ever get Karen to understand? The thought hung heavy on her mind as she scrambled the eggs and cooked them. Maybe she would have to go against her daughter's wishes and marry the doctor anyway. She could. Margaret was the mother. She didn't need either of her daughters to tell her what to do or to approve of her actions.

But living in the same town as Karen after becoming Mrs. Kaldenberg would feel tense. Margaret didn't look forward to a strained relationship with her daughter who doubled as the pastor's wife. The conflict would hinder the working relationship of their husbands. It might even affect hers or Karen's relationship with the people in town.

She set the table as she continued to mull over her dilemma. If only Karen would relax. Then she could see Matthew's admirable traits and how perfect he was for her mother. But no, Karen wouldn't change her opinion that drastically. The only choice Margaret had was to defy Karen and pursue a courtship. But they'd be in conflict.

The scenario chased itself in a circle with no resolution to mark the end of their differences. Margaret dragged her focus off of her troubling thoughts and onto breakfast preparation.

Helen Brinks, the orchard's housekeeper, entered the house, greeted Karen, and visited with Matthew about his adventures.

Then she came to the kitchen. "Good morning, Mrs. Millerson. Thanks for starting breakfast. I can take over now."

"These eggs are nearly done. I'll finish them and then wash a few dishes. I couldn't think of leaving you to get breakfast for so many extras without any help."

Helen laughed. "I've cooked for a lot more in my day. Really, I don't mind. Go ahead and visit with the doctor and Mrs. De Witt. I can manage here. It is my job after all."

"At least let me make the coffee."

"All right. That would help me out so I can cook a batch of pancakes." Helen smoothed the apron she'd tied around her waist.

Margaret smiled. "I'll be right back to work on the coffee." She slid the skillet of scrambled eggs off of the stove and went to the parlor.

Logan had joined the group. He visited with Matthew about his flights. As Matthew told stories, Logan shook his head and exclaimed in amazement.

Matthew for sure was a hero, risking landings and takeoffs in a flooded area to rescue children. When this story got out, he'd be famous. Margaret hid a proud smile and entered the conversation.

The house filled with the cozy smell of frying pancakes. It must have reached the rooms upstairs because footsteps sounded in the hall and down the steps. Two of the boys Matthew delivered in the night entered the parlor.

"You made it." The boy named Lance smiled at Matthew.

"I sure did, son. Safe and sound. Did you sleep well?"

"Yes. But I want to see your biplane. Will you give us rides again?" Lance's eyes lit up with excitement.

Matthew chuckled. "I don't expect to, but if you want to fly again, I can take you up someday."

Lance exchanged a glance with the other boy that said he couldn't believe what he was hearing.

"Will you take Bernie too?" Lance pointed to his friend.

"I suppose I can, if you liked it that much."

"I did!" Bernie's enthusiasm rivaled Lance's.

The rest of the children came to the parlor dressed and ready to start the day. Soon the room filled with excited voices chatting to Matthew about their rides with him in his biplane.

Helen came to the parlor. "All right, everyone. Breakfast is ready. Come to the dining room, and I'll help you find your seats."

Margaret went to make the coffee while the energetic crowd moved with Helen to the dining room and joined the Broekhuizen family at the table. The group eventually settled down enough for Logan to open the meal with prayer.

"Heavenly Father, we thank you for the protection you gave to each of us during the night. Thank you for guiding Dr. Kaldenberg as he delivered the children and the staff to safety. We continue to rest in your gracious hand. Amen."

Tears burned under Margaret's lids as she listened to Logan. The night could have turned out much differently. She added her own silent prayer of thanks for sparing Matthew's life and for using him to protect the lives of the children.

"When does Mrs. Garner hope to have use of the children's home again?" Logan asked.

"She didn't say, but I'd guess it won't be for several weeks. The water level must lower before any repairs can be done to the building. She's probably looking at a month or so." Matthew filled his coffee cup.

Logan clicked his tongue. "That's rough. Is there anything I can do to help?"

"The most immediate need is care for these children. I'd like to return to the orphanage to get a better look at the situation." Matthew stirred cream into his cup.

"I'd like to go along." Logan glanced at Matthew.

"I'd like to come too." Mr. Broekhuizen also looked at Matthew.

"Thank you. I appreciate that, and I'm sure Mrs. Garner will too. Let's travel to Clear Brook this afternoon. I'd like to go home first and catch a few hours of sleep."

Mr. Broekhuizen nodded.

"I don't see why the children can't stay here for a day or two. There's plenty of room and they can be outdoors. The boys could help Conrad in the barn, and the girls could—"

"I get the picture, Helen." Matthew held up his hand and chuckled. "You don't have to explain anything to me. Go ahead and make plans to keep everyone busy."

"Can we, Dr. Matt?" Lance asked. "Me and Bernie would like to look around in that barn, wouldn't we Bernie?"

Bernie nodded. "Uh-huh."

"Conrad will be here shortly. I'll tell him all about it," Helen said.

Ruby cast a shy glance at the parlor. "Will the babies stay here with us?"

Helen chuckled. "No, dear. I'm afraid the babies will have to go home with their mother and father."

Sadness claimed Ruby's face.

"But they'll come back to visit." Karen smoothed a hand over the little girl's hair. "Or maybe you can come visit us in town."

Ruby's eyes grew round. "Could I?"

Karen smiled. "Of course. Bring your other friends, and we can have tea together."

"That would be fun." Ruby leaned into Karen's side.

Karen put her arm around the little girl as if to say the date was set.

Breakfast ended when Conrad's team of horses pulled his wagon into the yard. The boys leaped from their seats and rushed to the window. Conrad disappeared around the corner of the house so the boys ran into the kitchen for another glance of him. Helen shooed them upstairs in search of their shoes, and within minutes, the boys were outside and headed to the barn.

"I'll go inform Conrad before he gets completely bombarded." Logan left the table. "If you'll be ready to leave soon, Karen, I'll get the buggy while I'm out there."

Karen nodded.

Margaret drank the rest of her coffee and went to the kitchen to prepare the dish water. Helen followed behind with the platter of pancakes. Mrs. Broekhuizen helped clear the table while Karen settled the girls in the parlor with drawing supplies.

The house in order, Margaret helped Karen wrap the twins in blankets. She waved to Mrs. Broekhuizen, who supervised the girls in the parlor.

"Come back soon." Helen emerged from the kitchen and held the door for Karen and Margaret as they carried babies to Logan's waiting buggy.

The drive through the cloudy morning brought them home to the parsonage. After the buggy was unloaded and the twins were unwrapped from their blankets, Margaret put away the dishes and cutlery still on the table. Yesterday's hasty run to the orchard had allowed her and Karen no time to put their own kitchen in order. Margaret worked on that now, glad for the quiet, simple task. Her heart reveled in this moment to reflect on risks taken and dangers averted. So much could have happened during those hours Matthew spent in the sky. She might be feeling the sorrow of tragedy right now instead of the peace of safety and security.

The doorbell rang. Karen was in the bedroom feeding a twin. so Margaret went to the door. When she opened it, she discovered Walter Brinks as their visitor.

"Good morning Walter. Are you looking for Pastor Logan? He is at the church."

Walter shook his head. "No, ma'am. I'm looking for you."

"For me?" Margaret rested her hand on her chest.

"Yeah. Dad just took a telephone call from Chicago and asked me to deliver it to you."

"A call from Chicago? Who was it? What did they say?" Margaret held her breath.

"A man named Henry called. He said to tell you his wife is sick, and they need you to come home."

26

"Fran is sick?" Margaret's insides quivered. She rested her hand on her abdomen. "What does she have? How long has this been going on?"

Karen joined Margaret in the foyer. "I heard the doorbell."

"Walter Brinks is here with news from Henry." Margaret pointed at the boy standing in the doorway.

He nodded a greeting at Karen. "Good morning, Mrs. De Witt. Sorry to bother you, but I had orders to deliver a message to Mrs. Millerson."

"It's about Fran." Margaret's brow wrinkled as she glanced at Karen.

"What's the matter, Walter?" Karen gave him a look of concern.

"A man from Chicago called. He's asking for Mrs. Millerson to come. His wife is sick. Pneumonia, I think he said." Walt adjusted the cap on his head. "I gotta go. See ya."

He bolted away, leaving Margaret and Karen staring at each other over the disconcerting news.

"Pneumonia is serious. Lillian Ellenbroek almost died from it a few years ago." Karen's quiet voice held a note of foreboding.

Margaret nodded. "I know of people in the city who have

died from it. Many people struggle to recover. I wonder how long she's been sick."

Karen shrugged. "Would you like to call Henry back and get more details?"

"I don't know." Margaret's hands fluttered at her sides and her attention refused to stay in one place. "Of course I should go. I can't imagine not being there if Fran ..." She gulped in some air. "I should pack."

"Before you leave for Chicago, let me give you some items to take to Julia and Aunt Fran. I've been accumulating them for the day when you'd return home." Karen hastened to the room that at one time had been Margaret's, but now served as a nursery for the twins.

Margaret wandered to the window, lifted the lace curtain, and looked out. The tone of Karen's voice stuck in her mind. Karen still viewed Chicago as Margaret's home. A sinking feeling claimed Margaret's stomach. Oswell City had become her home. She had family here. Friends too. At times, the line blurred between the people who were related to her by blood, and the ones that were related to her through love. Her heart had taken everyone in as belonging in her life, infusing it with meaning and association.

How could she ever get Karen to understand? What would make her daughter see the shift that had taken place?

Logan and Matthew met up on the sidewalk and approached the house. How could she ever leave Matthew? She'd only just begun to understand her feelings about him, but now she must go. Maybe she was too late and had taken too long. What if Fran's illness lingered for months? She might have to stay in Chicago, put Oswell City behind her, and relearn the old ways and manners of the former life.

One thing she would never take up again was the low expectations she'd always held of love. Matthew had shown her deep, satisfying caverns of its pools. She'd changed too much to accept the old life in Chicago as her only choice for existence.

The men entered the house talking over the plight of the children's home. Logan glanced up.

His brow furrowed when he saw her. "Hello, Mother. You look distraught. Did something happen?"

Margaret turned away from the window and gave a solemn nod. "I've received a message that Fran has pneumonia. Henry is asking for me to return to Chicago."

Matthew's eyes grew wide. "You're leaving?"

"I'm afraid so."

"Step outside with me." Matthew held his hand out to her. "Pardon us a moment, Logan. I fear I must delay this trip to Clear Brook until I've had a chance to speak with your mother-in-law."

"Why don't I save us some time and pick up Mr. Broekhuizen? I'll be back in half an hour."

"Fine idea." Matthew led Margaret outdoors while Logan went to the small barn where he stabled his horse.

"Tell me what has happened." Matthew brought them to a stop in the semi-private shelter of the large oak tree in the yard.

"Walt arrived from the hotel with the message this morning. My brother wants me. Fran's condition is serious. I must go." Margaret wrapped her arms around her torso as if to protect herself from the wind.

"What about us?" Matthew looked at her intently.

"I don't know. We can write. Henry has a telephone. You can call me from the hotel." The picture the suggestion painted made her smile. The idea of Matthew standing in the hotel office talking of quiet, intimate topics while Mrs. Brinks, her housekeeping staff, and guests bustled about seemed far-fetched.

He laughed. "Not sure I'd get by with that. Our chats would draw an audience."

"Write to me then."

"For how long?" Matthew frowned.

"I don't know. Depending on the success of Fran's recovery, I could be gone a long time." Margaret twisted her hand in her skirt.

Matthew sighed. After a moment of silence, he spoke. "I'll miss you."

A bead of moisture filled the corner of her eye. "I'll miss you too."

Light entered his eyes. He took a step closer and held both of her hands.

"Don't forget me." He tilted his face toward hers.

"Not a chance." She kept her focus on him ready to receive the kiss soon to be hers.

"Doctor!" A man's yell came from the direction of the street.

The sweet moment shattered. Margaret stepped away. The town's doctor shouldn't get caught kissing in the great outdoors for anyone to see. He gave her a solemn yet warm gaze before turning to the intruder.

The man came to a stop. "Oh. Sorry." His eyes took in their clasped hands and lack of distance between them. "Didn't mean to interrupt."

"It's fine. I, ah, was on my way to Clara's. I should get going." Margaret nodded at Matthew and then walked away.

Matthew's conversation with the visitor floated to her ears. They talked about an injury at the lumber yard. Margaret sighed as she followed the sidewalk to Clara's home. The scene mirrored their relationship. Just when Matthew had been about to kiss her, trouble had arrived pulling them apart. Trouble in the form of Fran's sickness called her away, pulling her from Matthew, from this town full of friends, and from her hopes.

At Clara's, she entered the house, told Clara of the new turn of events, and set to work packing her belongings.

"I don't know if I'll come back." Margaret said to Clara as they stood together in the hall an hour later.

"I'm so sorry to see you go. I've enjoyed sharing my home with you. We've gotten along quite well." Clara smiled at her.

"I agree. Thank you, Clara." She reached to give the elderly lady a hug.

Margaret returned to Karen's house in time to help with lunch preparations. She held a baby while she stirred the soup. Karen set the table while they talked of their family in Chicago. When Logan came home, Karen gave her a message from Matthew about the accident at the sawmill. Margaret asked him to take her suitcases to the train station.

"Since Dr. Kaldenberg is tied up at the lumberyard and must delay our trip to the children's home, I should have time." He turned to Mr. Broekhuizen, who also planned to go to Clear Brook. "Do you mind eating lunch with us and waiting here until Dr. Kaldenberg is ready to leave?"

"Not at all."

Karen set another place for him.

As she ate, Margaret's heart grew heavy. Leaving town required much thought and planning. Her choices affected so many. She'd become an important part of this community. Her absence would leave a hole just like her removal from the town would create a gap in her heart only Oswell City could fill.

After the meal was finished, Karen gave Margaret a hug.

"We are really saying 'good-bye' this time. Thanks for coming and staying with us, Mother. I don't know what I would have done without you." Karen held her for a moment and then pulled away. Tears sparkled in her eyes.

Tears filled Margaret's eyes too. "I'm so glad I could be here to help you. I've loved the time I've spent with you. Write me and keep me up to date on those babies. They'll change so quickly."

Karen nodded as she wiped her eyes.

"Ready?" Logan laid his hand on her shoulder. Margaret fastened her hat in place. "Yes, I suppose."

After one more hug from Karen, Logan led her out the door to Clara's house. The scene was repeated with Clara. The women hugged while Logan gathered her suitcases.

Leaving was so difficult, harder than Margaret expected. Maybe she should pay attention to the resistance she felt and decide to stay. No, she couldn't do that. Fran needed her. Margaret must stick to her plan to return to Chicago.

Logan accompanied her down Main Street past the shops, the bank, and the medical clinic. If only she could catch one more glimpse of Matthew. If they could just share that kiss and have more time for a proper good-bye.

She walked on at Logan's side. There was very little she could do to alter the unfolding events. Peace would only come when she accepted the changes and cooperated with them.

At the station, Margaret bought her ticket and found Logan in the lobby. "The train will be here soon." She held her ticket out to show him.

"Would you like for me to stay and wait with you?" Logan's forehead creased.

"Thank you, but no. You are busy with many other things to do." Margaret straightened. Standing taller might help her make this final break a little easier.

"Your suitcases are checked in, so you are all ready to leave." Logan glanced out the window at the overcast day and back at her.

"Thank you, Logan. For everything. Truly." The tears ran over her cheeks. This young man was very dear to her, as special as any son-in-law could be. Leaving town meant an end to her reliance on him and her dependence on the strength and assurance his presence brought her. There was no Logan in Chicago, just like there was no Matthew in the city either. This return to Henry's home forced from her daily existence vital communion with two irreplaceable men.

Logan must have understood her tears because he opened his arms to her ready to offer an embrace. His posture reminded her of the evening in his barn all those years ago when she'd needed convincing that he was worthy of her daughter.

He was worthy. Very worthy. These summer months she'd

spent in Oswell City had allowed her a rare and treasured glimpse into the deep levels of his integrity and compassion. She rushed into his arms and rested there in an effort to draw one last ounce of strength from him.

"Have a good trip, Mother. Write to us and let us know how Aunt Fran does." He spoke above her hat.

"I will. Make sure you and Karen write too. I want to hear all about John and Simon. It's nice to know I'm leaving them in good hands. You're a wonderful father, Logan. I couldn't ask for anyone better to share my daughter's life and raise my grandsons."

Logan pulled away and grinned at her. "You and I have come a long way, haven't we?"

Margaret nodded as she chuckled. From skepticism to fondness to admiration to this moment of not wanting to leave him, her relationship with her son-in-law had definitely grown from nothing. Now it thrived with vitality and a mutual respect.

He lifted his hat to her and left the station. Margaret picked up her satchel and went to the platform. Other people gathered about as they waited for the train. Her wait went quickly. Soon the train arrived. She boarded and found a seat near the back where she could look out the window.

Six hours of travel stretched before her. She should visit the dining car. Enjoying a meal there would help her pass the time. Then she might read from the magazine Clara had given her. And then she'd take a nap. A nice doze sounded heavenly after spending last night awake and worried about Matthew.

The train pulled away from the station and gained speed as it raced out of town. Miles and miles of flat, open cropland comprised the scenery as she headed east. Margaret made use of the dining car, her magazine, and her wish to nap before the train reached the outskirts of Chicago. It pulled into the central station where Margaret got off. She entered the large lobby and looked around.

Julia waved. She stood with her two boys and Henry's chauffeur. Margaret hastened in their direction.

"Mother! It's so good to see you again." Julia gave her an enthusiastic hug.

"Yes. I have a feeling I'm home to stay. It sounds like Fran's condition hasn't improved."

Julia grew somber at the mention of Fran. "It's so serious. I hope she survives. She needs time. And you."

Margaret smiled. "Well, let's have Hank run us home so I can see for myself how Fran is."

Julia fell in step with her and led her boys along as they followed Hank to the car. Was this a happy homecoming, or would Margaret be faced with grief and loss? She'd soon find out. Everything she'd left behind in Oswell City was about to be traded in for uncertainty.

27

Margaret stepped into the foyer of Henry's luxurious mansion. Everything looked just as she remembered in its well cared-for and expensive state.

"Come, boys. Let's get you settled with your toys, and then I will take Grandma upstairs to see Aunt Fran." Julia carried Sam and led Ben by the hand to the drawing room.

The house fell quiet. So quiet it felt eerie. Staff was probably working at the routine tasks in the large kitchen at the back of the house, but Margaret couldn't hear them. Maybe they kept the doors closed out of respect to the sick woman. Ida, the housekeeper, didn't even make an appearance to greet Margaret. Perhaps Ida was already upstairs helping the doctor or looking after her employer.

Julia returned while Margaret removed her hat and settled her satchel on a bench. "The boys are busy with a collection of blocks. Rita will take breaks in her household work to check on them."

Margaret followed Julia up the stairs and into Fran's bedroom. The doctor, a nurse, and Ida stood around the bed. Fran lay sleeping on the pillow. Everyone turned in her direction when Margaret entered with Julia.

"Mrs. Millerson, good afternoon. Welcome home." The doctor greeted her.

"Good afternoon, Doctor. How is she?" Margaret ventured near the bed.

"Slightly improved, I think, although she still runs a fever. I'm giving her the best treatment possible, the antipneumococcal serum therapy. If I began the treatment early enough, she will continue to improve. Only time will tell." The doctor bent over Fran, and with the use of the stethoscope around his neck, he checked her pulse. Then he listened to various places on his patient's chest.

Margaret held her breath as she watched.

"Steady heartbeat. That's a good sign. But her lungs are still quite congested." He straightened and looked at Julia. "You and your mother may stay in the sickroom for as long as you like if you are quiet. I'll check on her this evening when I complete my rounds in this part of the city. Good day." He packed up his bag, gave some hushed instructions to the nurse, and left the room.

"Nice to have you home again. Welcome back," Ida said in a soft voice as she adjusted the curtains to let more light into the room.

"Thank you. I was glad to receive Henry's call even though it contained troubling news." Margaret settled into a chair.

"Your room is ready for you, so feel free to retire there whenever you like. I'm going to check on the kitchen." Ida fluffed a pillow and left the room.

Julia settled into another chair and talked in a hushed voice. "Fran's health started to decline the end of last week when her fever climbed. We'd hoped the fever would break, but it grew worse. That's when Uncle Henry decided we should call you."

"I'm glad he did. What brought on Fran's pneumonia? Did she have a cough or a cold?" Margaret asked in a whisper. The doctor had told them to stay quiet, so she'd try her best to respect his instruction.

"She'd gotten chilled one day when walking in the wind and rain. Soon she developed a cough. Her condition worsened after that."

Margaret glanced at the still form of her sister-in-law resting on the bed. Fran looked comfortable. Maybe she suffered less than Margaret feared.

"Tell me about Oswell City, Mother. How is Karen?" Julia asked.

"Quite well. She had a big adjustment to make but she has succeeded." Margaret replied.

"I'm glad to hear it. And the twins?"

"Growing fast. They'll change so quickly. I don't know when I'll see them again. When I do, I'll hardly recognize them." She failed to keep the sadness from her voice.

"You miss them."

"Yes. They are too small to remember me. I'll be a stranger to them if I'm not there and a part of their lives while they grow up." Margaret swallowed to hold the tears back.

"I feel that way too," Julia said in a quiet voice. "I wish there was a way for me to stay closer to Karen and see her more often."

"It's hard to have my daughters and their children in two different states. I want to be in both places at the same time."

"I'd feel the same way if I were you. What do you think of Oswell City?"

"I love it. I've made so many good friends there."

Julia smiled. "That doesn't surprise me. You make friends wherever you go."

"One of them has become special to me. Have you read in my letters about the doctor, Matthew Kaldenberg?" Margaret took a deep breath. If Julia felt the same way Karen did, her life would become much more complicated.

"I have. It sounds like he wishes to court you."

"He does. Karen isn't in favor of it. I know that she doesn't want to see me get hurt. But if she could just understand what he is really like. If she could know that I wouldn't get hurt with Matthew. He's not like that. She'd change her mind. But I don't know how to make her understand. I fear we will always disagree and remain in conflict on the matter." Margaret rubbed her forehead.

"Mother, if it is any comfort to you, I think you should pursue a courtship with the doctor." Julia rested her hand on Margaret's.

"You do?" Julia's statement surprised her and pleased her.

"Yes, I do. What happens if Fran doesn't live? Uncle Henry could have just as easily been the one to get sick. If they were gone, you'd be alone. That isn't fair to you. I want you to have another chance to get married and find happiness."

"Oh, Julia. Thank you. That means so much. But what about Karen? I want both of you to be at peace with my decision."

Julia tilted her head. "What does Logan think? Is he opposed to your friendship with the doctor?"

"Not at all. Matthew said he talked to Logan about it, and Logan was fully in favor of it."

"You may not be able to please everyone, Mother. Do what you feel is best and what brings you peace."

Margaret bit her lip. She wouldn't find peace unless both of her daughters supported her decision. And yet, she didn't want to lose Matthew either. This move to the city had already put more distance between them than she was comfortable with. But if she hadn't come, she wouldn't have heard Julia's thoughts. And she might not have had another chance to see Fran.

Why did her life have to become so complex? Why did she have to care so much for Matthew? She'd met him the night of Karen's wedding. If she hadn't seen him again months later, she could have gone on living her life with ease and predictability. Whenever she wanted, she could have entertained his memory as a pleasant dream.

But if she listened to her heart, she'd find that course of action wouldn't satisfy for very long. The truth flowed far beneath her confusion, washing away the contentment she'd find in the predictable and the easy.

Margaret turned from Julia and watched Fran. The sick woman breathed in a regular rising and falling of the blanket covering her chest. The best thing for her might be to stay here in Chicago with quiet hours at Fran's bedside in which to sort out her life, deciding what she wished to keep and letting go of all that no longer mattered.

MATTHEW GUIDED the horse along the road from Clear Brook. Logan and Mr. Broekhuizen rode in the buggy with him. The seating was tight with two other men sharing the buggy. He looked forward to the arrival at home where he could get out and stretch his legs.

Turning to the other men, he asked, "What did you think of the situation in Clear Brook?"

"They have quite a bit of work ahead of them. The staff at the children's home should plan to house the children in another location while the damage is repaired," Logan said.

"I agree. The children are welcome to stay at the orchard. We can see what Mrs. Brinks says about that, but I know that my family wouldn't mind." Mr. Broekhuizen gestured to the wide cornfield at their left which lay in the direction of the orchard.

Matthew hid a smile. He could guess how Helen Brinks would feel about keeping the children at the orchard. She loved those kids and would probably do whatever was required of her to provide them with a comfortable home.

"I'll visit with Mrs. Garner about the matter," he mumbled as he drove.

Birds chirped in the grasses along the road. Summer breezes

swept in from the west and waved in the tassels of the corn. It was a beautiful afternoon with occasional cracks in the clouds that allowed the sun to shine through.

"Do you mind if we stop to take a look at Martin's inventory of new cars?" Logan pointed at the sign for Oswell City Auto when they approached the edge of town.

"I didn't know you were interested in buying a car." Matthew frowned as he processed this new information.

"Karen and I have been talking about it for some time. We can get by with the buggy for now, but as the twins grow, we're in need of a larger vehicle. I've also been thinking about buying a car for my calls out in the country. It would make my travel time go so much faster."

"Makes sense." Matthew guided the buggy toward the car dealership. A chance to get out and look around would give Matthew and his passengers a nice break.

Ezra Barnaveldt, a partner to his brother Martin in the car business, met them as Matthew parked the buggy. "Good afternoon, gentlemen. Anything I can help you with?"

"Logan is interested in looking at new cars." Matthew pointed at the younger man as he leaped to the ground.

A smile spread across Ezra's face. "Follow me."

Matthew walked with the other men to the area where the newest models of Ford cars were displayed. His attention stayed on Ezra as he thought about the man's wife. A new baby was expected in their family this month. The latest examination he'd performed on the mother told him she was in good health. He prayed a silent prayer that the delivery would go smoothy when the time came.

Ezra stopped and rested his hand on the shiny fender of a sleek blue Model T. "This is the model similar to the one the mayor drives. Three years newer, of course, but of the same line. Paul's was one of the first models we sold of the Ford Model T."

Logan walked around the car and studied it carefully. From

the slim tires to the cloth on the roof, everything received Logan's analyzation.

"How much are you selling these cars for?" Logan lifted his head and looked at Ezra.

"I'd be willing to give it to you for five hundred dollars." Ezra folded his arms across his chest.

"Hmm." Logan continued his walk around the car but said nothing more.

"Let me tell you about the engine and the suspension." Ezra launched into a compelling speech about the advantages a car owner would enjoy.

The salesman made a convincing point. Maybe Matthew should follow Logan's lead and consider the purchase of a car for himself. When the country roads dried out, if they ever did, a car might help him during the summer and fall months.

"Mr. Barnaveldt is asking for you. His wife is in labor and sent him here." Matthew's mother poked her head into the examination room to give him the message. She helped out with nursing duties at the clinic three days a week.

Matthew didn't know what he would have done without her. The past two weeks had been an unending string of births and medical emergencies. He barely found time to sleep. If he didn't have Millie to cook his meals, he would have starved.

"Let me finish up here, and then I'll come out and talk to him." Matthew continued the messy job of applying wet plaster to the broken arm of a ten-year-old boy.

"Fine. I'll let him know." His mother disappeared.

Matthew smoothed the plaster of the cast and crossed the room to wash his hands.

"There you go, Nicky. All fixed up." Matthew bent to examine the drying white cylinder enclosing the boy's limb. He turned to the mother. "He must wear this cast for six weeks. See that he doesn't use that arm for anything. I'll drive out in a few days and check on him. Any questions?"

The woman shook her head.

Matthew helped Nicky down from the examination table and led the way to the waiting room. Ezra Barnaveldt stood near the door looking agitated.

"My wife needs your help, Doctor." He ran his hand through his hair.

"She's in labor?"

"Yeah. Started this morning as I was getting ready to go to work. When I went home for lunch just now, she was worse."

"All right. You go on home and help her stay as comfortable as you can. I've got two more patients here. After I've seen them, I'll come to your house. Expect me in an hour."

Ezra's eyes widened. "I don't know if she'll hang on that long. That baby is on its way."

Matthew took him to an examination room for a private place to quiz him. After gaining more details, Matthew assured him that an hour was plenty of time. The expectant father left the clinic unconvinced, but with no other choices, he settled for Matthew's manner of handling the situation.

When Ezra left, Matthew called the next patient in and listened to her complaints of back pain. After examining her, he sent her home with a regimen of stretching exercises and ideas to keep her pain managed. The second patient was a teen with vision problems. A thorough examination told Matthew the young man was in need of spectacles. Matthew fitted him with a pair and scheduled him for a follow-up appointment.

Leaving his nurse in charge of the clinic to handle any basic ailments that might arrive, he went to the Barnaveldt's. Mrs. Barnaveldt lay in bed while Ezra hovered around talking with her and stacking towels nearby. Relief claimed his face when Matthew walked in.

"You look nice and comfortable," Matthew said to Mrs. Barnaveldt as he took off his jacket and rolled up his sleeves.

"I've tried." She heaved in a deep breath and exhaled it in a groan.

"Let's take a look." Matthew washed his hands in the basin on the dresser and then gave the woman a full examination.

He waited and watched throughout the afternoon hours for the arrival of a newborn. Finally around the supper hour, when a neighbor lady had the other children gathered for the meal, a baby girl was born. Matthew cared for the infant and placed her in bed with her mother. Then he went home and ate the meal Millie had fixed for him.

"Have you heard anything from Mrs. Millerson?" Millie asked as she worked at the sink.

"Yesterday I received a letter. She informed me that the danger is passed. Her sister-in-law is sitting up for a couple hours at a time."

"Good for her. When will you see her again?"

"Not for a long time. She's in Chicago to stay. That is where her other daughter lives, and Margaret will want to be with her."

Millie said nothing more, but Matthew felt her eyes on him as he enjoyed his meal. She probably wanted him to give her a reason to cook for two. He'd like to do that as well but Margaret's choice to move away made his pursuit much harder.

The doorbell rang so Millie went to answer it. Jake Harmsen, the newspaper editor, entered the kitchen.

"Good evening, Doctor. Sorry to interrupt. I didn't know you were still eating."

"I was waiting on a baby to arrive this afternoon, so I am a bit delayed." Matthew wiped his mouth with his napkin. "What can I help you with?"

Jake sat down at the table. "I'd like to ask you a few questions about your flight to Clear Brook for a newspaper article. You're a busy man to track down. This is the first I've caught you."

Matthew smiled. "There's not much to tell. Mrs. Garner, the matron of the children's home called me to reschedule appointments. When I asked the reason, I discovered a rather dangerous situation had developed. I offered to help out. That's pretty much all."

Jake took notes as Matthew answered questions about his biplane and flying in the darkness of an approaching storm. "Where are those children now?"

"They are still staying at the orchard. Helen Brinks takes care of them and I provide their medical care. Their teachers travel there as needed, and a boy with physical disabilities by the name of Albert has been brought to stay there. I've talked with Mrs. Garner. She says that the children's home hopes to have the building repaired sometime next month. Then the children can return."

Shaking his head in amazement, Jake scribbled notes in a rush. "Thank you for sharing your story. I hope to run it in the paper this week."

"My pleasure." Matthew shook his hand when Jake stood to leave.

The next morning, Matthew made his daily trip to the orchard to check on the children and then went to the clinic. He kept busy with a surgery, wart removal from the finger of a little boy, conversations with expectant mothers, and another broken bone. He worked at tidying the empty office when Conrad Van Drunen rushed in.

"What's the matter?" Matthew asked in response to the distraught look on Conrad's face.

"My little girl, Betje. She fell and hit her head. Now she is unconscious. My brother's wife is with her. They only live two blocks away. The children have been playing together this afternoon, so I sent one of them home for their mother. She relieved me so I could run over here to get you." The father panted out his words.

Matthew tensed. Surely nothing permanently debilitating had happened to precious little Betje. The family had already lost so much with the death of the mother and new baby in childbirth over the past Christmas. He gathered up supplies and stuffed them in his bag. In a matter of minutes he followed Conrad out the door. He didn't bother to take the time to hitch his horse to the buggy. Conrad only lived on the next street over from the church. Walking—or sprinting as Conrad was doing—was the fastest way to get to the side of the injured girl.

28

Matthew rushed into the Van Drunen yard and headed to the grass where little Betje lay. She looked like a crumpled flower. He must do all he could to help her. The thought of Conrad losing another child tortured him. Conrad's sister-in-law knelt on the grass near the injured girl. A cluster of children, probably cousins, hovered around the scene.

"Betje, can you hear me?" Matthew felt along the side of her head with gentle fingers.

The girl gave no response. Matthew continued to examine her until satisfactory answers surfaced.

"She has a concussion. We won't know the extent of the damage to her brain until she starts to wake up. Do you know how this happened?" Matthew turned to the anxious father.

"What can you tell us, Markus?" Conrad looked down at his son.

The boy wiped his eyes with the back of his sleeve. "I'd run up the ladder to the treehouse you built for me. Earl and his brother Wil were chasing me. We were playing pirates. Betje climbed up after me, but she fell off. I'm sorry, Dad. I didn't know Betje was behind me." He began to cry.

Conrad patted his shoulder. "It's all right. Don't blame

yourself for what happened. I should have been paying more attention and waited to cook supper until you'd both come inside."

"You did the right thing by not moving her before I got here." Matthew straightened and looked at the group. "All of you children, go home with your mother. We need to take care of Betje now." He turned to Conrad. "I have a stretcher at the clinic. I'll be right back."

Matthew hurried to his clinic and returned with the medical equipment.

Conrad helped him ease Betje onto the stretcher and held one end as he and Matthew carried her to the house. They put the girl on her bed and covered her with a blanket. Matthew asked for some ice. Conrad left and soon returned with a chunk.

"I'll finish cooking supper. Doctor, would you stay and eat with us?" Conrad asked.

"Yes. I want to monitor Betje for the next few hours. Markus, could you please take a message for Millie to my house please?" Matthew wrote a quick note on a slip of paper he pulled from his pocket and handed it to Markus.

When he returned, they gathered to eat the meal. Matthew went to the bedroom after the meal for another look at Betje. Nothing had changed.

He bent over her. "Betje? Betje. Can you hear me?"

She didn't respond. Matthew checked her vital signs and then returned to the main living area of the house. Markus played on the floor with a train set. Conrad had cleared the table and replaced the dishes and cutlery with ships in bottles.

"How interesting." Matthew sat beside Conrad and picked up a bottle with a ship inside.

Perfectly formed, the delicate model of a sailing ship had miniature white sails, tiny round windows, and a stern painted in bright colors.

"That's the *Zeelandia*. It's a Dutch ship from 1670. Built in Rotterdam and used in the battle of Solebay. See these little black sticks?" Conrad pointed with the skinny tool in his hand to the rows of tiny holes along the sides of the ship. "Guns. Forty-eight of them."

Matthew turned the bottle to closer examine the craftsmanship. "Amazing." He envisioned the real ship out on the seas, one in a fleet of many engaging the Dutch in battle against the English and the French.

"And this one over here. It's the *Duyfken*." Conrad pointed to another ship encased in a bottle. "It was used for exploration, not for battle. Legend says it made the first European discovery of Australia back in 1606."

Matthew picked it up and looked it over. Smaller in size, it was simpler than the *Zeelandia* with fewer sails and no guns.

"What are you working on now?" Matthew shifted his focus to the collection of miniature masts and sails in Conrad's hand.

"This one is the *Valkenburg*. Another battleship. Built in 1725." Conrad threaded a tiny string through the corner of a sail. "Watch. I'm ready to put this ship in its bottle." He reached for an empty bottle and with careful movements, thrust the flattened sails and slim hull through the bottle's neck.

He worked for a moment with his skinny tool to help the ship stand upright. "Now I pull on the strings and ... see that? The masts stand upright."

Fascinating. The process of putting a ship in a bottle was as much a work of art as the construction of the ship.

"This is my hobby, you know. I picked it up after Angelien died. I was so sad, but I was scared too. I mean, how was a man like me to raise two small children alone? They need a mother more than they need me. A mother can provide so many things that I cannot. I've learned to cook and to do the wash, but I'm not very good at nurture or at affection. Those were things Angelien did. And now with Betje hurt, I find I must build ships tonight. It helps me with my fear."

Matthew watched Conrad poke balls of a blue tacky substance into the bottle and press it around the base of the ship with his tool. It started to look like water as though the ship sat atop a calm ocean.

Conrad's art helped Matthew make sense of some things going on in his life. Building a ship in a bottle was like landing a biplane in a flood zone. They were both tight places calling for skill and precision. Similar to so many other medical tasks he completed daily without having to think about them. Skill and precision characterized Matthew's nature and his career, and had infiltrated his whole outlook.

His relationship with Margaret also fit into the category of a tight place. As Conrad's hobby and Matthew's flying experience proved, weighty, complex subjects required the confinement of a narrow space. There was certainly risk of damage, but there was also the great potential for marvelous beauty. The attractive qualities shone with a more obvious glory than they might if given a more comfortable environment.

If the ships Conrad built had plenty of space in which to stand, they wouldn't be near as fascinating. If his afternoon mission to the children's home would have had plenty of space for landings, it wouldn't have been so necessary. If his relationship with Margaret had no challenges or opposition, it wouldn't be as meaningful.

Conrad took a break from creating his model ocean and poked at the sails of the ship. "One of the sails caught on another during the transport, but I wanted to get the ship stabilized before I fixed this problem. Only have to do it once that way."

His careful movements spoke of Conrad's concentration on the hobby before him, but Matthew saw more in that moment. His vision seemed to tunnel deeper into the reality of Conrad's existence. Conrad didn't grieve alone. Neither did he raise his children without help. God was there comforting, healing, and guiding.

Even the physical construction of his model ships was evidence of God's work in Conrad's life. The imagination and patience necessary to complete that sort of artwork were qualities of God's character. He was here, in the midst of Conrad's everyday life sculpting and shaping while also helping him endure.

One word came to mind as the best explanation for this phenomenon: mercy. As a doctor, Matthew was responsible for showing this quality in easing suffering and administering healing. God was showing it to Conrad. The more Matthew observed, the more he discovered that God was showing it to him too. The mercy in Matthew's life was the reward of God's presence. Matthew didn't achieve the buoyancy required to rise above on his own. God supplied the strength.

Maybe precision and skill characterized God's nature, too. Matthew chewed on the thought while he watched Conrad work. The careful movement of the creator, the patience required to see a project through to completion, and the vision of what the final craft should look like were all a part of God's mercy.

"Finished." Conrad announced as he lay down his tool. He picked up the bottle and turned it so Matthew could see the *Valkenburg* from every angle.

"Impressive. I don't know of anyone who has that much patience. You are very talented, Conrad. Not only can you repair roofs and build furniture, but you can also make these delicate models of ships."

"I've had to learn it—both the patience and the hobby. Neither comes natural, I'm afraid." The solemn young man cracked a smile.

"At least you are willing to learn." Matthew had learned some important lessons over the past months as well. The trick of putting the ship with the flattened sails into the bottle fascinated him. Conrad had turned the ship the slightest bit to the side in order to get it to glide through the bottle's neck.

The lesson impressed itself on Matthew. Maybe he needed to employ the same technique in his own life. He must turn his love for Margaret sideways to protect this wide and marvelous work God had been doing in their lives from any damage. Like Conrad's model ship, parts of it could have been destroyed in the move to the bottle. Matthew's biplane could have also been damaged on his night of the rescue if he hadn't known how to steer it against the wind.

The biplane, with its wingspan, was not only fragile in itself, but capable of damaging objects around it. Careful steering had kept him on course preventing a crash that would have harmed both his biplane and the buildings or trees he might have run into.

He must practice the same care in his relationship with Margaret. It was deep and it was marvelous. Matthew must angle his heart and his love so that Margaret, her daughters, and the town he served didn't get hurt.

Maybe he didn't need to stand so unconquerable and stubborn in the face of death and pain. He could win in other ways. He should turn his attention away from his own ability to defeat and toward the tenderness required of him to love well. This maneuver might prove to be successful in his goal to ascend above the fears and the griefs that had weighed him down for so long.

Precision in love might triumph as well as precision in surgery or in flight. He'd have to give it a try.

He heaved in a breath and stood. "I'm going to check on Betje again."

With Margaret on his mind, He moved down the hall. Was there anything standing in his way of getting married again? He had a steady business that supported him. His career supplied him with plenty of financial resources to also support a wife.

He had a nice home and a housekeeper to go with it. His wife wouldn't have to do housework if she didn't want to. He had respect and standing in his community. His wife wouldn't bear any shame as a result of the condition of his relationships. Even the pastor's wife had to admit he was acceptable beyond reproach.

He also had a heart recovered from tragedy. Not forgetful of it, but restored from it. This was perhaps the best part of all. The gloominess that had burdened his soul for so long had lifted.

Matthew felt as though he could breathe again. Joy and cheer had punctured the darkness. Had purchasing the biplane and flying lifted his spirits? Had Margaret done it? Maybe God's presence in his life had raised him above the sadness and disappointments.

Maybe it was a combination of all three. God used the flying and the memories of Margaret to heal him and to reveal a new depth of mercy. There it was again. Mercy. Matthew checked Betje over with a smile on his lips. This assessment of his life turned up no obstacles to marriage. Maybe he ought to do something about that.

Matthew could trust that God's merciful presence was in his love for Margaret. The Lord had placed them in each other's paths. This meant God would move in Margaret's life until the way become clear for her to step into his life. God was on the move in Matthew's life too. Margaret wouldn't come back on her own. She'd need some nudging, especially now that she was in the familiar city enjoying luxurious surroundings.

He'd have to do something about that too.

He returned to the table where Conrad worked. "Betje hasn't changed. I'll come check on her again tomorrow, but try to talk to her occasionally overnight. That will help wake her up."

"Thank you, Doctor." Conrad shook his hand.

Matthew returned home in the dark. As he prepared for sleep he prayed, thought through some ideas, and considered the facts. A plan started to form in his mind. He smiled as he dropped off to sleep.

The next morning, Matthew greeted Millie in the kitchen while she fixed him breakfast.

"You look cheery this morning." Her eyebrow rose.

"I am, thank you." Matthew poured himself some coffee.

"If Margaret Millerson was still in town, I'd say you'd recently spent time with her." Millie set a plate of food before him.

"You are quite perceptive, but dead wrong." He grinned. This return of his sense of humor was something he could get used to.

Millie chuckled. "Your good mood must have something to do with her."

"Perhaps." Matthew speared a slice of bacon with his fork.

Millie groaned. "I know better than to try and get any information out of you, Mr. Confidentiality."

Matthew's smile grew. "You'll find out soon enough."

Millie rolled her eyes at him and went to the dining room. She returned with a newspaper in her hand.

"This came this morning. Read it." She unfolded the paper and pointed to the front page.

Matthew's name appeared in bold letters.

Dr. Matthew Kaldenburg Accomplishes Rescue Mission.

He set down his fork and read the article. Jake had done a nice job reporting the facts. Pride in the children he'd rescued swelled in his chest.

"You never said a word." Millie looked at him in confusion.

He shrugged. "Everything happened so quickly, and then I got busy."

Millie shook her head and went to the sink, allowing him to eat his breakfast in peace.

Throughout the day, patients came to the clinic with the usual ailments. But they weren't his only visitors. Jake's article in the morning paper had been a popular topic because many people with no health conditions stopped in to see him. Some shook his hand. Others told him he was a hero. Everyone wanted to hear the details. He told the story over and over, thrilling his listeners with the truth of the danger of that stormy night.

Late afternoon, another visitor stopped in. The last person

he expected to see in the clinic, she didn't appear sick or in need of medical attention. Matthew couldn't guess what she wanted unless she'd come to impose more restrictions on him. His insides tensed as he faced Karen De Witt.

"Good afternoon, Karen. What can I help you with?" He gestured for her to follow him to the room where he kept his desk.

She moved some papers and a medical journal from a chair and sat down. "I find that my views are growing more and more unpopular." She folded her hands in her lap with a grace that reminded him of Margaret.

"What do you mean?"

"You are a celebrity, Dr. Kaldenburg. Everyone has read the story Jake published in the paper."

"Why does that matter?"

"At the Ladies Mission Society meeting today, I was quite vocal about my disapproval of any sort of serious relationship between you and my mother. The subject came up because the women had seen her flying with you at the festival in July. Several of them sounded almost envious, I might add."

Matthew raised his brows at the bit of information. The husbands of these women had voiced their disapproval of his ownership of the biplane. Never had he suspected that any of the women in town envied Margaret's opportunities to fly.

"No one agreed with me. Everyone commented on your bravery and on your deep concern for those children." Karen inhaled. "I know those things are true about you. After being with those other women today, I went home and took a good look at my own attitudes. I came here to tell you that I haven't been fair to you or to Mother."

She leaned on her knees and stared at the floor. "I've been scared. I don't want her to get hurt again. But when I really thought about it, I realized that I've never heard anyone praise my father in the way those women praised you. I've compared you unfairly to him, and I'm sorry."

When Karen looked at him, Matthew saw the sincere apology in her eyes. He'd expected to have to do harder work than this to bring Karen around. He hardly knew what to say. God had removed the last possible obstacle from his path, and he'd done it so graciously. Here was another facet to the jewel of mercy God had settled into his life.

He leaned forward. "Thank you, Karen. This is most unexpected. I appreciate you coming and talking with me. Does this mean that you are comfortable with me courting your mother?"

She nodded. "It does. You are nothing like my father. I think she'll be very happy with you."

He raised a brow. One question still needed answered. "And what about my flying? Your mother loves to fly. She thinks it is fun."

Karen stood and paced the room for a moment. "I know that. She's told me of her enjoyment of flying. I think she likes it so much because she gets to do it with you. Riding in the passenger seat of a biplane would never have occurred to her as a good time if you weren't involved in it somehow." She drew closer and glanced at him. "If flying makes my mother happy, then I suppose she can keep doing it. I won't interfere anymore."

"Thank you, Karen. I've always understood your concerns, and I promise that I will take the best care of your mother that I know how."

"I believe you will. I've seen how much you care for the twins. I've trusted their lives to you, and I'll do the same with Mother's." Karen reclaimed the chair and looked at him with respect in her eyes.

Matthew smiled. "May I share something with you?"

Karen returned his smile and listened with her complete attention on him as he told her of his plan.

29

"You're looking quite well today, Aunt Fran." Julia tucked a quilt around the recovering woman.

"I'm feeling better. My breathing is improved, and my energy is returning." Fran held her hat against the soft breeze fluttering in from the lake.

"Glad to hear it. I was so worried about you." Margaret smiled at Fran.

"Henry was too. This is one time when I'm grateful he could afford to get for me the best medical care money can buy." Fran pressed Margaret's hand. "I wouldn't have pulled through without it."

"God has been good to you."

"That he has. Good to all of us. Good, merciful, and gracious." Fran spoke in a soft voice as she lifted her gaze to watch gulls swoop in the sunny air.

Margaret watched the serene woman enjoy their afternoon at the lakeshore. She couldn't imagine spending today mourning her loss of Fran. They'd been good friends as well as members of the same family for years. After sharing a home and her children and grandchildren with Fran, Margaret's life would look very different without her sister-in-law in it.

"Grandma, come watch." Ben motioned for her to join him where he built a sandcastle with help from his little brother Sam.

Margaret left her place on the blanket they'd spread out in the grass and went to inspect his work.

"See. Water flows here and here." Ben motioned with his hand to demonstrate how the moat around his castle worked.

At that moment, a wave from Lake Michigan gushed in crumbling a portion of their fortress.

"Oh, no!" Ben moaned and covered his face.

Sam used his small shovel to scoop wet sand into a bucket and dumped his load onto the damaged side of the castle.

"No! That won't work." Ben pushed Sam's bucket away. "Now we have to start over."

Sam sunk his shovel into the pile of sand he'd added to the castle and set to work. Ben stood and stomped down the crumbled sand making space for another load from Sam's bucket.

Margaret tousled Ben's hair. "Looks like the two of you are getting it worked out. Your castle looks very nice. It's so tall right here." She pointed to a packed mound.

"I made it." Sam pointed to his chest and gave her a wide grin.

"I did this part." Ben pressed the sand down around the moat.

"Nice work." Margaret smiled at the boys and turned to glance at the blanket. Julia opened a large basket and removed items from it. "Would you like to take a break for something to eat? I see your mother has found food in our basket." Margaret turned to the boys.

They jumped up. "Yeah!" Abandoning their toys and the castle, they ran up the beach to the women gathered on the blanket. Margaret collected the toys and followed along behind.

She settled on the blanket and accepted a sandwich from Julia. What a lovely time they were having seated outdoors, eating Evelyn the cook's good food, and watching Fran enjoy the company. Why wouldn't she want to stay in the city and pick up her life here? She had a wide circle of friends. Whenever an evening event or social function arose, she could count on plenty of people in attendance who she could mingle with and talk to. Bertha and Isabel were two women she'd known for many years. They worked together on committees and trusted each other as friends.

She mustn't forget to count her family as more good reasons to stay in Chicago. Julia, her husband Arthur, and their two boys were close to her as an important part of her life. Henry had offered his home to her. Fran filled both roles of sister-in-law as well as confidante.

Margaret could quite easily settle back into the ways and manners of the city. She could see it now. The years of quiet complacency stretched before her in which she could enjoy the luxuries and relationships her surroundings offered.

The picture should soothe her, but it didn't. It left her uneasy. She glanced around at the others. Ben munched on a sandwich. Julia fed grapes to Sam while she visited with Fran about an upcoming party. No one seemed to sense the quiver on Margaret's insides that interfered with her appetite.

The only thing that brought her peace were thoughts of Matthew. Julia had said Margaret should do what brought her peace. Remembering Matthew was most successful. He was the reason she couldn't stay in the city. She'd found love—real, deep love—with him in his ordinary small town. That was the place where she must go.

"Have some." Ben passed her a dish of crackers.

"Thank you." Margaret took a handful and set the dish in the center of the blanket.

Sam reached for the dish but received a chiding from Julia since he already had a pile of crackers on his plate.

A troubling thought dawned on her. If Oswell City was the

place where she belonged, then she must make serious preparations to go there. Cancel her account at the department store. Resign from committees. Consult about her bank account. The list went on. When they returned to the house the hour would be too late to put any plans in motion. Tomorrow she would make use of the hall telephone and get in touch with the necessary people.

But before she did any of that, she must have a conversation with her family.

She turned to her daughter. "Julia, would you and Arthur be able to come over a little while later this evening? There's something I want to discuss with you."

Concern furrowed Julia's brow. "Certainly, Mother. I'll mention it to Arthur when he comes home."

"Thank you."

The boys finished eating and played in the sand while Margaret and Julia put away their lunch. Hank arrived and helped them put Fran in the car. He took Julia and her sons home. Then he delivered Margaret and Fran to the Millerson mansion.

They enjoyed a quiet evening meal with Henry and then retired to the drawing room. Fran picked up a book to read. Henry read the newspaper. Margaret worked on a piece of embroidery. The soft evening breeze filtered through the open windows facing the street. Leaves fluttered on the trees. Children called to each other in a game across the street. A car puttered by. Streaks of sunlight announced the lowering of the sun to close the day.

Above the sounds of their serene city street, a whirr reached her ears. Margaret raised her eyes to the windows while her jaw dropped. A frown fought with a smile to dominate her face.

Henry heard it too because he lowered his paper and glanced around. "That sounds like ... I don't recall hearing of any military operations taking place in our area." His brow creased.

The whirring grew closer and sharper accompanied by the putter of a motor. The sound increased in volume until it seemed to come from the street.

Henry left his chair and rushed to the window. "Good heavens!" He bellowed as he flung back the curtains.

Margaret and Fran crowded in behind him to discover what evoked such a disturbance from her usually placid brother.

There, on Michigan Avenue, parked directly in front of their house, was a Wright Model B biplane. Dogs barked. A police whistle blew. People opened their front doors, crept from their houses, and looked around.

The pilot shut off the engine and left his seat. He stood in the yard with hands on his waist and faced the house. Even with leather helmet and goggles covering his head, Margaret recognized him at once.

"Matthew!" She took off on a run as light as a child.

"You know this person?" Henry's incredulous words followed her out the door.

She rushed across the lawn and straight into his arms.

He wrapped her in a tight embrace and whispered into her hair. "Hello, Margaret. I've missed you, my dear."

And then that kiss she missed out on her last day in Oswell City came forth, full and sweet and promising.

"How'd you do it? How'd you get here?' Margaret asked when she pulled away. Happiness radiated in her heart. Her face glowed.

"Easier than landing on a flooded hill, if you can believe that." Matthew smiled. "I circled around over the lake and came in from the south. Had to watch out for telephone poles and tree branches, but a little maneuvering helped me avoid both."

Margaret laughed and shook her head in wonder.

"I won't be able to stay long, though. I see the police are rather annoyed with me." Matthew pointed at a police car with light flashing and siren blaring while racing in their direction.

He turned his full attention on her. "I've come to ask you to ride with me. Will you, Margaret? I have something very important to say to you."

"Yes, I will."

"Ahem. Before you go, we'd like an explanation." Henry's voice came from behind.

Margaret had forgotten all about her brother. She turned to find him and Fran standing in the yard. "This is Dr. Matthew Kaldenburg from Oswell City. He's come to take me for a ride." Margaret gestured to Matthew.

"Doctor." Henry shook Matthew's hand and nodded. Then he glanced at the biplane and sighed. "I suppose you'll have to go somewhere in it. This contraption is blocking our street. It has to be moved." Henry probably didn't intend to sound so gruff. The landing of a biplane on his street had certainly unnerved him. "Find somewhere to park it when you get back. I want to invite you to stay so we can become better acquainted."

"Look for us in a couple of hours." Matthew nodded to Henry.

"Land at the steel works. I'll send Hank to pick up both of you."

Matthew nodded again and helped Margaret into the passenger's seat.

The police car pulled recklessly onto the curb. A door swung open. An officer emerged and yelled at Matthew. "Sir, you must remove this flying machine from the street immediately. You're blocking traffic."

"If you help by turning my propeller, I'll be gone right now," Matthew yelled back.

The startled officer stopped in his tracks. After receiving a command from Matthew, he stumbled toward the biplane and followed directions.

"Thanks!" Matthew waved to him, zoomed down Michigan Avenue, and left the ground just as a street car crossed the intersection.

Margaret clutched Matthew's arm and caught her breath.

"That was close." Matthew leaned over to look at the street below to make sure he hadn't nicked the roof of the car. It kept moving down the street as if the avoidance of a near collision with a Model B biplane was a common daily occurrence.

"All I had to do was turn a little sideways. That helped me angle in the best way to slip through a tight spot." Matthew smiled at her as though he enjoyed an inside joke. Then he swooped over Lake Michigan and soared into the countryside.

Twenty minutes later he brought them to a landing in a farm field.

"On my last stop for fuel, I asked if I might return here to take you on a picnic. Are you hungry?" Matthew reached over and loosened a basket from its secure location on the cloth wing.

"Sure." She couldn't bring herself to tell him she'd already eaten her evening meal.

"Good." He helped her down and led her to a grassy spot beneath a tree.

Margaret removed her helmet and goggles and sat on a stump. Matthew set the basket down, but instead of opening it to reveal the contents, he pulled a box from his coat pocket and knelt on one knee.

She held her breath. A man had done this for her in the past, before her daughters were born or scandal and shame entered her life. But Matthew was different. The moment had come to try again.

"Margaret, you know how much I love you. So, my question will come as no surprise. I've waited through challenges and indecision until a proper time came to ask it. Karen and I visited before I left town. She gave me her blessing. When I told her I wanted to take you flying, she looked nervous but told me she wanted you to be happy."

"She did?" Margaret held her fingertips to her mouth.

Matthew gave her a solemn nod.

"So did Julia. I have the approval of both of my daughters," she whispered.

Matthew smiled as he slipped a gold band from the box in his hand. "Margaret Millerson, will you do me the honor of becoming my wife?"

"Yes, Matthew." She cupped his face and placed a kiss on his lips.

Dusk crept over the city as Hank delivered Margaret and her fiancé home to the Millerson mansion. Julia answered the door.

"Mother, what have you been up to? Henry said you left on a biplane." A question hung in her voice as though she couldn't quite picture her mother accomplishing such a daring feat.

Margaret patted Julia's cheek as she passed by. "Yes, I did, my dear. And it was the most fun I've had since leaving Oswell City." She shared a grin with Matthew.

"I'm so glad you didn't wreck." Julia sounded troubled as she followed Margaret and Matthew to the drawing room.

"I do my best to maintain safety in the air. Especially when your mother accompanies me." Matthew claimed a seat near the grand piano.

Margaret settled on the couch and straightened her skirts as the rest of the family found places to sit. She took a deep breath. "I invited Julia and Arthur over this evening because I wanted to discuss with you the decision I'd made to return to Oswell City. That was before Matthew arrived. Now we have even bigger news."

The attention of her audience shifted from Margaret to Matthew.

"Would you like to tell them?" She raised a brow at him.

Matthew cleared his throat. "I came to the city today with the intention of asking your mother to marry me. She has agreed."

Julia clasped her hands and squealed. "Oh, Mother! Congratulations!"

Fran came to Margaret and hugged her. "I'm so happy for you."

"Thank you." Margaret returned the hug. Soon her time of living here in Fran's home would come to an end. She pushed those thoughts away so that the tears wouldn't fall.

"Wonderful news, Margaret. I'm happy for you, but Fran and I will miss you. We've enjoyed sharing our home with you." Henry smiled at her. "But I'd like to give you a wedding gift. Something big. Something really special." Henry looked at Matthew. "Do you have a car to drive on your house calls?"

Matthew raised his brows. "Uh, no. I don't."

"Could you use one?"

"I've thought about it, but can't decide. My horse and buggy are more dependable than an automobile on muddy country roads." Matthew straightened the tie at his neck.

"Well, if I were to give it to you as a gift, could you find places to drive it?" Henry asked.

"Yes. I'd also share it with Logan. We looked at cars together a while ago. He would like a larger vehicle now that the twins have joined their family."

"Ah. That's a good idea. If I give you and Margaret a car, it could stay in the family as a help to everyone." Henry leaned back in his chair as though satisfied with the direction of this conversation.

"Yes, it would. Thank you, Mr. Millerson, for your kindness and generosity. We'd put your gift to very good use in Oswell City." Matthew left his chair and shook hands with Henry.

"Let's make plans to travel. How soon do you want us in Oswell City for the wedding?" Julia turned to Margaret with excitement glowing in her eyes.

"Why don't you come to Oswell City for the festival to celebrate the completion of our new bandstand? There will be activities and food in the park. You'll be able to see the new babies." Matthew suggested.

Fran's eyes lit up at the possibility of spending time with Karen's babies and Julia clapped. Soon they were all engaged in plans for the family from Chicago to travel to Oswell City.

30

"Spread that corner out over there." Matthew pointed to the edge of the banner lying in the hayfield near Paul Ellenbroek's home.

"Like this?" George Brinks flapped the fabric so that it flattened.

"Looks good." Matthew nodded his approval.

James Koelman and Artie Goud walked around the biplane inspecting every part of its frame, its wheels, and the propellers. Alex Zahn leaned against the lower wing as he chewed the end of a grass stem and smoothed his hand over the fabric.

"You have plenty of gas, and the engine is ready to go." Tim gave Matthew a report.

"Thanks for your help, everyone. I hope to make this flight across town in celebration of the new bandstand a success." Matthew pulled his helmet into place.

"Glad to. You're famous in this part of the state. We're proud to have you as the doctor to our town and one of our most celebrated citizens." James stepped over and shook Matthew's hand.

"Let's get back downtown in time for Paul's speech." James looked at the other men.

"You got the propellers under control?" George glanced at Tim.

"They're becoming my specialty." Tim saluted to the group.

Alex chuckled. "Come on. I left Mildred in charge of the doughnut stand. She'll want my help."

He led the other businessmen away leaving Matthew and his brother-in-law alone in the hayfield with another banner to fly and a biplane that had saved his sanity, taught him lessons about love, and recovered his respect with the town.

MARGARET STOOD with her daughters in Oswell City's downtown square. A bright blue sky arched overhead. Hints of golds and yellows mixed with the green of the leaves. Slight breezes fluttered the flag near the new bandstand. A lovely September day to spend outdoors.

"Ben is learning fast." Julia commented as she watched her oldest skip over squares in a game of hopscotch.

"He might win a prize," Karen said. Her children were too small to participate in the games set up on the grass for the children, so they stayed in the buggy.

Margaret looked around at the other families clustered about. Mothers helped children throw bean bags at a target. Others jumped rope. A group under the tree fished for little toys in a shallow pool. A person dressed up in a clown suit walked by waving at the children and handing out candy. Grace Koelman and her daughter inflated balloons. A group of men operated a popcorn machine. The smell of buttery popcorn wafted on the air.

A cluster of children gathered around with their hands held out to accept bags of the freshly popped corn. One of the boys used a cane. The smallest girl wore spectacles.

"Karen, isn't that the group of children from the orphanage in Clear Brook?" Margaret pointed to them.

Karen looked over at the children." Why yes, I believe it is. We should say hello."

"We'll be right back," Margaret said to Julia and then walked across the lawn with Karen.

"Good afternoon, children." Karen caught their attention with her greeting.

Ruby's eyes widened and she tugged on the sleeve of her friend. "Jane, it's Mrs. De Witt and Mrs. Millerson."

Jane glanced at them. "I'm so glad to see you!"

"Are you girls and your friends settled back in at the children's home?" Margaret asked.

"We are. I missed Miss Worley. She's nice." Jane smiled up at Miss Worley as she accepted a bag of popcorn from her teacher.

"Can we have another tea party?" Ruby looked up at Karen.

"That's a lovely idea. Let's do that sometime." Karen smiled down at her.

"When does the mayor give his speech?" Margaret asked Karen.

"Anytime." She glanced at the large clock that hung between two of the brick buildings. "We should probably go meet Logan."

"Good-bye, girls." Margaret waved at them and returned to watch the boys play their games.

Ben finished his hopscotch, chose a prize, and cooperated with Julia when she led him away from the games. The group maneuvered through the crowd gathered in the area where the mayor's podium was set up. Logan and Arthur stood with Henry and Fran in the shade. Karen guided Margaret and Julia in their direction.

"Are you tired?" Margaret asked Fran.

"No. I'm doing quite well. I'm so glad Henry and I decided to come along on this trip." Fran picked Simon up and held him.

"Mother, we brought along some wedding gown sketches from Miss Rose. You'll need to start making decisions on your gown," Julia said.

"This is my second marriage. I don't plan to wear a traditional white gown."

"Miss Rose gave me a variety of styles. You could find one you'd like." Julia held up a hand to indicate she'd brought along at least five sketches.

"Thank you, dear, but I don't think so."

"Have you and Dr. Kaldenburg decided on a date? Logan will want to get that scheduled." Karen jiggled John on her hip as she spoke.

Margaret nodded. "We have a day in mind."

Julia squealed. "Oh! This is exciting! When is it? Will you tell us?"

"When Matthew comes." Margaret patted Julia's arm.

"Where is he? I hope he didn't get called out on an emergency." Julia looked around at the crowd.

"Shh. The mayor is starting." Margaret held her finger to her lips as Paul Ellenbroek approached the podium.

The assembly quieted as Paul spoke. "Good afternoon, everyone. We gather today to dedicate our new bandstand to the town's use. As you know, construction began on it this spring and continued through the summer. I want to give credit to Jake Harmsen, editor of the *Oswell Journal*, for keeping us informed of the progress over the summer months." Paul gestured to the place where Jake stood in the crowd while everyone clapped.

"We've planned for this day for many months, and I'm happy to announce to you that the bandstand is finished and ready for use."

People applauded again while James and Brandt Koelman, the town lawyers, shook Paul's hand. Then James gave Paul an oversized scissors he used to cut a wide red ribbon encircling the new structure.

The click of the scissors as it sliced through the ribbon brought more applause. Men with shiny brass instruments emerged from the crowd. They took their places alongside a woman with a clarinet and two others with flutes. When the ensemble was settled, a director led them into a song. It was light and rhythmic. Soon people were clapping along with the band.

They played three more songs. All the tunes were lively, adding to the festive mood of the day. During the last song, a whir came from above. Margaret looked up to find a biplane flying overhead. A banner stretched behind displaying the words *A Day to Remember*. She smiled. Matthew had mentioned this flying mission to her. She'd chosen not to go with him in exchange for staying downtown with her family.

As she watched him fly over, her chest swelled. She was so proud of him successfully completing this assignment. It stood as a sort of second chance, a way for him to recover what he'd lost in July when his biplane crashed.

The crowd cheered as they watched the show. Matthew's biplane disappeared from sight as the band started another song. When the song ended, Matthew emerged from the crowd and stood at the podium. He waited for the applause to die down.

"Good afternoon. It was truly an honor to fly the banner today. As you probably noticed, I didn't crash. I can believe you are as relieved about that as I am." He laughed along with the group.

When they quieted, he continued. "I'd like to give the bandstand its first public event. As you know, Margaret Millerson and I are engaged. We've been working on the guest list for our wedding but we're having trouble trying to decide who to invite. We gave up on the list and decided to invite the whole town. We're getting married today. Right now. Logan, could you come here, please?" Matthew paused in his speech as an astonished murmur ran through the crowd.

Logan left his place where he stood behind Margaret with Arthur and Henry and approached the podium.

"And now I need Margaret. My bride." Matthew held a hand out in her direction.

Karen gasped.

Julia whispered, "Oh, Mother!"

Margaret left their side. The crowd parted for her as if she were royalty. Logan moved to the bandstand. Instrumentalists clustered on the lawn. Clara handed her a bouquet of fall flowers tied with wide ribbon. Then she worked with Cornelia to fasten more bouquets to the posts. The decoration transformed the structure into a gazebo, a little dream world she'd enter into with Matthew.

The crowd shifted until it surrounded the site for the wedding. Band members played the wedding march as Margaret walked to meet her groom. Her floral print dress and stylish hat were a perfect outfit to wear on this special day. She didn't need the fancy designs Miss Rose had created for her.

How much she'd changed over the past months. The charm of this town had worked its wonder on her. Love. Friendships. Faithfulness. Those were the things that mattered. Those were the things she wanted to keep in her life. Not faddish styles or write-ups in the society column.

Matthew looked nice dressed in a dark suit. He clasped her hand when she met him. Together they faced Logan, her pastor son-in-law who, now that she really thought about it, had begun the shift in her values. He'd shown her what integrity looked like. He'd proven to her that marriage lasted. Stronger than reputation or disappointment, it was a safe and joyful place. He smiled into her eyes as if to tell her he understood the battles that had been fought in her heart over the past months.

"Dearly beloved, we are gathered here today in the presence of God to witness the joining together of this man and this woman." He continued with the wedding liturgy, prompting them in the exchange of vows and of wedding rings. Then, with a grin on his face, he invited Matthew to kiss the bride.

Margaret's inbred modesty caused her to blush. She enjoyed Matthew's kisses, but receiving one here in front of the whole town required all of her courage. She lifted her face and let him place his lips on hers for one unforgettable moment.

"It is my pleasure to introduce to you Doctor and Mrs. Matthew Kaldenburg," Logan announced.

People clapped and the band played another song as Margaret left the bandstand-turned-gazebo with her new husband. A shiny new Model T Ford drove up to the curb and parked. Ezra Barnaveldt got out of the car and handed the keys to Matthew.

"Congratulations on your wedding gift," Ezra said with a smile as Matthew slapped him on the back.

Logan, Karen, and the family from Chicago joined their group. "What a nice car." Logan whistled and he studied the shiny windows and leather seats.

"It is Henry's wedding gift to us, but we want you to have it." Margaret laid her hand on his arm.

"What?" Logan raised his brows in utter surprise.

Matthew nodded and handed the keys to him. "Yes. Take it. Store it. Use it on your pastoral visits or whatever other trips you and Karen need to make. I'll come get it whenever I need it."

Logan shook his head as if he didn't know what to say and wrapped an arm around Karen's shoulders.

"Thank you, Mother. Thank you very much." Karen offered a huge smile.

Margaret went with Matthew to another area of the park designated for the community picnic. Women organized food on a table. Mabel Zahn brought out a cake decorated in white frosting and pink flowers.

"Come cut the first slice, Doctor," Mabel called.

People cheered and slapped Matthew on the back indicating to Margaret how much the townspeople enjoyed watching their beloved and famous doctor celebrate a new marriage.

"Mother, we didn't know. None of us had the slightest idea you had this planned." Karen looked at her with wide eyes.

Margaret smiled. "Matthew knows how to keep secrets. He is the model of confidentiality."

"I'll say." Julia laughed. "Did Logan know about the wedding?"

"Yes. Logan, Mildred, Clara, and the band members were the only ones. We wanted our special day to fit into the flow of the celebration without a lot of fuss. I'd say it worked, don't you?" Margaret raised her brows in a knowing smile.

After they'd eaten, Matthew announced their departure. Margaret hugged her daughters, Fran, and Arthur.

"Thank you, Logan. You are very special to me," she said when he embraced her.

"We love you, Mother," he said back. "Thank you for the car. I still don't know what to say."

Then she hugged each of her grandsons. Two of them would be going back to Chicago before she returned to town. She and Matthew must find a way to stay involved in their lives.

"Good bye, dear. Grandma will see you soon," she said to Ben as he wrapped her in a little boy hug.

"I'll miss you, Grandma."

"I know. I'll miss you too." How she'd love to stay and spend every last minute with them until their train carried them back to Chicago. But Matthew had made plans for her to go with him. They'd be traveling to a peaceful lake for the weekend, and they must arrive before dark.

"Come, Margaret." Matthew led her away after shaking hands with the other men.

Beyond the lumberyard, just on the edge of town, the biplane waited. She slipped off her hat and replaced it with her helmet and goggles. Then she moved to help spin the propeller.

When both propellers were turning rapidly, Matthew helped her to her seat. He shifted the controls to put the biplane in motion. Soon they left the ground and glided over the town.

Margaret looked down at the mass still gathered for the picnic. She recognized her family and many friends in the crowd. God had been good to her. She could just as easily not have any of these blessings in her life. Daughters with good husbands.

Grandchildren. Friends who loved her. Matthew. She waved to those on the ground and turned to him.

He was the definition of mercy in her life. If she ever needed a reminder of God's graciousness to her, all she had to do was look at him. Steady. Faithful. Dedicated. Together they would rise above the sorrows of the past. To them belonged a new beginning. One filled with ascent into new heights of love with daily proofs of God's rich mercy.

ABOUT THE AUTHOR

Michelle lives in Iowa with her husband and two teenage sons. She is a graduate of Northwestern College in Orange City, Iowa, with an associate's degree in office management. She is also a graduate of Central College in Pella, Iowa, with a Bachelor's degree in Religion with a Christian Ministry emphasis and Music. Michelle is the spiritual services provider for Christian Opportunity Center, an organization that offers services for people with physical and mental disabilities. She is also a chaplain for the local hospital, Pella Regional Health Center.

You can learn more about Michelle by visiting her website: michelledebruin.com.

ALSO BY MICHELLE DE BRUIN

Hope for Tomorrow

When Logan De Witt learns of his father's sudden death, he returns home to the family's dairy farm. During his stay, he discovers his mother's struggle with finances and his younger sister's struggle with grief. Concern for his family presses Logan to make the difficult decision to leave his career as a pastor and stay on the farm. As a way to make some extra money, he agrees to board the teacher for their local school.

Karen Millerson arrives from Chicago ready to teach high school but her position is eliminated so she accepts the role of country school teacher. Eager to put her family's ugly past behind her, Karen begins a new career to replace the trust she lost in her own father who had been in ministry when she was a child.

Logan and Karen both sense a call from the Lord to serve him, but neither of them expected that one day they would do it together.

Can Karen learn to trust again? Will Logan lay aside his grief in exchange for God's purpose for his life?

Promise for Tomorrow

Living a life of faith isn't going the way Logan and Karen hoped until some special visitors arrive and offer them their future back.

Karen Millerson dreamed of teaching high school but now finds herself boarding with a farm family and teaching country school. She is engaged to marry Logan De Witt and is getting prepared to share in ministry with him. But when she gets blamed for the tragic fire at the school, Karen's future grows uncertain.

Logan De Witt is working to clear his family's name with the bank. But when he breaks his leg, hindering his ability to work the farm, Logan is faced with life-changing decisions. When his best friend can't offer the help he requested, can Logan find a way to care for his family and court Karen at the same time before his love for her destroys all of them?

Dreaming of Tomorrow

Popular and eligible, Logan De Witt must convince the women in town that he is engaged to be married. A quiet, simple ceremony is what he has in mind for his wedding day, but when the date and time of his bride's arrival is published in the newspaper, the whole town joins in the celebration proving to Logan and his new wife their sincere friendship and support. Added to the excitement of Logan's marriage is the question of what the congregation should do with the unexpected donation of an orchard.

Karen Millerson is counting the days until her long-distance engagement comes to an end and she may travel to Oswell City to marry Logan. More than anything, she wants to share in his life as a help and support, but keeping a house and finding her place in the community requires much more work than she ever expected.

Learn, laugh, and love with Karen and Logan as they start a new marriage and work together ministering to the citizens of their small town.

MORE HISTORICAL ROMANCE FROM SCRIVENINGS PRESS

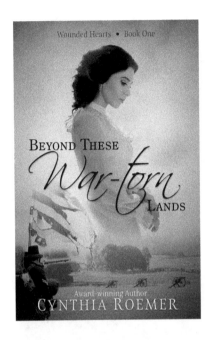

Beyond These War-torn Lands

Wounded Hearts - Book One

By Cynthia Roemer

While en route to aid Confederate soldiers injured in battle near her home, Southerner Caroline Dunbar stumbles across a wounded Union sergeant. Unable to ignore his plea for help, she tends his injuries and hides him away, only to find her attachment to him deepen with each passing day. But when her secret is discovered, Caroline incurs her father's wrath and, in turn, unlocks a dark secret from the past which she is determined to unravel.

After being forced to flee his place of refuge, Sergeant Andrew Gallagher fears he's seen the last of Caroline. Resolved not to let that happen, when the war ends, he seeks her out, only to discover she's been sent away. When word reaches him that President Lincoln has been shot, Drew is assigned the task of tracking down the assassin. A chance encounter with Caroline revives his hopes, until he learns she may be involved in a plot to aid the assassin.

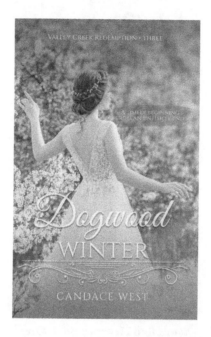

Dogwood Winter

Valley Creek Redemption - Book Three

By Candace West

After a springtime swim, Ella Steen is stricken with a dire illness, leaving her without the use of her legs. Meanwhile, Dr. George Curtis, the man she secretly loves, faces ruin. For over a year, the crusty New York City bachelor and vivacious spinster have exchanged dozens of letters and formed a wary friendship.

Neither are willing to open their hearts completely. Until they face each other. The past looms between them, however. Does George still love another or is his heart completely free?

A trip to Valley Creek holds the answers. Instead, when George and Ella arrive, they encounter obstacles that force other truths to the surface. Is George brave enough to confront what he fled in New York? Can Ella confess why she hates dogwood winters? Will their hearts survive?

If only their pasts would keep out of the present.

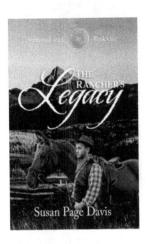

The Rancher's Legacy
Homeward Trails - Book One
by Susan Page Davis

Matthew Anderson and his father try to help neighbor Bill Maxwell when his ranch is attacked. On the day his daughter Rachel is to return from school back East, outlaws target the Maxwell ranch. After Rachel's world is shattered, she won't even consider the plan her father and Matt's cooked up—to see their two children marry and combine the ranches.

Meanwhile in Maine, sea captain's widow Edith Rose hires a private investigator to locate her three missing grandchildren. The children were abandoned by their father nearly twenty years ago. They've been adopted into very different families, and they're scattered across the country. Can investigator Ryland Atkins find them all while the elderly woman still lives? His first attempt is to find the boy now called Matthew Anderson. Can Ryland survive his trip into the wild Colorado Territory and find Matt before the outlaws finish destroying a legacy?

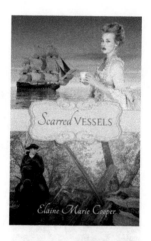

Scarred Vessels

2021 Selah winner for Historical Romance

by Elaine Marie Cooper

In a time when America battles for freedom, a man and woman seek to fight the injustice of slavery while discovering love in the midst of tragedy.

In 1778 Rhode Island, the American Revolution rallies the Patriots to fight for freedom. But the slavery of black men and women from Africa, bartered for rum, is a travesty that many in America cannot ignore. The seeds of abolition are planted even as the laws allowing slavery in the north still exist.

Lydia Saunders, the daughter of a slave ship owner, grew up with the horror of slavery. It became more of a nightmare when, at a young age, she is confronted with the truth about her father's occupation. Burdened with the guilt of her family's sin, she struggles to make a difference in whatever way she can. When she loses her husband in the battle for freedom from England, she makes a difficult decision that will change her life forever.

Sergeant Micah Hughes is too dedicated to serving the fledgling country of America to consider falling in love. When he carries the tragic news to Lydia Saunders about her husband's death, he is appalled by his attraction to the young widow. Micah wrestles with his feelings for Lydia while he tries to focus on helping the cause of freedom. He trains a group of former slaves to become capable soldiers on the battlefield.

Tensions both on the battlefield and on the home front bring hardship and turmoil that threaten to endanger them all. When Lydia and Micah are faced with saving the life of a black infant in danger, can they survive this turning point in their lives?

A groundbreaking book, honest and inspiring, showcasing black soldiers in the American Revolution. *Scarred Vessels* is peopled with flesh and blood characters and true events that not only inspire and entertain but educate. Well done!

- Laura Frantz, Christy Award-winning author

of *An Uncommon Woman*

Stay up-to-date on your favorite books and authors with our free e-newsletters.

ScriveningsPress.com

CPSIA information can be obtained
at www.ICGtesting.com
Printed in the USA
FSHW021522280721
83592FS